The Guamanian Princess

Dana L. Evans

The smell of diesel fuel was overwhelming as Jade-R clutched her legs against the pain of her father's savage beating. After years of looking down the hill at the loading docks in Agana Harbor, she was now in the cargo hold of one of those ships, with no hint of its final destination.

As an only child, daughter of the governor of Guam, growing up in the governor's mansion, she had a life of terrible loneliness, yet extreme luxury, but always felt safe and loved. Now, that was shattered!

Sixteen years old and pregnant, she was fleeing her father's rage and threat of a brutal forced abortion. Curled against enormous bags of rice, she removed her shoe and blood poured onto the dirty floor. Terrified and exhausted from her escape, the vibration of the ship's engines finally lulled her to sleep.

Her ensuing journey would take her across oceans and countries, barely surviving:
Death, murder, and a life tiered in terrible deceit!

The entire work in this novel is fiction. The names, the characters, dialogue, and events taking place in any of these cities, towns or countries do not exist and are strictly created by the imagination of the author. Resemblance in any way to any actual persons, living or deceased, is completely coincidental.

ISBN 978-0-578-45108-4

Printed in the United States of America

www.DanaLEvans.com

Original book cover art by Dana L. Evans

Acknowledgments

My deepest love to Joe, my husband, for his support, allowing me to disappear many hours a day while writing this novel.

I am also grateful to the following people; Christa Shewbridge, Judy Gillespie, Joni Evans, Dan Felix and Coleen Brennan. Last, but not least, to my ever-resourceful brother Paulden, many thanks always.

Dedicated to
Terré, Kevin and Joe
with all my love.

DE

PROLOGUE

Moonlight bounces across the tumbling waves. At a distance two people are struggling in the surf: a man and a woman. A sudden wave knocks them over. The woman breaks away and runs screaming toward the beach. The man grabs her from behind and drags her back. She thrashes as he holds her under water until there is no more movement. The tide takes her lifeless body out to sea as he calmly walks onto the shore.

CHAPTER ONE

That horrifying image of what he did, will it ever leave me? Jade-R paused, her heart pounding.

Entering the hospital, she took a deep breath, adjusted the collar on her blouse and headed down the long corridor. Moments later she stood beside him. Sunlight streamed through the window and fell across the bed. Her father's face had lost the powerful look it once had, and his thick dark hair was gray. It was the first time she had seen him since that lurid night. His eyes, transfixed with terror, stared up at her.

Suddenly clenching his fist, he began gasping for his last breath. With a feverish chill she reached out and touched his arm. He did not respond, and soon the nurses removed his oxygen tube and IVs. Now it was over. The black framed clock on the wall showed 11:00 a.m. A quick thought flashed through her mind as they covered him with a white sheet, *Will the gates of heaven or hell be waiting?* She wiped a burning tear as it rolled down her face, put on sunglasses and walked out of the hospital to the waiting limousine parked at the curb.

Official flags fluttered on the front of the black government car, and people stood watching in the blistering heat as the limo sped through town.

Turning onto the loop in the road she could finally see the mansion, drenched in sparkling sunshine, sprawled across the hilltop. She smiled at its remembered elegance. At the guardhouse they stopped long enough for Napo, the chauffeur, to give his usual nod to the man on duty. Winding up the long driveway past lush green plants, they arrived at the entrance.

Napo jumped out to open her door. “Glad

you're home," he said.

She patted the cuff on his navy blue suit and replied, "Thank you," noticing the freckles across his nose had lightened. Or maybe she had forgotten. But his wide smile and polite manner, as always, were comforting.

The living room with its polished blue marble floors still seemed enormous. The rich sweeping view through walls of glass to the tropical turquoise sea was endless, with white clouds floating above. Picking up a photo of her gorgeous American mother, she admired how her arms were gracefully crossed. Quickly Jade-R placed her hand over her heart and sighed. In that picture, her mother was wearing a familiar diamond and emerald ring with matching bracelet.

Heading on to her grand piano, she stopped for a moment and ran her fingers down the genuine ivory keys and listened as the sound echoed through the room, reminding her of the long hours she was made to practice.

Pushing the doors open to the formal dining room, which had always been her favorite spot, she recalled the summer when she was eight years old, lying on the floor watching the artist hand-paint a white coral motif around sections of the ceiling, eventually running it down the corners. Now more than ever, the chandelier seemed to sparkle, with blue crystal prisms intertwined with huge pieces of natural coral. Flopped across a bamboo chair was her patched tabby cat named Max.

"You grew up to be a big boy. I told you you'd be beautiful!" She rubbed his head as he rapidly swished his distinctive striped salt-and-pepper tail. She had interrupted the cat's nap and Max was irritated. Amused, she watched as he darted off and then remembered, *Dogs have masters; cats have staff.*

Making her way to the kitchen, she found the faithful servants listening to the radio just as the announcement was made:

"The governor is dead." Immediately one of

the older servants bowed her head into her starched white apron and began to cry. The cook dropped a stainless steel pan that went crashing to the floor, and then covered her mouth in disbelief. Suddenly both servants looked up at Jade-R, stunned, completely dazed, as if they were seeing a ghost. Tears flowed as she hugged them, but still in shock they continued to stare at her.

Later, walking the long hallway lined with matching chandeliers, the one so many times as a kid she had roller-skated down, Jade-R finally reached her room. To her surprise nothing had changed. She wrapped her arms around the custom post on her bed and looked up at the ornately carved wood pineapples resting on top. Her large dramatic bed jutted out from the oval end of the room. Draperies on the tall glass doors were pale pink silk with a subtle palm tree design.

She grabbed a handful of fabric, pressing it against her face, to enjoy the softness. She had forgotten how pretty, how elegant they were.

Glancing toward the dresser she noticed her youthful keepsakes, such as the whimsical poem with frayed paper edges, ripped from her favorite book, still taped to the mirror; and the coconut she had hand-painted one rainy day long ago.

On a table, stacks of unopened books caught her eye and she stood fixed on them, knowing all those years of reading had helped her survive that terrible journey. She dropped her head and fought tears, sick with the memory of those tragic events, and how it all began in 1959...on the Island of Guam.

Her father the governor, always loving, spent plenty of time doting on her with a constant stream of gifts. He gave her a pony she named Oatmeal. He built a huge swimming pool, but no one was allowed to come swim. When she would ask, his answer was, “They are not worthy.” Boasting, but somewhat irritated, he would add, “You are my only child. I teach you at home, and I hire the best. I won't allow my daughter to associate with other kids," pointing his finger, adding, "not of your level."

He made sure her dresses were tailor designed and from the finest cloth imported from Hong Kong. The local jeweler created custom buttons in 18 karat gold, all of which were either shaped like island flowers, or "P" for Princess, inlaid with diamonds, rubies and emeralds, the only ones to be sewn on her clothes.

When political functions were held at the governor's mansion, her governess, a sweet lady named Kimea, would help her into a gold silk dress, and then escort her to her father. She loved how tightly he held her hand, while proudly introducing her to his guests. However, before long she would be sent back to her room. One such night it was warm, so she pulled back the drapes to let in some air. The band was playing, and through the open window she could hear the beautiful music and see people dancing. At the buffet line she noticed the lieutenant governor's son, her age, standing and laughing with his parents as she watched from the lonely darkness of her room.

Only a collection of plastic spoons was a tangible reminder of the one day a week she was allowed off the compound. On those days, Napo would drive Jade-R and the governor to the local Dairy Queen. One afternoon her father telephoned to say he couldn't make it, but that evening surprised her. It had never happened before, the excitement of being out at night together!

While she ate peppermint ice cream from a cup, next door a movie began to play on a huge screen. She didn't know this existed! Cars were parked side by side, with speakers resting on their windows.

Thrilled, and quickly taking it all in, Jade-R begged to stay and watch the movie. Gruffly her father answered, "A drive-in? No. That will never be for you."

The ride home was quiet. They passed a

small hamburger place and from the car window she could see young kids her age having fun.

Most nights being isolated made her wonder, *What would it be like to have friends and just do teenage things?*

However, as time passed, she continued respecting her father's wishes... until one night.

CHAPTER TWO

It had been dark and stormy all day. That evening, Jade-R sipped on a caramel-colored cola, lying on the floor listening to music. Angrily her father barreled into the room, drink in hand, yelling. He banged the glass down on her dresser.

She jumped up as her kitten tore off.

"I will stop your allowance! Don't order anymore of those! I told you not to listen to that Goddamn rock-and-roll music shit!" He kicked the turntable across the room, busting off the arm, then spotted a stack of 45 rpm records beside her. In that rage, he stomped on them several times with the heel of his left shoe. His mysterious brown eyes stared straight at her.

He yelled again, "Nothing but classical, do you hear me? Or read a book!" He straightened his red tie in the mirror nearby and picked up his drink.

Kissing her forehead, he said "Good night."

She crumpled to the floor, quickly gathering small pieces of the broken records, lumped them in a pile and began to cry.

Evenings alone changed. Always so important, her music was the one thing that made her feel like a normal teenager, and now it was gone. Weeks went by.

At breakfast one morning, a new portable player, with a big bow wrapped around it, sat on the table. Her father smiled. He pointed. "Those are what you should listen to." Quickly she sifted through the records coated with shellac.

Quietly, she said, "Thank you, Father." He finished his juice, kissed her forehead and left for his office.

That evening she gathered the grown-up records. With disappointment she listened, but soon turned the player off. An hour and fifteen minutes passed. She told herself, *I've just turned sixteen. What am I supposed to do? Sit here alone every night? Learn about the world out there by reading the latest book?*

Acting from boredom, she sighed as her kitten bounced around batting something. Suddenly she jumped up. It was a record, one her father hadn't seen! It must have slid under the chair. She held it to her heart with joy, then peeked out her door into the hallway. The chandeliers were off. Excited, she placed the record on the turntable, lowering the volume and pulling her chair close. Her kitten curled beside her purring. The night was warm and the air was soft.

The song was "Blueberry Hill." Listening to the words, she shook her head and sighed. *What have I done? Nothing. I'm not even allowed to see a movie!* As the full moon rose outside the glass doors, romantic and bright, it seemed to whisper playfully, "Come, come have fun."

Sweeping a brush through her glossy dark hair, she slipped out the tall sliding door. Closing it carefully behind her, she sneaked through the lush green bushes. As she reached the pool cabana, there were voices. Her father was talking to Ditch, his close childhood friend and fierce drinking companion. The two men laughed as her father continued.

"Listen, I keep telling you if you only have sex with them in the rear, you're safe. They can't get pregnant! It's for sure midnight girls aren't worthy of my seed. And we won't have as many kids running the streets like we did. At our place they better not complain, they better do whatever!" Clinking their rock glasses together, they both laughed again.

She was shocked by their conversation. When they quit laughing, her father added, "The young guys today are not like us, with our sense of ambition, ready to castrate or kill. Sometimes I think, late at night... I think about all we did... Now look at us. We're respectable! I'm the Governor and you're a successful businessman."

Laughing again, they both said, "Hmm . . . those were the days!"

"Remember, by age ten, we could knock out teeth and bust back bones? We were tough!" added Ditch.

Heartsick and unable to listen, she headed toward a tropical paradise of natural plants, squeezed through a secret opening in the fence, discovered a path, and hurried down the hill toward town. Feeling free, she finally came to that quaint restaurant she had passed in the car one night. A brightly lit sign declared in huge letters, “Island Burgers. We guarantee the best burgers on the island.”

Under the canvas awning, she straightened her dress but felt nervous as Jade-R entered. Directed to a booth, she ordered a root beer float. She spooned the creamy, bubbling foam into her mouth while looking around. Light green walls and the yellow island flowers on the tables gave the rather small place a cheerful look. Concerned, she quickly unfastened the clip on her purse and checked her money.

Suddenly the door pushed open, and a handsome young man in a sporty, tailored jacket sauntered in. Catching her looking at him, he gave her a flirtatious wink and she quickly turned away. Trying to appear disinterested at first, she slowly glanced back.

With a watchful eye she followed him as he headed toward the jukebox. He pushed buttons. The song "Stardust" softly filled the room.

For a moment she ignored his attention, then peered over to the next table. He smiled. She hesitated, but felt a flutter in her stomach. A tempting feeling came over her as she turned his way, and again he smiled.

Feeling awkward, she fussed with the sleeve on her white pearl dress. A few minutes later she grew nervous and decided it was time to leave. When asking for the bill, the waitress replied, "That young man in front of you took care of it."

She watched as the hot cheese on his burger rolled down the sides onto the crispy lettuce as he took his first bite. Not quite sure, she finally decided it would be proper to thank him. Walking toward his table she politely tilted her head and smiled. He grinned and handed her a note scribbled on a paper napkin. She reached out, shyly taking it, looked at him once more, then hurried off.

On the way home there was a frightening

sound of something moving about the banana trees. Quickly she hid behind a large palm tree, fighting back a wave of fear. Eventually continuing on, she simply shrugged it off ,telling herself, maybe it was the sound of one of Guam's ancestor ghosts, like the stories the servants enjoyed telling when she was little, sitting on a stool in the kitchen, half-scared to death.

Before long the night air felt warm again and the magic from the evening returned. She smiled at the stars drifting above and wished she could pick them and forever save them in a box. Carefully tiptoeing back inside her room, she locked the glass door and pulled out the note.

"I will see you in my dreams, and be here at the same time, waiting for you, tomorrow night!"

Her heart was bursting. He was so handsome and to think, he was attracted to her. She stood back and looked in the mirror. *Yes, my lips are full and I am pretty. I know my legs are long. Kimea my governess, would always say, "When you have on your swimsuit, your legs are long and beautiful. Just like your mother's were!"*

She opened the note again and read it over and over, memorizing it. Smiling proudly, she finally hid it in her closet.

The next day the fun and memories of the previous night were wildly spinning in her thoughts. She could hardly wait to see if those new feeling could happen again. *What would it be like to sit near him?*

At noon she poured a glass of water and wandered out to the pool. A brightly colored butterfly with yellow tips on its wings landed on her lounge cushion as if to sun itself. Watching, it seemed almost friendly and for a moment she thought it might cuddle next to her. But soon it fluttered away.

A light breeze scattered the scent of perfume from the roses, while Max, her kitten, stalked like a little panther something moving under the bushes.

She dove in the pool, but swimming was not on her mind. Instead, all she could think about was which dress she should wear that evening.

As she floated on her back she abruptly recalled the conversation from her father last night. It hit her, when Ditch came to the mansion, it was usually late and they always sat outside. Now that she thought about it, he had never been invited for dinner. Only a few times had she said hello to him. Maybe his crudeness was the reason her father kept distance between them. At some point she convinced herself, *Those terrible things her father was saying, he must have been drunk and probably joking.*

The day lingered on as she watched the clock. After a quick dinner with her father, he hurried off to what he always called, a "business meeting." Most evenings being alone bothered her, but not tonight.

Filling her marble tub with bubble bath she soaked in the warm water waiting for the sun to set. With relief she heard a knock. It was the head servant checking on her one last time before retiring to her quarters.

Finally the drapery of darkness arrived.

With the clean smell of soap and a few dabs of Island perfume, she slipped on her shoes that matched her blue dress, patted gloss over her full lips, and smiled at her reflection in the mirror. She was ready.

Her heart was pounding as she hurried down the hill toward the night ahead, filled with excitement.

Like a gentleman, he quickly stood when she entered. “Stardust” was playing as he gallantly extended his arm and invited her to sit in his booth.

With a grin, he said, “All day I wondered what I’d say if I were lucky enough to see you!” He handed her a white gardenia. She sighed and put it to her nose, then brushed the petals with her finger and whispered, “Thank you.” His voice was almost hypnotizing as he spoke and right then he had taken her heart away.

Handsome, he’s so handsome. For a moment she could only hear her own thoughts. Suddenly she realized he was asking her a question.

"Do you live nearby?"

As the waitress set glasses of iced tea on the table, she answered, "Not far, just up the hill," then asked, "Where do you live?"

"I live in Hawaii."

"Hawaii," she repeated. "What brought you to Guam?"

"My grandfather's company builds cargo ships. We delivered one here yesterday. Before I saw you, I'd been driving around the island and on my way back to town spotted a sign. It dragged me in when I read, 'Island Burgers.' For me a juicy burger, that's my favorite. Nothing better!"

"So you arrived by ship?" she asked.

With a wry smile, he answered. "My grandfather and my father decided this summer, I'm not climbing on and off tennis courts, or in and out of golf carts, or hanging around the Country Club! In a stern voice, my grandfather informed me: 'You will accompany our new freighter on its maiden journey.' Quote, unquote." His eyes became fixed on her. "You don't look like the people

I've seen so far on this island. Where are you from?"

She answered quietly. "This is home and my father is Guamanian. My mother was born and raised in San Francisco. She came here to teach." Her smile spread across her perfectly straight teeth. "This is what my father told me. When they met, she was so beautiful he used all his charm. Six weeks later they were married." She paused, then said, "Being able to go anywhere, being free like you are, that seems so nice."

"Well, that's the family business!"

"How did they get into that business?"

He stretched his arms out, his chest swelling with pride, as he explained, "During college, Grandfather, who goes by the name Wills, worked doing manual labor for a shipping company in California. One summer vacation he came to Hawaii. He liked it and made it home. Lucky for us, he met this guy while playing tennis, the president of a local bank and they became close friends. Within a year, Grandfather got a loan from that bank and bought out a failing shipping company.

He's the smartest man I've ever been around. It took years, but he turned it into what we have today."

Smiling, he said, "Your hair, it's so shiny it doesn't look real."

She laughed. "That's because once a week, growing up, I had to sleep with it wrapped in olive oil."

"Olive oil!" He grinned. "I put that on my salad. Ha, maybe I'll try it on my hair." His reply made her laugh again. Then he stared. "And your eyes? "

She answered, "A gift from my mother."

He rubbed his hand through his thick blonde hair. "Well, they're beautiful."

It was quiet again. He looked up from the table. "What you said about traveling, I've never really thought about it. There's not much action aboard a cargo ship. But actually, straddling a deck chair with all the fresh air, and miles of open sea, it's great!" He paused. "Excuse my manners. What is your name?"

"Jade-R." She answered.

"Pretty. Is that a family name?"

"No, my father loves jade. He is certain it brings him luck. The R is for Reign, my mother's name."

"Different. It's nice. I don't have an interesting story. I'm just Connor." Then he smiled. "However, I am William Connor Bodwen, the Third!"

"Impressive," she said, smiling. Fearing it was getting late she added, "I must go."

He stood. "Can I walk you home?"

"No. But thanks."

"Will I see you tomorrow night?"

She lowered her head bashfully and nodded.

And so it went; each night was magical! Dazzled by his charm, she listened intently to his stories.

"My parents are different. Mom likes to play bridge at our country club all day, and if we get lucky, once a week she'll cook." He shook his head. "Even when we were kids she liked dining out, which ticked off my father. My guess, they wouldn't be together if it weren't for my older sister and me." He laughed, "You'll enjoy this. When my sister was born, my parents named her Cathy. Grandfather quickly started calling her little Catfish! It became his endearing term. It really annoyed my mother. Years later, she said he got paid back. Grandfather sent my sister to the most expensive French school in Paris. Then no one expected what she did next."

Jade-R shook her head and asked, "What did she do?"

"Cathy came back very educated and married the tennis pro at our country club! She could have done that without all the fancy schooling." Connor ran his hand through the side of his hair as he said, "I agree with my father, the guy is somewhat lazy. He thinks our family should foot the bill on everything. Grandfather bought them a nice house. He'll do that for me someday. Then he furnished it. Well...hired an interior designer. Oh, and he gave them new cars. My brother-in-law never says thanks. That's what bugs my grandfather."

"Do they have children?"

"They do. Two and they're really cute." He seemed in deep thought, then continued, "Well, I guess someone has to help them."

One night "Stardust," number 13 on the jukebox, was playing as they sat talking. He smiled. "I want that to be our song."

She blushed and dropped her head, "I'd like that."

He slid out of the booth and extended his hand. "Let's dance to our song."

"I don't know how."

He looked at her.

"Dancing slow is easy. I'll show you."

Leading her to a secluded corner near the jukebox she stumbled into his arms. His grip around her tiny waist tightened at times, as he glided her over the old wood floor. She could smell the scent of his cologne, and her heart leaped toward his every word.

That night there was a moment she wanted to relive a thousand times. He said, “We were made for each other.”

On her way home, she thought about her feelings. He was exciting, smart, she had never heard words like “copacetic,” “groovy,” or “can you dig it.” He was wonderful, everything a girl could dream of. She could barely contain herself. *This must be what love feels like.*

When she was safely in her room, she looked up at the crescent moon. “You’re the only friend I can talk to. Is this love?”

CHAPTER THREE

The next evening she reached the restaurant first and sat waiting in their booth. A new waitress with a cluster of yellow curls piled on her head and held with black bobby pins, asked, "Would you like to order something?"

"Thank you, but not yet. I'm waiting for someone."

Minutes later, he arrived, bursting with excitement.

She leaned forward.

"I just thought about this," he said. "I have a car outside. I was going to cruise down the hill. How about it, a walk on the beach, you darling girl, Jade-R?"

She smiled sweetly, pulled her long shiny hair to one side, straightened the pink collar on her blouse, and said, “All right!”

It was thrilling riding down the hill alone with a young man. They parked in a private area on the beach. The moon seemed to be glowing over the water. They left their shoes in the car. The sand sifted across their feet while they walked. As he took her hand, the sound of a soft gentle breeze rippled around them.

Connor picked up a shell and held it to his ear. “When I’m gone, oh sing to me, please, of faraway islands like Guam and of the beautiful maiden Jade-R.” He handed the shell to her as the full moon shone down on them. “I fly out tomorrow! College starts next week.”

Surprised, she quietly repeated. “You leave tomorrow?”

“Yes, but next year I’ll come back.” Tracing her lips with his finger, he said, “You have the perfect pout in those beautiful lips. It makes me crazy. From the moment I saw you, I was blinded by your beauty.” And there, under that full moon, she had her first kiss. The kiss was long. He paused only to say, “You’re so delicate, so beautiful!”

Again he gathered her in his arms and at first it was tremendous. She shivered with excitement. But then he said, “I must be with you,” as he pulled her to the ground.

“No.” She begged. “I don’t want to do this! You’re the first boy to kiss me! No please!”

He wouldn’t listen as he pushed her skirt up, and pulled her panties down.

Wiggling around, she tried to slide out from under him, but his weight was on top of her. She felt the heat of his body as he wildly thrust himself inside her. He pawed at her breast while she cried, “Please stop.”

Breathing heavily, he whispered, “Don’t worry. I have feelings for you. You’re beautiful! You’ll enjoy it!”

When he was finished, he ran his hand across his thick blonde hair and in the moonlight she could see his naughty smile.

“You were wonderful!” He said, zipping his pants. “I could tell it was your first time!”

There was a long horrible silence between them.

At last he added, “I admit I like you, and I feel something.”

She was trembling as she fussed with her wrinkled skirt and tried to straighten her hair. Suddenly, she felt sick.

Tossing his sport jacket over his shoulder he put out his hand to help her up. Standing quietly, she could feel semen running down the inside of her thighs. He reached down and picked up the shell next to her blood in the sand.

“You will remember tonight forever,” he said, then kissed her check.

The ride back was silent. She barely blinked. He rolled down the window and lit a cigarette. When he dropped her at the restaurant, he said, “I’m sorry, I probably shouldn’t have done that. But you are irresistible!” He handed her the shell and added, “Please don’t hate me.” She shook her head slightly, unable to look at him, and walked away.

The path home that night was different, more frightening than ever. A thunderstorm suddenly broke open, drenching her troubled heart. Near the house she spotted her father's car pulling up the long driveway. As he entered the side kitchen door, she hurried into her room. Not even the piping hot shower seemed to wash away her sorrow. Lying in bed, the rain had ended and there were stars darting across the sky as if they were playing tag. Usually she enjoyed watching, but not that night. Completely sick going over what Connor had done, she turned her head to the dark side of the wall, and soon her pillow was damp from what used to be a virgin's tears.

CHAPTER FOUR

Day after day she watched the rolling whitecaps on the sea, each day angrier than the last. He had taken advantage of her, but she also felt guilty for not trying harder to push him away. Terribly confused, she knew she still had feelings for him, maybe even love.

Nights at home, from out her window she'd look up at the sky but the magic in the moon was gone. No longer did she play her favorite record or have a desire to read. Snuggling in her chair with a blanket, remembering the talks and laughter they shared, occasionally it made her feel better.

Weeks passed. She woke up sick one morning, and days later with the absence of her monthly period began to think, *Could I be pregnant*? Then she constantly worried about her father's reaction. *What would he do? What will he do?* She remembered the night, the rage, when he broke her records and had never seen him so mad. Slumped in a chair holding the shell Connor had given her, she desperately wished for someone to confide in.

Each day alone with no one to shepherd her through the mess, she grew more frightened. Her clothes became tighter, her body was changing, and it was constantly on her mind. To stay calm she told herself her father loved her and will love this baby. It would be impossible not to! This would be his grandchild. Everything would work out.

One dreary rainy day, she spent the afternoon baking a cake. She had just finished swirling the vanilla frosting over it as the rain stopped and the sun briefly broke through the clouds. After dinner she sat playing the piano while her father smoked his cigar. He sipped his cocktail, listening. When the song ended she turned and froze, seeing the look on his face. He knew. With fear, she waited. The servants had gone to their quarters. Only her kitten lay at her feet, playing.

There was fury in his voice as he said, “How could it be only your tummy is getting round?”

She hung her head. “I’m sorry Father, I’m pregnant! It wasn’t my fault. A young man forced himself on me.”

Glancing back up, the look across his face quickly became worse, and it terrified her. Immediately he ripped off his belt and began slashing it across her soft delicate legs, yelling, “What cheap prick did this to you?”

She didn’t answer and her mouth went dry as she grabbed at the welts on her legs. Raising the belt again he yelled, “Answer me! Who screwed you?” She began crying and shook her head.

She stood. He pushed her to the sofa. “You’ll tell me and I’ll find him. I’ll break his kneecaps! No one else will get near you until I’m dead! By noon tomorrow, I’ll have the doctor here to cut that bastard out of you!”

She noticed the sweat beading on his brow. She pleaded again, “No, Father, please, no!” She stood back up and begged, “I want my baby, please. It is mine! You can’t do this!”

Belt still in hand, his face was scarlet with rage, and a horrid, insane look came over him.

He grabbed her arm and screamed. “I killed her, I drowned your mother. She was leaving, said I was too possessive. Hell, you were two and a half. One night we went to the beach. I pulled her into the waves. She ran; I grabbed her, held her under.” He tossed his hand like it was nothing, and added, “The tide took her.”

His voice went chillingly calm. But his eyes still looked dangerous. “This bastard will be cut out of you tomorrow! You’re a disgrace.” Then he turned and stormed out of the house.

At that moment she hated him. She had never felt such anger.

Back in her room, alone, she couldn’t stop crying. The sorrow was endless, realizing he had drowned her mother. He had killed her! Crying, she wondered what tomorrow would bring, then looked at the welts on her legs. He had been firm, even mad, but had never before laid a hand on her nor had she seen that insane kind of madness in him. It was late when he returned. Bludgeoned with fear, she realized that in order to keep her baby, she must quickly disappear. Frantically, again she thought about everything. While staring out her window, she noticed a ship down the hill at the docks. Lights were on, with smoke billowing from the stacks. From years of watching ships come from around the world, she knew it would soon be leaving.

Sneaking into her father's room, she could hear him lightly snoring as he lay in his towering carved bed. She was terrified, but slowly opened the drawer and took her mother's velvet pouch that held an emerald and diamond bracelet with matching ring that were being saved for her. Glancing back over her shoulder, she carefully entered his closet. She had watched him put money in dozens of shoeboxes for years. She reached in with trembling hands and grabbed a stack and stuffed it into one of his green leather duffel bags, then quietly backed out of his room. She tightly rolled up some clothes, shoes, and her own pink baby blanket from the back of the chair. She placed them in the bag along with tissues.

From the kitchen pantry she gathered cans of nuts, beans, crackers and a thermos of water. Tiptoeing through the living room, she paused one last time to look around, picked up her favorite picture of her mother holding her as a baby, then hugged her kitten good-bye.

With daylight coming, she headed away from the guardhouse, down past the pool and through the pasture where several carabaos stood watching. The ground was wet and slippery from the day of rain, and the path ahead unknown. Close to the end of the field, she grabbed a wild yam, and then moved toward a patch of darkness where she started running down the dirt road. Suddenly she stepped on some rubble as something caught her foot. "Ouch" she yelled. It was painful, and she could see a rotted old board with large wood spikes sticking up. Tugging, again and again, she freed herself.

Minutes later, a silhouette crossed near the road and quickly she dropped behind drooping tree limbs. When the man was out of sight, she ran hard telling herself to hurry to get to safety before the town awoke.

Hearing something, she turned the corner and hid close to a row of huts with tin roofs until the headlights from a car passed. While trying to slide underneath a fence of bamboo poles, she became tangled in dead bushes. Working frantically to free herself again, she waited quietly until a dog stopped barking at a nearby house.

Filled with panic that time was running out, she felt an urgent need to keep going before her father found her missing.

At last, she could see the docks and stopped for a moment to think. Feeling the excruciating pain in the bottom of her foot she glanced down. Blood was coming out the side of her shoe. However, the intense desire to get aboard that ship before it left was far more important. Watching, she saw two men on deck smoking. Not knowing what to do, she waited and finally they tossed their cigarettes over the side and left. Quickly she raced up the gangplank and ducked behind a lifeboat.

Before long she felt the ship backing out and was overwhelmed with relief just knowing it was leaving, and gave no thought to where it was headed. Over the horizon the peach-gold sun was coming up. She took one last look at the island, the only place she knew. The governor's mansion was beautiful in the morning light, her home on the hill that she loved and where she had always felt safe. Suddenly alone, she whispered good-bye and immediately tears rolled down her cheeks from her pale blue eyes as the Island of Guam slipped away.

With land fading in the distance, she realized she needed to get below before anyone saw her. She discovered a set of narrow iron stairs that led down. In the cargo hold it was hot and stuffy, and with very little airflow, she began to feel faint. As she looked around and her eyes adjusted to the dark, she could see rows and rows of crates and containers. At last she slid behind one in a corner.

By now the pain in her foot was throbbing up her leg as she slowly removed her shoe. Never had she felt such agonizing pain. It frightened her when blood oozed all over the floor. Just touching it made her want to scream. Then her legs started burning from her father's beating, and everything seemed almost unbearable. Undoing the lid on her thermos, she slowly let water trickle over the injured parts, and wished she had thought to bring alcohol. Unable to see clearly, she decided her foot must have a bad cut or puncture wound. Digging around in her duffel bag she found one of her nice silk blouses and gently wrapped it. Exhausted, she sat trying to figure out what to do, and then spotted a dirty canvas. With her duffel bag as a pillow she finally curled up and went to sleep.

CHAPTER FIVE

When she awoke her head was wet with sweat and her body burning with fever. Her sight was blurred; and she could hardly open her eyes. Feeling confused, she had trouble remembering where she was. For a few minutes her mind played tricks on her, wondering how this happened. Scared, she glanced around. Her mouth dry, her tongue was swollen, and she could barely swallow. Fumbling around with the thermos, desperately she tried to sip water, spilled it on her neck, but finally was grateful when some reached her mouth. Quietly she lay there. Only a murmur or soft moan came; no tears. *I've never been so sick. I hope I don't die.* Fading in and out of reality, she could feel warm urine running down her legs as she drifted back to sleep.

Soaked in sweat, she woke to the sound of

sharp voices. Afraid, she gathered the duffel bag and pulled the dusty canvas fully over her. Remembering the blood on the floor, she tugged one last time to cover it. Remaining perfectly still under the suffocating tarp, she suddenly felt a man's shoe next to her injured foot as he stood talking to someone. Fearing she would yell if he stepped on her, she put her hand across her mouth and clenched down hard with her teeth. Moments later the men moved away. Slowly she lifted the corner of the canvas and could see them swaying around while peeing on gunnysack bags of rice. Before long they hid something and left. Slowly she crawled out from under the canvas gasping for air. Carefully she looked back and forth, then took a deep breath and began to tremble. Finally putting her dirty hands to her face, she began to cry, telling herself, "Somehow I will be all right."

Sipping water, she hoped it would steady her, but there was the sound of her stomach growling from hunger. *I can't remember the last time I ate.* Weak and trying to open a can of beans, she eventually settled for a cracker and a small bite of raw yam. *I need to think.* As she leaned against the bulkhead, a large rat quickly ran close to her and disappeared between the containers. The throbbing in her foot shifted her attention as it grew more intense traveling up her sore, bruised leg. Frightened, she remembered reading about a man in the French West Indies having his infected foot cut off from the lack of medical care. *What would happen if I go to the ship's doctor, if they even have one? No, I don't dare.* When she turned her head she spotted something behind a crate. Scooting over again and again, she finally reached a bottle. It was whiskey, alcohol! That would disinfect her wound. As she poured it over her leg, it burned like acid soaking into the cut and she wanted to scream.

Again taking a deep breath, she sat thinking. *I need to get out of here. If those men come back to drink and I don't hear them, they could find me. Maybe put me in jail, or worse.* She feared they might send her back to her father. Then she remembered a recent dream she had. A woman running toward the beach and a man grabbing her. Jade-R quickly tried to shake that horrible thought of what happened to her mother. Tired, alone and sick, tears began rolling down her cheeks. It was quiet as she sat wiping her nose and wondering how many days had she been here? Scared again, it hit her how serious everything was in her life.

Jade-R tried to figure out where she could feel safe when sleeping, and soon thought about the lifeboat! Gathering her things, and slowly dragging the duffel bag behind her, she crawled past the large wood and metal crates, and then carefully began climbing the rusty stairs. She clung tightly to the railing hoping not to pass out. "No," she told herself. "It's just humid, I can make it. I'll feel better with fresh air." At the top of the stairs she could see it was nighttime, with no one in sight.

Moving as quickly as possible, she turned and looked back at the planks on the deck, making sure there was no trail of burgundy blood. Too weak right then to do more, she hid. For a while the night air and light wind felt good, even with the smell of diesel smoke pouring from the stacks. But soon she became chilled with her fever, then somehow, with her hands shaking, managed to undo the rope on one side of the lifeboat. With very little strength left, she climbed in. By now her teeth were chattering uncontrollably as she covered herself with her baby blanket. Burning with fever, she quickly fell asleep.

It was late that night when she was abruptly awakened by a loud crashing sound. As she listened, she heard the raging sea slamming hard against the huge ship. The tarp was flapping loose and before she tied it back down, she could see crewmen holding onto the rail as they walked in a row with heads bowed against the wind. She swallowed nervously. It was eerie. Then streaks of lightning slashed like a knife tormenting the troubled sky. In her mind she recalled the many typhoons she had lived through growing up. But here, she was isolated and afraid.

Faintly hearing a whistle blow, she recalled reading a story about a captain and his whistle. He was trying to alert the crew that danger was coming. She worried. *Would this be the freighter that ends up sinking to the bottom of the ocean?* Chains were clanging loose from somewhere. *No. I'll be safe,* she thought. *If they have to lower the lifeboats, they'll find me.*

Searching around the floor for water, she touched a square metal box. It was dark, but she discovered it contained gauze, tape, and ointment with other supplies, and realized it was a first aid kit. Immediately she started cleaning her injured foot, but with all the swaying from the storm, her stomach felt sick. Before long she began violently throwing up. Wind constantly whipped against the tarp as rain ran down a loose corner and into the bottom around her. Moving up to a bench, she lay there thinking. Back home the servants would fill large trashcans and bathtubs with water; she remembered the noise when storm shutters dropped, and how boats were moved around to the Harbor of Refuge. For a moment she felt comfort remembering home. She could almost hear the soothing song Kimea would sing to her during those storms and then recalled how their arms were sore and ached from wringing out towels when water came under the door a few times. Power would go off and generators would come on at the governor's mansion. Always when the storm would start, the servants would say: "Is this the one... the monster that's due to destroy us one day?"

Terrified, she soon heard metal banging and tin rolling around the deck. She held on tight to the wood bench she was lying on as the storm continued and the huge ship pushed through the long, scary night.

CHAPTER SIX

A flaming sun rose shattering through the brilliant clouds. The danger from that horrible typhoon had finally passed. Looking down she smiled faintly, pleased there was not more water in the bottom of the lifeboat, but to stay dry, she would have to continue lying down on the hard narrow wood bench. She glanced at the top of her filthy hands, then turned them over. The insides were brown and dirty from rust and sweat. *I need a bath and I smell so bad.*

She poured a small amount of water on tissue and wiped her face. *If only I could clean the vomit out of my hair,* she thought, *but I forgot to bring soap.* Searching through the first aid box, she applied more ointment to her foot and the welts on her legs.

Listening to the chant of the ship's engines

proceeding through the dreadful hours at sea gave her plenty of time to reflect on how rapidly her life had changed in that evil moment with her father, the father she trusted and thought would protect her always.

I wonder, how long did the police investigate and search for my mother?, she questioned. Then she answered her own question. *Being governor, and what he told them at the time, probably not long. I know her body never washed ashore! That's what he said, several years ago when he explained to me what happened. What a lie! Maybe what I overheard out at the pool cabana that night from my father and Ditch, talking about beating people up, busting their bones, did happen.*

She tucked a life jacket under her sore leg, propping it, hoping it would take pressure off and stop the throbbing. Moments later she fell into sadness again. *How could he kill her? How could he do that?*

"I hate him!" she said out loud, as tears ran down her face. *I can only imagine what my mother was going through in the last minutes of her life. I'm sure she was fighting him and worried about me. I never got to hug her, or hear her laugh, or see her smile at me. He stole that away when he killed her.*

Trying to calm down she closed her eyes and remembered Kimea's soothing voice, then focused on how she enjoyed petting her little kitten, Max.

The day passed slowly. Her thoughts wandered to the devastating night Connor took advantage of her on the beach. *But maybe he did have feelings for me.*

She rubbed her stomach and whispered to her unborn baby, "I love you and will protect you always." She dozed off thinking about peppermint ice cream and a soft bed. Again, that wretched dream came back.

Moonlight bounces off the tumbling waves. At a distance two people struggle in the surf. The woman gets up and runs toward the beach. The man grabs her from behind.

In a sweat she abruptly woke up feeling helpless, thinking about the tide taking her mother out to sea. So clearly again, she could see the insane rage in her father's face, as though he were standing in front of her yelling, "I killed her, I drowned her!" The thought made her feel sick, as the enormous vessel slowly rolled back and forth through thick, heavy seas.

Under the canvas tarp a delicious odor drifted by one evening, followed by a muttering sound. She remained still. Footsteps trampled across the deck, then stopped near the lifeboat. "I was hunting for you! There's a hot card game going. Come on!"

She heard the men walking away, and then peeked through the slat. One more drift of night air sent the smell of food streaming toward her again. With only small bits of nuts and crackers left and one can of beans, she had started rationing her food. She rubbed her stomach and whispered, "Just think about something pleasant. At least you still have water." Moments later hunger pains took over. She glanced around, then scurried hastily to the small ledge and grabbed the bowl and cup he had left behind. Darting quickly back she pulled herself into the lifeboat.

Wiping off the chopsticks she gobbled down the food. Cleaning the brim of the cup with the hem on her dress, she took a gulp, but right away spit it out. It must be some sort of sake. She looked down at the floor with small particles floating around. Thinking it might help disinfect the dirty, vile water, she dumped the rest into the bottom of the lifeboat.

CHAPTER SEVEN

One morning the vibrations from the engines began slowing. She raised a corner of the lifeboat cover. A tugboat was heading toward them and she could see land in the dark blue distance. The entire sky was shades of gray. She ducked back in and thought, *What should I do next?*

Before long it seemed, men were securing huge ropes from the ship to the dock.

Fifty crewmen scrambled to undo iron hatches as a crane moved slowly over the cargo hold. Carefully she peeked through the slit of the tarp watching the process. All day it was noisy and the warm water in the bottom of the lifeboat made the humidity almost unbearable. *What country is this? I'm a stowaway and need to get out of here soon.*

The grip of night finally covered the ship, as it began pouring.

This is it. I must go! Climbing out from the lifeboat she spotted a straw hat and shoved it on her head just as the sound of an iron door slammed. From the middle of the ship, racing toward her, a man yelled lewd and disgusting things. Weakened with fright, blood pumped through her body as Jade-R hurried down the gangplank. With torturing pain in her foot, she ran across the dock and hid in the shadow of an old building. Painted in faded letters were the words, "Formosa Packing Company." She thought, *At least I'm somewhere in Formosa*, then crouched against the side in the drenching rain. Resting a minute while looking around, it seemed safe and so she started down a street toward lights. Out of the darkness, a man jumped toward her, grabbing at the strap on her shoulder, trying to steal the duffel bag. As she screamed, "Help me please!" he pushed her to the ground, ripping and tugging at her bag. Jade-R held tight, kicking at him with all of her strength. From a corner restaurant, a woman came running, flapping a huge broom against the rain. She began whacking the man, yelling, "nuofu, zhu, gou!" The man yelled back, batting at her with empty hands.

Jade-R rolled to one side and the woman continued poking him with the straw spikes on the broom. Holding his eye, the scrawny guy staggered to the left, then took off in the opposite direction.

The woman helped Jade-R up, and led her into the closed restaurant. Spotting something the woman went running back out and waved down a man pedaling a bike with a cart attached. Jade-R remembered reading about rickshaw taxis. He wheeled around and headed their way. Still out of breath, the woman muttered and pointed toward town as she took Jade-R's hand. Mumbling and shrugging her shoulders, almost scolding her, she helped Jade-R climb in the back. As water ran down her face, the woman flagged the taxi driver on. Shaking uncontrollably, Jade-R clutched her bag and rubbed her neck where the man's sharp elbow had landed. Stressed from that dangerous event, a wave of nausea washed over her. The natural palm leaf top provided some shelter as she wiped her tears still mixed with rain, and felt blessed that someone had come to help. The constant heavy downpour along the ride made it nearly impossible to see anything but the blurred streetlights. Finally the driver wheeled under a large covered area. Important-looking in a green uniform with gold braids across the shoulders, a man stood ready to open the hotel door. She hesitated when she saw the beautiful lobby through large windows, and how nicely people were dressed. Timidly, she leaned forward, shook her head, and motioned to the driver as she said, “A smaller place.”

He pedaled on in the rain, eventually turning down a side street and up to a broken glass door with tape across it. Nodding her head, she said, “Thank you,” handing him money and the crumpled wet straw hat from her head.

Behind the counter a man with thick glasses spit tobacco into a can as he listened to a radio, then finally climbed off his stool. Softly she asked, “Do you have a room?” but could hardly understand his reply.

Slowly he repeated, “How many nights you stay?”

"I'm not sure." For a moment she felt disoriented, then repeated, "I'm not sure; maybe a month." She leaned her arm on the counter, helping steady herself, her body still weak and trembling.

"You sign name and you pay!"

She hesitated, thinking maybe she needed a different name, but finally wrote on the torn page, "Jade-R." She handed him money.

"I take, but tomorrow you go bank!" He gave her a key attached to a thin oval board and pointed to the stairs. "Go up, room seven."

Walking away, she tried to contain herself, and adjust her wobbling sea legs to land. She stopped and turned. "Do you know where I can get something to eat?"

He pointed next door. "Good food!" Then paused. "Maybe I have young son bring." Looking her up and down he said, "We add bill. Food taste good!"

"Thank you," she replied as she looked down at her dirty clothes and touched the collar on her wet blouse.

At first there was trouble with the key. It seemed rusted, but at last it opened the door. She clicked on the light. The room had a sour smell, and a cockroach ran across the floor. She sat down with her duffel bag on the bed and looked around, still frightened. Before long there was a knock. "Who is it?" she called.

"I have noodle soup!" came a very young boy's voice. Without hesitation, she greeted him at the door. Quickly she removed the paper lid, and steam poured out. She pulled up the blind and opened the window as he left the room.

The rain had stopped and there were colorful lanterns on the building across the street. Every so often, a big red dragon in neon lights flashed on and off, giving her something to watch as she ate. The noodle and meat soup was what she needed to regain her strength.

The hot water in the shower soon turned cold. The one tiny bar of soap was almost gone by the time her hair felt clean. Hopping over to the bed it seemed to be rocking as if she were still aboard the ship. She checked her foot and it scared her seeing the color of the fluid oozing out and she said out loud, "I must get to a doctor soon."

Taking out her pink baby blanket, the one her mother had crocheted, she hugged it tightly to her chest, then looked at her duffel bag. *I'm lucky I still have that. I hope I thanked the older woman that helped me*, then tried to rid herself from that awful event.

As she lay down the mattress springs squeaked, and a bug ran across the lumpy pillow before she clicked off the light.

CHAPTER EIGHT

Morning came fast. She fussed around looking at the walls, then slumped against the flat pillow, and soon her thoughts went to Connor. She remembered his grin and it made her smile. But thinking about it, that night on the beach had ended badly. She told herself, *He's young, and was out of control. Maybe by now he's remorseful? Perhaps he came back to Guam looking for me?* She remembered the feeling of love and their song, "Stardust," number 13 on the jukebox. Her sentimental favorite! Soon she began humming it, wondering what their baby might look like.

As she dressed, a pretty flash of sun seemed to puff across the old linoleum floor. Smoothing the bed covers, she spread out the items from her green duffel bag. First, she picked up the picture of her mother holding her as a baby. For a moment, she felt less lonely in this strange unfamiliar place. Her mother was wearing a pretty white dress and looked so beautiful. Jade-R took a deep breath, putting her hand to her heart.

Cleaning the dry crusted blood from the inside of her shoe, she again told herself out loud, "I've made it this far, somehow, things will be fine."

She tore the buttons off her stained blouse, which had protected her seriously injured foot. She hid the gold and jeweled buttons on her clothes by folding them inside out, and neatly placed them in the drawers.

Pulling out the last can of beans, she set it on the dresser along with the shell Connor had given her. Digging through the bag she realized one of her brand-new, favorite yellow linen shoes was missing! *It must have been lost in the rush to escape. How long ago had that been?*

Touching the small yellow heel, so sleek and pretty, she remembered begging her father to let her order them from a magazine; her first pair of high heels, and daily she waited. It took weeks for them to arrive. The excitement Jade-R felt when she undid the box and first saw them would never be forgotten. Looking at the single shoe, she sadly shook her head.

Again reality hit while glancing around the room for a hiding place. Finally pulling out the drawer to the nightstand she tucked most of the money and the velvet pouch with her mother's ring and bracelet in the back, then slid the drawer in place.

Checking the room one last time, she fumbled with the rusted key in the lock and left.

While politely waiting for the woman behind the counter to finish sharpening pencils, Jade-R noticed her dark hair was pulled so tight in a severe bun it looked uncomfortable. Her eyebrows were penciled in with a slight upward turn at the ends, and she had a very stern look on her face.

"Hi, I'm in room number..."

Jade-R was quickly interrupted when the woman said, "Yes! I know room! My husband say you come late in rain. What I help with?"

"I need directions to a medical clinic, please?"

"You sick?"

"No, I just need my foot checked." The woman leaned over the desk and stared at her wrapped foot.

"Okay. Go out door. Go left, then left again at corner. One just down street and bank too! You need change U.S. dollars for Taipei currency. They help, good bank! You pay bill every day and food last night!"

"Yes" Jade-R answered. "I will."

The town seemed lacquered in gold and vivid Chinese red. Shops made of wood boards roughly pieced together stood upright like colorful shacks lined up in a row. While she hobbled along, the language of the land flowed around her and hands reached out begging her to come in as she passed. Almost everywhere, there was a slight stench in the air from the open sewer along the road.

By the time she got to the clinic the pain was severe. The toilet paper Jade-R wrapped her foot in had slid down and her shoe was rubbing against the wound. The woman at the counter scratched information on a yellow piece of paper but stopped often to look up at the gold and ruby buttons on Jade-R's dress. Luckily only one person was ahead of her. It was a small waiting area with no windows and the only place she could sit was across from an elderly man. He kept picking his nose with his long fingernails while he browsed through a magazine.

Before long she was led to a room. She sat on a brown chair covered with some kind of plastic while waiting for the doctor. The smell of antiseptic was strong. Trying to take her mind off a feeling of dizziness, she glanced around the tiny room at scuffed walls, a table covered with white paper, and a metal tray with instruments that didn't look very sterile. For a moment she felt concerned, but within minutes a heavyset man knocked and entered the room, wiping his hands on a towel. At first he spoke to her in Taiwanese.

Jade-R shook her head.

He seemed confident as he switched to broken English and introduced himself.

"I'm the doctor. They tell me you have a bad foot?" In a relaxed manner he asked, "May I see?"

When he undid the toilet paper bandage, she noticed his eyes widen. "Yes, you do!"

With a serious tone he explained, "You have a puncture wound. It's badly infected. How did you do this?"

Grimly she explained, "I stepped on something, maybe a board. It was rather dark. I couldn't see what it was!"

"I must flush it out now," he muttered. "I'll give you a couple of shots, one for the pain."

Injecting the antibiotic into the wound hurt, but did not take long. As he bandaged it, he warned, "I want you to stay off of this as much as you can. Keep it elevated with pillows." Then he glanced down. "I'll give you some good ointment for the welts on your legs."

Sitting upright when he was finished, she tugged several times at her dress uncomfortably stretched tightly across her stomach.

"Are you pregnant?"

She looked down and quietly answered, "Yes."

"Would you like me to check you?"

Timidly she said, "Please. I have not been to a doctor."

While she put on a gown in the bathroom, she could hear the doctor whispering something to the nurse.

Even for medical reasons, she was embarrassed having a doctor probing and pushing between her legs.

While examining he questioned her. "Where are you from?"

She quickly replied, "I was born in the Philippines. My father is an American." She stumbled on her words adding, "Also my husband."

He answered, "That's where you get such light eyes!"

As he continued with questions, the nurse wrote something on a pad. Once again Jade-R could not look up when she lied about being married. Then quickly added, “My husband will be here in a few weeks.”

Now finished he said, “Everything is fine, you’re close to five months along. Does that sound about right?”

She nodded.

“Your foot is bad. When I scraped skin away I was glad there was no gangrene. You’ve not been taking care of yourself! I insist. You must rest. This is important. Be sure to come back in one week, so I can check your foot!”

By the time she got to the corner, her stomach was growling. She fanned away fumes from a dirty bus passing by as she picked the closest restaurant. It was beautiful inside. The hostess seated her near a fountain and the sound of water trickling nearby was soothing. The menu with painted cherry blossoms around the sides unrolled like a scroll. A waitress with reddish brown hair tucked behind her ears spoke with a thick English accent when she asked, “What would you like?”

“Everything sounds nice, but maybe you could bring me your favorite?” Jade-R answered. A slight smile spread across the waitress’s face when she walked away, as the row of jade bracelets slid down her arm jingling together like a pretty wind chime.

Sipping on hot orange tea, Jade-R ravished her way through the last bite of chicken and rice in the bowl. Having a full stomach felt wonderful. Looking at the bill, she realized that, although the food had been delicious, she could not afford to come here again.

It was easier than expected at the Bank of Taipei to exchange money. The comfort of air-conditioning as she waited helped her relax. Once they called a translator over, he showed her a chart on the rates, and then carefully started explaining every detail. The sight of his good-humored face was pleasant as he constantly smiled. Jade-R caught on quickly and for a few minutes didn’t feel like she was among strangers.

Nudging her way into a store, she found the bar of carbolic soap the doctor suggested she use. Wandering the narrow isle she came across hair shampoo, toothbrush, lotion, and detergent to wash clothes, then beamed with pleasure when she found the last item; a travel-sized hand iron. Holding it, she smiled at how small it was.

Before long shooting pain spread across her foot again. The shot the doctor had given her was wearing off. With thick bandages wrapped around her foot, it throbbed from being crammed in her closed shoe. She searched at another place down the street for rubber sandals worn by most of the locals. The only pair that fit was red and she immediately put them on and felt instant relief.

Walking slowly among the crowd of men and woman with woven coolie hats, she knew she needed different clothes; ones that were loose and felt good and would make her blend into the collection of people in this part of the world.

She passed a shop filled with snakes twisted and wound together in glass cages. One struck the window as she hurried by.

A foul odor saturated the next food stand that displayed strange animal bones hanging from the ceiling.

At one place she heard a baby's tiny voice in a playpen, then noticed another flung across its mother's hip. Sifting through a woven basket of clothes, she found some that were fairly priced and looked like they would be comfortable for the next few months. She picked several nice loose cotton dresses in solid colors hanging from the plastic hangers next to the wall. While paying her bill, she glanced down and saw both babies, now in the playpen crying. Jade-R smiled at the shopkeeper. Suddenly she saw the feeling of hopelessness come across the young mother's empty brown face. Sorrow cut straight to Jade-R's heart. With benevolence and a smile, she left much more money than required for the sack of clothes.

Heading back to the hotel, she became amused at the sight of an old man dressed in only his underwear. He was riding down the middle of the street on a bike held together by wire, and holding a chicken tucked tight under his arm. Every so often a car horn would honk at him and then someone would yell something, but he looked straight ahead, pedaling on and paid no attention.

It had been a full day and she was feeling exhausted carrying her heavy bags. Suddenly a skinny dog brushed against her leg as it ran past, then turned and stopped with its tail vigorously wagging. It was small and looked helpless. It stared at her, obviously begging. She said, “I have no food to give you.” The dog turned, looked ahead and trotted on. It was thin and all alone, and she wondered if that poor little thing called these busy streets home.

That night she washed her dresses and hung them wet, dripping in the shower. Propping her foot on a pillow, she picked up her pink baby blanket and hugged it to her chest, telling her unborn baby, *I love you and will take care of you always*. Turning off the lamp, she sat up in bed and looked across the street at the red dragon in neon lights. She knew she must quickly learn that just outside that window, good or bad, the world continued on and she would have to figure out how to live in it.

Most of the following morning was spent trying to rest, as the doctor suggested. The faded yellow and green wallpaper with one section pulling loose in the corner caught her attention. She studied the picture of her mother and thought about her kitten Max. But shortly after three o'clock she couldn't keep recycling the grief in her heart. She must find something new.

CHAPTER NINE

People scurried past her in the cool breeze as she hunted for the bookstore the desk clerk had told her about. It was nearly impossible to find her way down those narrow streets searching among the small clusters of shops. Finally she spotted the address the clerk had written down. She could see shelves of books through the grimy windows. Just steps from the door, a strange man with weird-looking eyes popped in front of her. A huge green lizard was wrapped around his shoulders and flicking its long tongue against his arm. His voice was bitter as he yelled something in her face she couldn't understand, then laughed and darted off.

Unnerved, she almost fell, stumbling over the doorstep to the shop, but quickly peeked back through the screen door. The drowsy shopkeeper seemed disinterested as he blew dust from the book in his hand. She asked, "Are any of these in English?" He pointed to the back wall. Only one light bulb hung from the center of the rather dark and dreary room, but the shelves were packed with interesting old books. Sifting through them, she picked several. Reading had been the biggest part of her life and she was anxious to learn about the culture of Formosa. Hesitating to leave the relative security of the shop, she waited as long as possible before stepping back out, then looked carefully up and down the street hoping the crazy man with his lizard was gone.

On her way back to the room she was eager to explore the pages of those books. It would be the distraction she needed to help dispel her dreadful loneliness.

For several weeks she left her room only to see the doctor or eat at the small restaurant next to the hotel. With no understanding of Mandarin, the official language, pointing at pictures on the menu worked. However, after just a few days she was able to identify her favorites, and could avoid the less-appetizing items.

Weeks passed. Ready once again, she ventured out to experience some of the culture from the pages of those books she had been reading.

The warmth of the morning sun on her face was soothing. The humidity was low as she strolled past shops and watched people bartering over their goods. Nearing the end of the street, something was fluttering around in a shop window. Drawing closer she smiled and was delighted to see their bright colors provided some visual relief in an otherwise dreary city. Small, ornate, wicker cages held dozens of exotic birds flapping their wings; ones that looked and sang like canaries. She enjoyed watching the interplay among the birds as they flitted from perch to perch.

In the middle of the room was a large aviary built on bamboo poles that had several large birds with long blue tails and yellow eyes. Feathers drifted through the air as a thin, grey-haired lady began throwing insects and rodents into the cage. The door opened again and the shopkeeper turned to see who had wandered in, but quickly turned back, moving with seeds from cage to cage. “You’re in my way,” were the only words she spat out.

Stepping aside, Jade-R said politely, “I’m sorry,” then added, “Your birds are beautiful!”

The older lady turned around and grumbled, “Some people enjoy dogs; I like cats and birds!” Her dull grey hair was long and straight, draping over her dry and weathered skin. A deep scar ran from above her eyebrow down her cheek to the side of her mouth. As she came closer, Jade-R caught the fragrance of rose-altar oil. Occasionally, the bird lady would scratch her head, find something and crush it between her thumbnails. She kept busy as she drank from a tarnished old cup and fussed with papers by the cash box.

Jade-R said, “Excuse me... I’ve been reading about a Gold Temple almost two hundred years old. Would you know if it’s close by?”

The lady stopped what she was doing and looked up. She stared at Jade-R’s face and down toward her bulging stomach, then shut her eyes for a moment. “Next back street,” she finally answered. "You will see it at the end."

"Thank you," Jade-R replied. "I'll come back and see your pretty birds again!" She closed the door slowly behind her.

Sun shadows lit the Gold Temple as she made her way across the road, past huge trees. Crossing a small bridge that arched over a gurgling stream, she could hear the sound of trickling water as she passed through open doors to the temple. Instantly there was a comforting sense of peace as she glanced around and took a seat. Hand carved steps, rugged and worn, led up to the large, beautiful gold Buddha. Candles were lit and surrounded the ornate base at the altar, with bowls of oranges and exotic fruit on platters mingled between small groupings of flowers. A plant was growing through the open window as if it had come to pray. She had read this temple was different. It didn't allow the burning of fake money, called ghost or spirit money, which was thought to benefit ancestors in the life hereafter. In their religious rituals this temple wanted people to worship with their hearts.

A hunchbacked old woman rose from the front row and smiled proudly as she passed by on her way out. The temple was quiet as Jade-R thought about the books she had read about temples around the world. Now she was finally in one. It was wonderfully calming; and all of her troubles seemed to lift from her shoulders. Right away, she decided this was her favorite place in Taipei. Silently she sat on the wood bench, closing her eyes and enjoying the smell of floating incense.

On her way out of the temple, she noticed a bronze pedestal engraved in Mandarin characters. She admired the letters, and wished she could understand, when an old Chinese priest approached from behind and gently touched her shoulder. He looked at her with kindness, then slowly rubbed his hand across the writing and whispered, “These grounds have been blessed.”

CHAPTER TEN

That evening the pre-monsoon heat sent bugs swarming into her room. Beetles and insects kept up a buzz like a clock ticking hour after hour as she read. The cover of the book was a soft blue and the title had enticed her into it. However the story soon took a gruesome turn about a tradition that began during the Song Dynasty and how it lasted for ten kingdoms. In those days it was a status symbol among the upper class, the affluent families, to engage in binding of the feet, in an effort to create "Lotus Feet." The feet of a young girl were soaked in hot water with herbs and animal blood. The feet, toes and arches were then severely broken and reshaped to resemble hooves, then wrapped painfully tight. This was done to girls at four years of age and they could never walk again. Girls were praised for this in the well-to-do families. With foot growth being stunted, and limited exercise, their legs soon looked like sticks! For centuries women endured the pain and had to be carried everywhere they went. Captivated with such history, learning about these young ladies' lives, she continued reading until midnight. Swallowing hard she closed the book thinking, *No longer do I want to hear about the cruelty they endured, all for the sake of status in this part of the world.* Later as the week came to an end she found herself still going over the sadness in that book.

Walking had become a favored pastime, and with not much else to do, one morning she decided to head toward the other end of town. It was easy to loose track of how far she had gone when she came to an outdoor stand. The fried meat was unidentifiable. A rugged man, teeth missing on one side, smiled as he basted what appeared to be pig blood over chickens' feet on a primitive old grill. She watched him sprinkle a dust of ground seasonings over the top. Two minutes later he flipped them to one side. Forking a well-done piece, he pointed it at her. She smiled and shook her head. "No, thank you," she said, backing away, and then continued on.

Finally there was a neighborhood where children were playing. A broken-down, rusted wheelbarrow was their source of entertainment as they took turns jumping in and out. An old man wearing a torn, dirty, woven hat flipped water from a cut-off garden hose from plant to plant in his yard.

With the window open, really loud music pounded across the yard. As if they couldn't hear it, a young couple sat completely entranced with each other, curled together on the outdoor stoop.

Further down the block was a small, bright pink-colored beauty parlor. A woman, her hair stretched tightly around plastic rollers, sat under a blue hair dryer reading a magazine. Another lady with wet hair patiently waited in the chair getting a fresh cut, occasionally glancing down to watch her long strands of hair bounce onto the floor.

As Jade-R continued on her walk, at a house nearby a man had the hood up on his car fixing something. Every so often the young lady that sat behind the wheel tried to start the engine. One too many times he yelled something that appeared to make her angry. She got out and slammed the car door. He threw down his wrench and chased after her, irritated.

Jade-R rubbed her hand across her tummy telling herself, *Enough walking, I need to rest.* She spotted a strange-looking tree with holes in the leaves and stopped. It was huge and definitely in need of water as leaves constantly fell to the ground. Again, a wave of fear washed over her. She questioned, *How can I provide a home or give my baby anything? I'll end up in worse shape than some of these people. Why didn't I take more money from the shoeboxes? But terrified as I was that night, it seemed like a lot. I sure had no idea how much it cost to live. I better figure out something quickly, some way, to get money.*

Jade-R rubbed her neck and looked up. Coming from a quaint-looking teahouse, a lady passed by and shuffled slowly down the street in her tight kimono and platform shoes, her padded hem trailing the filthy walkway. Her dark hair was piled in several large buns on her head, with orchids falling down around them. Her face, painted white, matched her white umbrella. Covered in mystery, she reminded Jade-R of a story about a beautiful geisha trained in the art of singing and dancing for banquets. The young geisha in the story was desperate for a love that never came. The white powder used on her face, neck and back, heavy with lead, caused her to have severe health problems. In the end, tragically, she threw herself in front of a car that dragged her down the road to her death.

Jade-R watched until the woman faded out of sight, hoping her life was better than that in the story.

On the long walk back she came to a strip joint, where a young boy stood at the door passing out pictures of naked men and women. *That's awful. Where is his mother?* she thought.

Next door was an acupuncture shop and through the window, she could see a man lying face down on the table. Needles ran across his back like hundreds of tiny feet on centipedes, and he appeared to be sleeping. *That's creepy*, she thought, but remembered reading that it was suppose to help with pain.

All around her, the air seemed laden with unhappiness, and she could sense that people's moods were different along these ravaged streets.

Discouraged and tired in the oppressive heat, it seemed to take hours to get back to her room. She set a small bag of mangoes on the dresser next to the seashell Connor had given her. It was stiflingly hot in her room and even after a cooling shower she still felt uneasy.

That night there was no reading and no watching the red dragon light up. She cried out for home, but didn't know where home would be, then snuggled her pink baby blanket to her heart.

CHAPTER ELEVEN

The Gold Temple was the only place Jade-R had found real comfort. Day after day she spent hours listening to the gentle water and trying to decide how to care for her baby when it came. One morning, she tried to imagine what Connor was doing back at school. Lonely, her thoughts turned desperate, thinking maybe somehow, someday, they would meet again!

After crossing over the bridge to leave, she glanced back at the Temple, took a deep breath and silently said, *Thank you for comforting me!*

It was late on a cold afternoon. She passed the Bird Shop, then turned around and went in. A tin sign in front of an iron cage said, "Formosa Blue Magpie." She knew it was a member of the crow family from the book she was reading called *Native Birds of Taiwan*. In another cage there were zebra finches glowing under ultraviolet lights and she was amazed at the fascinating little creatures.

The same older woman was putting a brightly-colored parrot in a wood- and wire-structured cage. The bird flapped its wings and tried to nip at her arm. She spoke to it softly and it calmed down. Wet coughs rumbled from the grey-haired lady's chest as she hacked up something and spit it into a paper towel. This continued, so Jade-R asked, "Do you need anything?"

Gruffly the old woman paused; then answered, "No."

When Jade-R left, she stopped at the first restaurant she came to and ordered a large container of hot-and-sour noodle soup. She circled back to the Bird Shop. Harsh movement in the air churning through the troubled sky was now blowing and Jade-R could hardly get the door open. Driven by wind, it quickly slammed behind her. A surprised look crossed the grey-haired lady's face when Jade-R set the bag on the counter. "Hot soup. It always makes me feel better!"

She smiled.

The lady muttered, “Thanks.” It was the first time in all the months of stopping by the bird lady seemed to look at her. Except, of course, that first day when she peered down at Jade-R’s tummy, closed her eyes and gave her directions to the Gold Temple.

On the way back to the hotel, another heavy gust of cold wind suddenly blew her against a wall. As Jade-R stood, regaining her sense of direction, she suddenly noticed a man watching her. Instantly she recalled seeing him before, and remembered the strange tattoo under his eye. He was the same man staring at her the other day as she left the doctor’s office. The man stomped on his cigarette, stared at her again and finally moved on. Engulfed in fear she sensed an evil darkness about him. Glancing back several times, she hurried away. Her feet moved faster and faster and then she ran, too afraid to look behind her.

A touch of relief came over her when she was safely in the room. But for several long minutes she sat on the bed asking herself, *Is he following me?*

Finally, she paused, pulling her arms close to her chest, then around her tummy to protect her baby.

By evening, the whistling subtropical wind caused blackouts in the hotel and down the street. In the loneness of that dark room her baby kept kicking under her rib. She sat straight up on the side of the bed and rubbed her back; soon it eased the discomfort. Once more she whispered to her baby, "I love you and one way or another, I will take care of you always, somehow, everything will be fine."

The following morning was calm. Sitting on the only chair in the small lobby, she enjoyed watching a family checking in. But soon she looked down at the money in her hand. *I need to open the black velvet pouch and count the exact amount left in the room.* Quickly, the adorable children distracted her worries. They were hanging on their mother's leg, until they spotted the stairs and began racing up and down.

Her attention was suddenly drawn away by several men who were pulling out the last section of broken glass blown out by the dreadful windstorm. She turned again to watch the children still bouncing around, as their parents started dragging over-stuffed luggage up the narrow stairs.

After months of paying her bill, and unsuccessfully trying to befriend the clerk, today was no different. The woman behind the counter always seemed busy doing nothing.

Outside, heavy dust was still floating from shopkeepers scurrying around to clean things up. An old woman sat on a stool, eating a banana, enjoying the activity.

Jade-R bought a couple of hardboiled eggs from the place next door and walked for her daily exercise while she nibbled on them.

A new shop had just opened and on tiny little hangers were baby clothes! With delight she sorted through, and for a few minutes imagined how cute they would look on her newborn, then bought two outfits in soft white cotton, and headed off to her doctor's appointment. She checked in and sat down for what was usually a short wait. But today time passed as she thumbed through several magazines. Just as she was beginning to think about what she should have for lunch, the door opened from the doctor's private office. Out stepped a pretty blonde lady wearing huge diamond earrings, a red suit and red lipstick. She smiled at Jade-R and with an accent said, "Hi!" Behind her was a nice-looking older man in a brown double-breasted suit.

Her doctor, standing beside them, said, "Jade-R, sorry it took so long. How do you feel today?"

Quickly she stood and replied, "I'm fine. I feel good."

The lady seemed almost giddy when she said, "You are so beautiful!"

The man with her also spoke with an accent when he added, "Yes, you are."

Jade-R smiled and said, "Thank you."

The nurse led her to the examination room, and before long the doctor came in.

"Those are friends of mine from Sweden.

Just came to visit for a few days." When he was finished checking her, he said, "Well, you are ready to have this baby!"

For some reason on the way back to the hotel she felt uneasy and didn't understand why.

That night in the room, she fussed with the scarlet-tipped sleeves on her nightgown and waited as workers turned on lanterns in the street below. Soon the red dragon lit up in neon lights. Adding up the hotel, doctor bills, food and other items for the last several months, it came as a great shock. Worried, fear became her violent enemy.

For the best of reasons, she knew, she couldn't leave her little baby with a stranger and head out to find work. *Besides*, she questioned, *what kind of work can I do?*

Abruptly she sat up in bed and listened, then realized someone was softly knocking. She tiptoed over to the door, grabbed the handle and called out, "Who's there?"

A voice answered in a quiet whisper, "Dora,

from the Bird Shop. Open the door!" For a moment she hesitated, then eased it open.

Before she entered, Dora said, "Don't turn on the lights."

Once inside she added, "Get your things quickly and come with me! And hurry!"

Jade-R asked, "But how did you know where I was?"

Dora answered, "I just know. You're in danger and you have to trust me or we're both in trouble! I'll explain later. Hurry, come in your nightgown, there's no time to dress!"

Jade-R gathered her things into her green duffel bag and pulled out the nightstand drawer to get her mother's jewelry.

Dora whispered, "Let me look out first, then follow close behind me and be really quiet."

The light in the hallway was dim as they slipped out the back and down the creaky old stairs. Dora pointed at one of the steps and whispered, "That one is broken, go to the side," then took the duffel bag from her.

"Walk as fast as you can to my car, it's at

the end of the alley." Afraid, Jade-R could feel her heart pounding when they both stopped for a moment, and then realized the noise they heard were cats clawing and hissing as they dumped over a trashcan.

Rolling down the street, Dora left the headlights off for almost a block.

As they drove on a dirt road through the night, the car would backfire periodically, and a broken spring in the seat was constantly poking her.

Dora lit a cigarette and the air from outside blew smoke back into the car. They headed toward the south edge of town.

For a while there was silence; then finally Dora said, "You're in trouble! They have men watching you and are going to kidnap you tomorrow. As soon as your baby is born they will sell it on the black market! Your doctor is in on it! That's how they do it."

With disbelief, Jade-R asked, "How do you know this?"

Dora answered, "Because years ago, I was one of them."

Stunned, Jade-R couldn't speak.

Time passed until they finally turned off the main road and pulled up to a rundown dump of a house, tucked among tangled vines with the smell of rotting wood. Dora kicked open the door with her foot. The floor was dusty and the house cluttered. "Henry," she yelled, "Wake up, you old bastard!"

She yelled again and started shaking the rickety opium bed he was sleeping in. With drool rolling down the side of his mouth, he slurred something; then he turned his half naked backside away from her. Knocking ashes off her cigarette, she kicked the bed again.

Finally he muttered, "All right, all right; but you know I like my damn privacy." When he sat up, he popped some pills in his mouth and washed them down with whiskey. "What the hell do you want?" He looked at Jade-R standing there in the small glow of light. He slipped on a robe, then started clanging bottles together and asked, "Does anyone want a gin sling?" He went to a small icebox and pulled out a tray and dumped it in a bucket. “You know I make the best. I add extra cherry brandy!”

“No,” Dora answered. “I want a passport!” “Passport!”

He said. “Who the hell for?”

Dora pointed at Jade-R. “For her and her baby!”

He laughed. “I don’t do that anymore. Hands are too shaky!” He held his trembling hand near her face.

She knocked it aside. “Shaky hands and all, you’re still the best at passports.”

“I told you, I don’t do them anymore!”

“Then how do you earn money to keep up with your woman and drugs?” she asked.

“Hell, Dora, I’m over eighty! My health is bad! Women don’t interest me anymore. Can’t get it up. Shit, I’m glad to take a piss and not see blood! So I don’t need much. Some booze, a few pills, that’s it. You ask about money? My dump rental out back, they pay on time, that’s it!”

Dora watched him mixing his cocktail for a moment, then said, "Come on, Henry! You and me have done the worst of things! You know what we've done! Give her and her baby a chance. We've both seen what will happen to them, and how she'll end up in a whorehouse!" After a moment of silence she added, "You owe me. The things I've done for you! Look at the scar on my face."

She pulled her hair back on one side and showed him her missing ear. "Have you forgotten about my ear! I live with this painful reminder! I saved your life that night. Remember?"

He stood looking at her missing ear. Still holding her hair back she insisted, "Come on, for old times, one favor. The men are after her! They already have a buyer for the baby! In fact, they met her today at the doctor's office. They're from Sweden. Let's help! Let's do something good just once!" He stood there, still staring at her missing ear.

There was silence.

Finally he grumbled, "Shit!" He squinted his eyes at Jade-R and her bulging stomach.

"Okay, just this time," he answered. He went to his desk and tugged to get the roll top up and was finally able to pull out his camera. He yanked down a white sheet as a backdrop on the wall.

Dora said, "Jade-R, go that way to the bathroom and put on a dress for your picture."

When she came back Henry said, "I'm sure you're running from something, so we'll give you a new name. What do you want to be called?"

She hesitated.

"Well, you think about it; but for now go stand over there. I'll take your picture!"

"And the papers for the baby?" Dora asked, "Won't she need those?"

Rubbing his whiskers, he dug through stuff in a box, saying, "Where are those damn forms? Oh, found them. I'll type out the separate document and when the kid comes, just put on the blank lines, in black ink only, its name and birth date. That's all you'll need. Let's see, also...Oh good, I have two left. These are International Certificates of Inoculation and Vaccination. They're approved by the World Health Organization!" He dug further. "Good, these even have the embossed stamp all ready for the Federal Security Agency. It shows you have been inoculated against yellow fever! I paid extra money for these."

Dora added, "Yes, I remember. I was with you!"

"So what is your new name?" Henry asked.

Softly she answered, "Catherine Jewel Reign."

Dora smiled.

Then he asked, "How old are you?"

"Almost seventeen," she said timidly.

He looked at Dora and said, "Let's make her older! Now, where were you born?"

She stared past him.

"Never mind" he said, as he scribbled on paper. "We'll say you are from the United States. Your English is good. Maybe San Diego, California! It's a big town near the ocean."

She nodded, adding, “I like that!”

Intentionally, he gulped down the last of his drink and popped a small sheet of thick paper in his vintage typewriter. He lit a cigarette and put it in the corner of his lips and puffed. “I’ll have these by noon tomorrow,” he grumbled.

Dora leaned down and kissed the blotchy skin on his cheek adding, “I’ll be here. Just make sure they’re ready!”

Through the haze of scented smoke, he just looked at her.

CHAPTER TWELVE

Very little was said on the way back toward town as light rain washed the hot dirty streets. Soon they slowed in front of a cemetery and turned down the road next to it. Four small houses were spaced along the gravel road, and Dora parked in the driveway at the last one.

Together they got out and Dora unlocked the door, glancing over her shoulder constantly. She quickly closed the window blinds before snapping on the light. The living room had rattan mats on the floor, a pair of flowered upholstered chairs, somewhat faded, and a small TV with rabbit ears. An old brown cat with patches of missing hair lay sleeping. They sat for a few minutes at a Formica-topped kitchen table, then Dora stood and started boiling water for tea. She opened a cupboard and pulled out a pair of light-colored cups and poured a cup for each of them.

Jade-R was shaking as she took a few sips, and then said, “Thank you for helping me!”

Dora looked down and stared at the liver spots on her hands for a while. She seemed tense. She finally spoke. “I’ve done terrible things in my life!” Then she looked back down again for a moment, in deep thought.

“I grew up in Missouri. Had a stepmom. She and my dad, well, they had their own kids. Dad was weak, and she hated me. She made him take a strap to me almost every night. I finally ran away when I was thirteen, met this Marine, and he got stationed on an island near here. I came along. It was there I met Henry from Kansas. He was almost ten years older. I had never been around someone like him, but eventually he got me into drugs. He knew this guy in Formosa. So we came here. It seemed we always needed money for the drugs, so that’s when we started working for real bad people. We did unthinkable things.”

At times she looked away while she talked. Then she would look back at Jade-R. “We sold any and everything on the black market.

Stolen jewelry, guns, and babies, drugs...” She looked down again for a few minutes. “Then, you grow old. You can’t prostitute anymore, especially with my face. So they let you go, but expect you to still be their eyes and give them a cut of your money!”

There was a long pause. She fussed with her tea bag and gazed into space. In a sad tone she said, “I once had a kid!” There was another long silence. She added, “But somehow you learn to live with what you did!” She looked right at Jade-R. “Maybe this is the only good I’ll ever be able to do. At least in this life!” She held her gaze on Jade-R for a long minute and then began to gather the cups. “You must be tired. Morning will come soon. Take my bed. Most nights I sleep on the floor anyway. It’s good for my bad back!” She pushed her hand against her back for emphasis as she stood. “I’ll leave early. There’s food, but be quiet and don’t open the blinds. They’ll be looking for you! If I don’t show up at the Bird Shop... they’re smart and they’ll put it together. I’ll leave a note late morning on the shop door ‘going to get fresh bird food’ like usual, but I’ll go pick up your passport! I’ll be back here by one o'clock."

The twin bed with faded orange sheets felt comfortable. It was humid and the swamp cooler did little to cool down the room. Throughout the night Jade-R felt feverish and sick with worry. She kept remembering the excited look on the Swedish woman's face, not realizing at the time the woman was there for her baby.

CHAPTER THIRTEEN

It was light when she heard Dora lock the door and leave. Jade-R drank a glass of milk and watched the old cat eat out of a can of freshly opened food. Branches on a tree kept banging against the house and the sound of people's voices outside were swallowed up by the wind. She went in the bathroom to shower when fluid suddenly burst from between her legs. The next few hours she doubled over from agonizing pain. She worried about what to do if Dora didn't get back in time. She knew from reading her books that many mothers delivered their own babies.

She started taking deep breaths and laid a towel across the white chipped tile on the bathroom floor. Rummaging through the drawers until she found a pair of scissors and a bottle of rubbing alcohol. The cramps were constant and hard with no relief even for a moment. She was scared when she finally lay down on the towel, propped her legs against the wall and pushed, then again, harder and harder. Sweat covered her face. Her breathing was heavy. Tortured by pain she wanted to yell, but bit down on a washcloth and braved the savage waves of pain in silence. Exhausted, she finally pushed hard one last time and saw her baby entering the world.

She had just cut the umbilical cord and looked down at her beautiful baby girl's little face when she heard the front door open. Relief flowed through her tired body as she cried out, "Dora, I'm in here!"

When she looked up the man with the tattoo under his eye was standing there!

He lifted his lips in a nasty smirk and said, "I found you, bitch!" Panic hit as he kicked her side, then reached for the baby between her legs. In that split second she grabbed the scissors beside her and plunged them into the vein in his neck, stabbing him quickly again and again. Blood splattered the wall until he fell to the floor hemorrhaging. Her hands were shaking so much she could hardly pick up her newborn as the blood began pooling across the bathroom floor.

Faintly she heard her baby's first cry. Trying to calm her breathing from the trauma, Jade-R's eyes flooded with tears.

Trembling, she heard the door open again, but remained silent. This time she looked up and heard Dora saying, "Oh damn, shit, are you hurt?"

Jade-R shook her head.

"You get in the shower and wash the blood off. I'll clean the baby in the kitchen, and hurry, we got to get the hell out of here fast!" Dora picked up the baby from her arms and kicked away the man's leg to clear the door. Nervous, Dora said, "I'll shove him in his car and burn it late tonight, just hurry! Hurry!"

When Jade-R stood, the afterbirth oozed out on the floor as she held onto the towel rack for support.

Dora said, "Don't worry, that's normal. I'll mop everything up when I get back."

With the baby wrapped in a fresh towel,

they started out the door. Dora turned, ran back and grabbed a stack of clean dishtowels from the kitchen drawer.

"Here, you will need these for diapers and some more rags for yourself."

Outside a stiff wind was blowing as they quickly traveled the back streets through town. Jade-R held her baby tightly and crouched down, then lay flat across the back seat. At a stop she could see big leaves on a tree that she had studied so often and knew it was the entrance to the Gold Temple. Quietly she whispered under her breath, "Good-bye."

Dora drove in tense silence. Words finally sputtered out, "Don't be afraid. Soon you'll be on a ship to safety!"

Pulling into the dock area, she held the baby as Jade-R climbed out. Then she handed the baby back along with a ticket, passport and a few U.S. dollars. "It's not much money," Dora said, "but it will get you some food."

Jade-R replied, "Thank you! You have already done so much!" Dora touched the baby's head again. "Maybe send me a picture or postcard someday? Now go. Please go quickly. Hurry!"

Jade-R hugged her tightly then hustled up the wood gangplank. When she got to the top, the crew pulled it up and at last, she thought, *I feel safe.*

She turned to wave good-bye just as a black car with tinted windows sped up the dock next to Dora. Three men in suits jumped out. The beating was brutal as the men delivered blows to her ribs and chest. Stumbling forward Dora fell face down but the toughness inside of her rose up as she kicked and desperately fought to survive.

At that moment one of the guys pulled out a gun as they circled around her and came in close for the kill. Pointing it to her head, two deadly shots rang out and blood poured from Dora's face. An unholy darkness surrounded her as the killers hurried to escape. Jade-R could no longer see her limp body mixed in the pool of blood now covering the ground.

She hid on one side of a door and was silent, putting her hand over her mouth to muffle the scream; "No, no, Dora!" The ship slowly backed out of port, blocking the horrific scene from her view. Suffering from unthinkable shock, she wandered the passageways completely dazed. Then she heard a kind voice.

"I'm the steward. Are you looking for something?"

"Please, I can't find my room." She handed him her passport and ticket.

"Follow me. It's right here." With kindness he unlocked her door.

In despair she sat on the bed with her new baby, numb from everything, as visions of the day's horrible events swirled through her head.

Suddenly, she felt a warm tiny hand wrap around her finger. She glanced down at the baby angel in her arms and began to cry.

With her mind ready to break, and exhausted from having just given birth, the sound of the ship lulled them both to sleep.

She awoke frightened. Wiping away the

crust from her tears, she quickly undid the towel and looked at her baby, rubbing her tiny feet and staring at her perfect little body.

In the bathroom, warm water ran over her hand and washcloth while she gazed into the mirror in disbelief. Quickly the water turned hot as steam fogged the mirror. She again felt the need to clean and rinse the tragic day off her newborn's fresh, sweet skin, then kissed her. She had never dressed a baby, but eventually got one of the white cotton outfits buttoned. Wrapping the child in her own pink baby blanket, she hummed softly as she rocked her for the first time. Soon the baby fussed, looking at her. She thought, *I know; you're hungry*. She questioned, *Am I doing this right?* Her natural instincts guided her as she breastfed the baby, who eventually seemed content. Watching her, deep love filled her heart. She knew she was blessed to even be holding this precious little girl.

"You need a name," she said out loud, while touching her soft skin, amazed at how beautiful she was.

Along with a tap on the door, a man's voice

said, "Dinner is being served in twenty minutes."

Through the door she answered, "I'm rather tired; I won't come tonight."

The steward answered, "We do have room service aboard the ship."

Surprised, she answered, "That would be wonderful," then unlocked the cabin door.

His voice was kind when he said; "I'll be back with a tray in about 20 minutes, give or take."

Softly she asked, "If you have a glass of milk, I'd really like one, or maybe even two?"

"I'm sure we do," he said with a gallant smile.

A few bites of food gave her comfort, then she quickly doubled over from cramps in her stomach. As the baby slept, she ran hot water and soap over her own tired body, trying to wash the evil of the day off.

As she put on a clean robe she heard the baby's sweet cry again. In her arms, the tiny baby stirred and curled her little hands tight as she nursed. Jade-R touched her golden blonde hair and noticed her thick lashes. Out loud she said, “You look like your father. I know what I will name you, Cherish Bodwen Reign, for I will always cherish you. Bodwen is your handsome father’s name, and Reign was my mother’s name. Yes, Cherish Bodwen Reign!”

She clicked on the bathroom light and left the door open. The room was cozy, with wood walls and a built-in bed. She cuddled next to her warm little baby. But terrible thoughts kept her from settling down. She then resolved in her mind the best she could. Stabbing that man with the tattoo she felt was a mother’s right, and she knew she would do it again to protect her newborn baby. With the night so dark, fear still seemed close by. Tears came to her eyes as she relived the day of blood. *And what if she had not had the scissors to grab in time?* She would never have seen her baby again. Feeling cold and scared, she tried to fill her head with pleasant thoughts to calm her shattered nerves. Then the image of Dora bleeding on the dock broke her down again.

It was late into the night when she glanced at Cherish. She remembered reading that children sense a mother's fear. She thought, *My precious baby just came into the world and was introduced to trauma from the instant of her birth."*

The more Jade-R thought about the day, the more it sank into her mind and became real. Again sorrow filled her heart as she thought about what had happened and whispered, "I'm sorry, Dora, so sorry. I will never forget what you did. You gave your life helping us. Thank you. Thank you again."

CHAPTER FOURTEEN

Early morning light shone through the small porthole window. She kissed her baby's soft pink cheek and hummed a song while nursing her. For a few minutes her breast, filled with milk, didn't ache as much. She said out loud to her baby, "I haven't drunk much water or milk. How could I make so much?" Then the baby gave a little hiccup, and Jade-R said, "Hmm, that's the answer for your mommy." And it made Jade-R laugh. Looking at her she said, "I loved you from the moment I knew you were growing inside of me. Now I can't imagine my life without you."

She dressed the baby in another clean little outfit and set out to find the dining room.

When they arrived they were seated at a large round table covered with a starched white cloth. In the center sat a platter of fluffy scrambled eggs, along with several bowls of fruit. A middle-aged man with a dark thin mustache sat next to an attractive, older woman and her kind-looking husband. The woman wore a light blue dress with big sunflowers that ran around the hem. Her skin was soft and healthy, with rosy cheeks and lips. Her husband smiled cheerfully as he introduced them. "We are Mr. and Mrs. Ruvo. We're glad you're aboard."

The man with the thin mustache got up to assist Jade-R with her chair. When he spoke, it was with a British-sounding accent. "That's a new one," he said, looking at the baby.

She answered, "Yes, only a few days." It was the first time she had thought about it and quickly said, "My name is Catherine Reign, and my daughter's name is Cherish."

The older couple repeated her name several times; then Mrs. Ruvo said, "We like babies and that is a pretty one," as she buttered her toast. Jade-R smiled and beamed with pride as she looked down at her baby.

A distinguished-looking man, calm-mannered and with lots of white hair, joined the group. When he removed his hat, his hair poofed out and seemed to rule over the top of his head. His important white uniform was spotless and the gold buttons were very impressive.

In a deep voice he said, “I’m Captain Anders, and this is my Chief Purser, Thomas, as he prefers to be called.”

Sitting down, the Captain looked at the baby and joked, “I don’t think this passenger will eat much!” Then he winked at Jade-R, adding, “You have a nice little one! I saw on the logs you get off at our first port?”

“Yes,” she replied, wondering where the first port was, but afraid to ask. *After all, I should know where I am heading*.

Breakfast had almost ended when the purser announced, “Yesterday they radioed us from shore that a woman was shot on the dock about the time we were leaving, and I guess she died. I hope none of you happened to see this.”

The older couple said, “No, we didn’t. How terrible!”

The Captain turned, “Young lady, and how

about you?"

She thought quickly and reminded herself that her name was now Catherine. She shook her head and said, "No, as soon as I got aboard, I was busy looking for my cabin. The steward was helpful and took us to it."

The Captain said, "Good, I was hoping nobody had to witness that."

Most of the day she rested and gave her baby her first long bath, getting to know every inch of her soft little body. She held her head in her hand and was amazed at how tiny her lips were and how beautiful and sweet she was.

Outside the small porthole window, gray clouds hung low near the water and the sun appeared too weak to even burn through the gloom. The dreariness of the day seemed to match her grief for Dora.

Roast beef at dinner was delicious, followed by peppermint ice cream, one of her two favorites, served in a pretty glass dish. While she ate, she kept one hand on Cherish lying on the chair next to her. Jade-R listened to Mr. and Mrs. Ruvo telling their vacation stories about wonderful Hawaii!

Mr. Ruvo said, “Young lady, you’re sure quiet!”

His wife quickly smiled. “But, Father, she’s shy, just like I was at that age. Besides, we do all the talking. We probably ate all the air in the room along with our dinner!”

She added, “It is too bad we can’t stay for a few days in Paradise! This will be the first time we didn’t.”

Mr. Herb, the Englishman with the thin mustache, seemed to hold a strong opinion when he said, “Why don’t you stay, then fly home?”

Mrs. Ruvo answered, “Well, it was our choice to stay longer with our grandkids in the Philippines this trip.”

Mr. Ruvo spoke up again, “I need to get home to Long Beach. I miss our dog, and by now, she misses us!”

Overhearing the conversation, Purser Thomas spoke up, “We only have several containers to drop off, and will be in port a few hours, then we’re on our way home to San Pedro. But I do know what you mean about missing your dog! We’re out to sea so long sometimes, I get home and my dog doesn’t even get out of his bed to greet me! He’s either mad at me or has forgotten who I am!”

The next day Jade-R sat on a deck chair enjoying fresh ocean air and clear sky. Cherish had her eyes open, looking up at her mother, as Jade-R said, “Maybe it’s fate! We’re going to that wonderful place, Hawaii. It’s where your father lives! I know he would think you are adorable. I saved a shell he gave me. I saved it to give to you. But I must have left it in Formosa when I packed in a hurry. Perhaps though, someday, we’ll see your father.”

Later that afternoon she borrowed a black ink pen. In the cabin she filled in the baby’s name and birth date on the papers. “Now it’s official,” she said. Then she showed her the picture of her mother. “See, this was your grandmother holding me. Wasn’t she beautiful? As soon as I can, we'll have our picture taken just like that." She kissed her feet and touched her tiny arms as she talked to her, and watched her open and close her pretty eyes and give a little yawn.

Coming back from dinner she told Cherish, "I laughed tonight. Did you hear your mommy laugh? See, Captain Anders is Norwegian. It was funny when he said, 'Norwegian blood is mixed with Sami.' That's when the nice older Mr. Ruvo said, 'Sammie? That's my dog.' That's when we all laughed! The Captain joked for a while, but soon clarified it, as Sami people, not Sammie the dog. Someday when you are older, you too, will think it's funny. And you know I'm your mommy, and you can tell I feel so happy tonight!" She stopped and turned her baby toward the full moon. "See how beautiful! It changes shape every night. But it always comes up in the east and sets in the west. My sweet baby, if we had a car and that is, if I could drive, and if there were a road --— I know that's a lot of ifs — but I would put you on the seat right next to me, and it would take approximately 135 to 138 days traveling at 70 miles per hour to get there! Your mommy has read a lot of books on the powerful sun and my very favorite, the magic moon! I'll teach you. Stars that drift around the moon are magic! They twinkle just like your big beautiful baby eyes!" Then she kissed her on the ear.

In the cabin she pulled out one of her good dresses with buttons in gold and the P inlaid with small rubies and diamonds. It was clean but wrinkled. She did not dare put her iron to it. It was silk and with no dials on the iron, she was afraid it would get too hot. Out loud she said, "I know what I'll do." She lifted the side of the mattress, and said, "I will lay it out flat and sleep on it."

Happily, she laughed to her baby, "That will be the iron. And maybe tomorrow I'll wear it! You will think your mommy looks so nice."

She washed diapers and her baby's outfits and hung them on the towel bar in the bathroom to dry. Content, hugging her newborn, and wrapped in drowsiness, she soon drifted to sleep.

CHAPTER FIFTEEN

It was their fifth day aboard the big ship. That morning huge, ribbon-like clouds curled across the azure blue sky. After breakfast she watched from a deck chair, then sang her favorite Guamanian song to Cherish as she fell asleep. When she was finished, she kissed her on both of her pink precious cheeks and said, "Cherish, I love you and always will."

Soon the older couple, Mr. and Mrs. Ruvo came and sat near her. Mr. Ruvo started dealing out cards as he said, "Get ready, Mrs. Ruvo. I feel lucky today! Let's play gin rummy!" They both laughed.

Before long Mrs. Ruvo turned and said, "Cherish is so quiet today. Even at breakfast, hardly a peep!"

Jade-R looked down and saw the baby was turning blue! She started screaming, "My baby, help me, help me!"

The couple jumped up and rushed over. Hearing the screams, Purser Thomas came running. He grabbed Cherish and laid her on a table, took a deep breath and blew it steadily into her mouth and nose, then with his fingers tapped them on her chest. Jade-R was crying out, "Mommy wants you to breathe! Please breathe!" Over and over again, they repeated the procedure.

The Captain had appeared and was now assisting. Finally he touched the purser's arm, shook his head and whispered, "Stop." Jade-R fell to her knees in shock. Moments later, the Captain covered the baby with the pink blanket. Again she began screaming, "No, Mommy can't live without you!" Jade-R crawled to the table, almost hysterical. She sat rocking back and forth as she held her baby's lifeless little body tight, sobbing, "Cherish, I love you and I always will."

Within hours everyone gathered at the stern of the ship. Jade-R cradled the body wrapped in her pink baby blanket, then placed in sailcloth, and sewn closed. Captain Anders stood beside her and said, "I was raised in a

Christian home, but for years I have not been a religious man. I don't understand this tragedy. This infant, this baby girl, will never live a full life. She was beautiful and innocent. We can guess what several things could have caused this, however, we will never be sure why she died. For years and for all of us, especially her mother, this will be hard. But for now I ask, please God, watch over this young mother and someday let them be joined again in Heaven." Captain Anders then turned and said, "Would you like to say something before she's immersed?"

Sobbing and shaking, Jade-R finally said, "My precious daughter Cherish Bodwen Reign." Then she paused, hugging her baby. Finally saying the words, "I love you and I always will," she kissed the sailcloth again and said, "I want my arms to be the last to hold you." For a while she stood there, hugging the small bundle tightly. She tried, but could not throw her baby over the side. Sobbing harder, she handed her to the Captain, bowed her head and closed her eyes.

Seconds later he put his hand on her arm

and squeezed. She dropped down by the railing and could see the sailcloth floating on whitecaps in the ocean. Quietly Captain Anders said, “We’ll leave you alone for awhile.” Hands touched her shoulder as they passed by.

Crouched against the rail, she cried as the last view of the sailcloth disappeared. She watched miles of ocean come between them as darkness fell. The night grew cold and the wind picked up. She could feel Purser Thomas place a thick blanket over her shoulders. He asked, “Can I help you to your cabin?”

She shook her head. In a weak voice she replied, “No. I must stay with her. She’s alone out there.”

“All right, but I’ll come back and check on you constantly,” he added.

Jade-R remembered Connor saying when he was born his parents rushed him back to the hospital. It was related to his heart!

Hours of thought passed as she wiped her constant tears. Sometime, well after midnight, she called out in the darkness,

"Mother, I know what happened, I know the truth about your death. When I got pregnant, father snapped and in a horrifying rage he told me he drowned you. I'm so sorry. Sorry he did that!" Crying, she said, "But I need your help!" Wiping her tears and nose she said, "I had a baby and she's out there all alone in the ocean. Please, mother, try and find her. She's wrapped in the pink blanket, the one you crocheted for me! I'll feel better if I know you have her." Still sobbing, she said, "I want you to have each other. She's adorable. Take care of her for me, please, I beg of you!"

Dawn had almost arrived along with the wet dampness that covered the deck. Jade-R's limp body was still huddled against the railing. Captain Anders put his arm around her and gently pulled her to her feet. "You can't stay out here anymore," he said.

Her eyes were swollen shut from crying; her breasts were full and leaking milk onto the front of her dress. He held onto her as they walked slowly to her cabin, softly patting her head and closing the door behind him. She pulled the drape across the porthole window and felt her life had stopped as she hugged the remaining little white outfit, breathing in the smell of her baby and crying until she had no more tears.

Daily, the Captain had room service delivered, but only a few bites had been eaten when the tray was collected. Faithfully, in the late afternoon, she would wander across the deck to the stern and quietly sink down to watch between the rails. She stared at the white foam and endless miles of ocean until the sun was gone. The Captain and the other passengers were worried. She was fading before their eyes, not eating, and had become dreadfully thin. Her shiny hair was dull and dirty, in need of washing. And now, her face and soul seemed empty.

The day before arriving in port, Mrs. Ruvo knocked again on her cabin door, and this time Jade-R answered.

“Dear, I must talk to you.” They sat on the side of the bed as she spoke. “I’m a mother and a grandmother, and I’ve never seen anyone be better to their baby than you. You doted over her and she knew you loved her."

She took Jade-R's hand. There was silence. "It's tragic what happened. Only God has the answers and knows why! But don't let this destroy your life. Take her memories with you and keep them always. This is important. Somehow, find a peaceful place for them."

Tears were rolling down both of their faces as they embraced. Then Mrs. Ruvo added, "I will pray you will be all right, and that someday you'll see your baby again in heaven."

Breakfast was almost over when Jade-R walked in. Her dress was clean and her hair shiny and pretty. However, her beautiful pale eyes were without the smile she once had, as she choked back tears, struggling to thank Purser Thomas and the other guests. She lingered with the Captain to one side of the room in private and gave her special thanks to him.

An hour later the ship docked in the Honolulu port. The green duffel bag resting on her shoulder, she turned and waved good-bye again to Captain Anders. He stood on deck watching until she cleared customs and headed up the street away from the ship.

CHAPTER SIXTEEN

With sunlight beaming down, she wandered slowly to the first corner and sat waiting on a wood bench. Before long, just as the Captain had told her, she saw a bus coming. Above the window the sign said, "Waikiki Beach." Air flowed through the open windows, and she enjoyed watching palm trees swaying as they drove along. For a moment, it reminded her of Guam. Then the loneliness hit her, and she was sad as she thought about the safety and comfort that no longer existed in her home on the hill.

It was a short trip when the driver announced Kalakaua Avenue, downtown Waikiki. As the bus drove away, she stood across the street admiring the large hotels, lush hibiscus and plumeria along the entire walk as tourists hurried by.

She turned around. The sign outside said

"Kamora Jewelry Store." In the store a lady was watching her and smiled, then went back to arranging the window display. A pink coral and diamond necklace hung from her hand as she glanced back up and smiled again. Jade-R smiled back, then noticed the lady continued to watch as she walked away.

The sound of horns from traffic distracted her, but soon she headed into a combination souvenir shop and convenience store. Spending a few minutes browsing through books and magazines, she soon continued to the little deli section, and picked a chicken sandwich and container of fresh pineapple. Waiting in line at the checkout, she glanced at the pin-up calendars, with bright pictures of girls making leis. Silkscreen tee shirts and scented coconut shell candles covered the aisle.

It was her turn and she asked the sales girl, "Do you know any small hotels nearby?" As she paid for a book and her food, the girl responded with a hurried, "Yes. Four blocks up, turn right," then handed her the receipt.

"Thank you," Jade-R whispered back.

Heading up the sidewalk she passed an interesting tailor shop where colorful men's suits and ties hung in the window. At an eating-place she lingered as the savory smell of soy sauce and fish floated out the open door.

She continued on, and then spotted a sign, Hawaiian Shangri-La Hotel. The vacancy light was on next to "daily, weekly, or monthly rates." At first she had doubts when she spoke to the strange clerk, but the price seemed fair.

With a toothpick, he dug food from between his teeth as he explained, "We don't have maids. You do your own towels and sheets. We have coin-op machines, so buy detergent!"

His foul breath reeked across the counter. Every so often he would wipe the toothpick on the front of his shirt. His eyes darted left and right as he continued, "We have an ice-maker in laundry room. Usually ice-maker works, sometimes not; try and kick it!"

His hand suddenly knocked his soda all over the counter. He looked at it, then said, "That right hand was always clumsy. I should have cut it off years ago." Then he stared over her shoulder into empty space.

Walking under the thatched roof down the open-air hallway, Jade-R thought about how unstable he seemed.

The room was dark and sparse with only a twin bed, nightstand and chair, but on the wall in a blonde wood frame was a pretty bird-of-paradise print. When she pulled back the curtains, kids were splashing in a kidney-shaped pool, floating on a plastic inflatable whale.

The room was humid. She sighed with relief when she spotted a wall air conditioner, but the knob broke off as soon as she touched it.

Carefully she hung her dresses with the jeweled buttons inside out, the cotton ones from Formosa over the top. To her surprise, in the bottom corner of the duffel was the shell that Connor had given her. She rubbed her hand over the smooth top, sighing as she set it on the nightstand.

The bed had an unpleasant, unidentifiable odor as she finally curled up, hugging her baby's tiny outfit and looking at the picture of her mother on the nightstand. It was late when she turned off the light.

Through the wall she could hear party-goers in the room next door as they laughed and talked through the night.

The quietness of early morning had become her favorite time of day. It was peaceful, walking block after block to Kalakaua Avenue. A bus was waiting as she approached. The door cranked open and the driver looked at her questioningly. “No, thank you,” she said. “But maybe you can tell me where the beach is?”

With a big smile he pointed, “Right across the street, miss.”

A lady yelled, “Wait!” as she raced to catch the bus. Out of breath, she grabbed the rail and clambered on just before the door closed.

Jade-R walked along as giant birds-of-paradise with lush flowers and pink and white-striped canvas awnings caught her attention. They were pretty and covered the tops of most windows.

Reverently, she stood watching while the ocean gently rolled along the beach. A young man was wiggling umbrellas into the sand, setting up for the day. Further down she found a secluded spot just as a cloak of sea mist surrounded her. Its sudden appearance seemed like her baby was reaching out to her.

She whispered, “Cherish, I miss you. I love you and I always will.” She remembered her baby’s golden blonde hair and thick lashes and beautiful little face. Closing her eyes, Jade-R could feel her cradled in her arms. Stricken with grief, the memory was almost unbearable. Watching the waves, the thought raced through her mind again; the terrible thing her father had done to her mother and the disdain and fear she felt. But strangely, again for a moment she missed him.

Then she remembered reading a book about other people’s shattered dreams. *After all, I suppose like everything, dreams can break.* All day the sun did not appear, and suddenly, troubled waves crashed furiously against the sand. It was late when she imagined the pink blanket floating on whitecaps beneath a cloudless sky, as lonely tears rolled down her face.

Heading back, past the luxury hotel near the sidewalk, she noticed guests returning wet beach towels, now piled high in a bin. She stopped to watch a young couple sitting on a chaise lounge eating ice cream with their baby, and her broken heart stood still.

That night in the room she counted what money she had. Scared and disappointed, she thought about the plan she came up with in Formosa, to get money to care for her baby. She would sell the buttons off her dresses. Hugging her baby's outfit she stared at her mother's picture. Again it hit her. No longer did she have to worry about caring for her baby. Now it was only herself... if she wanted to survive.

It was early. Already the yellow sun was peering through the window. She finished brushing her teeth and turned the rusted faucet handle off. Pulling out the drawer, she unzipped the velvet pouch. Briefly looking at her mother's emerald and diamond bracelet, *No,* she thought. *I will starve before I sell those. That's all I have; they belonged to my mother.* She hugged them, then picked up the buttons with small fabric pieces still attached, the ones she had torn off of her bloodstained blouse, used to protect her injured foot that terrible night. Wandering to the bathroom, she took scissors and started cutting all the buttons off her dresses. Finally, she tucked the handful of jewels in her straw clutch next to her passport and zipped it closed.

As she passed down the open-air hallway, a door stood open. A large man with huge arms and lots of muscles wearing a t-shirt was digging through his suitcase. He nodded, and said, "Hi," while kids jumped up and down on the bed.

"Good morning," she replied, then hurried on.

Before long she found her way back to Kamora Jewelry. As she entered the store, a nice-looking couple in their early twenties were trying on watches. While waiting, she turned to admire trays of rounded diamonds mounted into rings and double-crested bracelets in the showcase. Moving clockwise she read a little card: “Coral is rumored to have supernatural powers when left uncut.” Next to it was a beautiful sapphire and white coral necklace. On down an array of South Sea pearls caused her to stop. Their luster outshone the lights in the case.

Fully mesmerized, she didn’t notice the couple had left. The saleslady moved in front of her and in a quiet manner asked, “May I show you something?”

“Your pearls are beautiful, especially that strand!” Jade-R stammered as she pointed to them.

“Would you like to try them on?” the lady asked.

“Oh, no thank you. But I have a question. Do you buy gold pieces?”

When the lady smiled, her dimples deepened and her almond-shaped eyes looked gentle and kind. Jade-R unzipped her clutch and placed the handful of tissue on the counter. Immediately a medium-height man with dark hair, silver streaks beginning around his temples, and immaculately dressed in white linen, came from behind a glassed-in area. He glanced at her, then opened the tissue as eighteen buttons rolled around sparkling in the lights.

The lady gasped and exclaimed, "How beautiful!"

The man appeared more reserved as he said, "Let me get my magnifying loupe!" Carefully holding them with a long pick, he inspected each one, turning them from all angles.

"Whoever made these did a good job! The flowers are nicely done with the unusual way they pavéd the rubies and diamonds! Are they buttons?"

"Yes," she answered.

He breathed in, then sighed, as he asked, "How much do you want for them?"

"I don't know their value. I want to be fair, but I do need money!"

He paused as he took out his handkerchief and cleaned his rimless glasses, then said to the lady standing next to him, "Maybe I could turn these into earrings or a brooch." She smiled with approval. Soon they agreed on a price.

While waiting, the lady said, "I'm Mrs. Kamora, and that's my husband. I saw you in front of our store a few days ago when you got off the bus. Are you on vacation?"

Jade-R nodded her head gently, with assurance; "This now will be my home. I'm going to stay here."

Smiling, she extended her hand, "I'm Catherine Reign."

Mr. Kamora was back with crisp one-hundred-dollar bills and started counting them on the counter, then handed her the stack. "Now, young lady, don't spend it all; save some!"

"Yes, thank you for the advice," she replied. Before leaving, she shook hands with both of them.

At the door Mrs. Kamora said, "Aloha," and waved her good-bye.

Across the street Jade-R stopped and

bought white flowers, then headed down the path by the hotel. Sand gathered in her rubber sandals as she walked along the beach, but eventually she found a secluded place to sit.

Watching the water, she spoke enduring silent words, then hugged and kissed the petals on the white flowers, finally releasing them into the water.

Suddenly a rainbow appeared! It was beautiful, the largest she had ever seen, and mostly pink in color. It grew wide over the top and protected the orchids as they floated out to sea. She knew in this land of cultural family ties, that rainbow had come to join her in love, sorrow, and celebration!

At that moment she didn't feel alone, while tears ran down her face.

CHAPTER SEVENTEEN

The next day, threatening skies were on the verge of dumping heavy rain as she dashed toward the corner coffee shop. After breakfast she ordered a couple of macadamia nut muffins before walking to the jewelry store. Pushing on the door it quickly opened and Mrs. Kamora looked up and smiled.

"I thought you and Mr. Kamora might like these. They're made fresh every morning. I had one hot, straight from the oven myself." Then Jade-R handed her the small box of muffins.

Mr. Kamora came out from behind the glass enclosure. "Why aren't you home? A storm is coming," he said sternly.

As Mrs. Kamora opened the box, as the aroma came billowing out. "They're our favorite and we haven't had muffins for some time," she said. "We may be slow and have time to enjoy them with weather like this!"

Quickly Jade-R asked, "Would you like me to run get tea or some coffee for you?"

"No, thank you, dear." Mrs. Kamora replied. "We have a hot plate in back. I can fix tea."

Mr. Kamora growled, "Go. Get home before the storm hits," then took a muffin and went back to what he was doing. Leaving, Jade-R waved to Mrs. Kamora, then headed toward the Shangri-La Hotel.

Just before the rain started pouring, she ducked under the thatched roof and unlocked her door. Lying on the bed she watched the rain and dark sky and listened to the storm's fury. She realized if she were going to tell people she was from California, she needed to read about it. Then something hit the window and she pulled back the curtains. A chunk of the thatched roof was lying nearby and umbrellas were in the pool. With the scary storm approaching, the chatter of neighbors through the common wall seemed a little more comforting.

Late that night was the first time she welcomed their loud music, while hearing the sound of rolling thunder. Sitting on a chair munching an apple, she soon found herself watching a pair of cockroaches walking on the ceiling upside down. She thought to herself, *They're probably from next door, trying to escape the deafening noise of that lively party.*

Bold streaks of red and saffron spread across the sky into a grand finale by the time she got to the shop near the corner. The tailor, a trim little man with a measuring tape draped around his neck, was assisting a customer with a suit jacket as she entered. He glanced at her, nodded and gave her a brief greeting. Thumbing through a stack of ties, she chose a nautical blue and a yellow polka-dot. *These would work as a belt to cinch in her loose-fitting dresses*, she thought. *They will look good*, as she wound one around her waist and smiled.

When the other man departed, the tailor with his measuring tape still hanging around his neck turned to her. "Those are on sale, good quality," he said. "Your choice is nice; your husband should like them."

She smiled and asked, "Do you know where I can find a book store?"

"Yes," he answered. "There's a large one. It's not that far." Kindly, he found a piece of paper and wrote down directions.

A cluster of motor scooters with tourists laughing whizzed by her as she walked toward the marketplace. In front she stopped to look at the huge, dramatic banyan tree shading like a natural awning, a bazaar full of little curio shops and food stands. It was a tropical place with Hawaiian heritage and character. A couple stood with a look of surprise as they pried open an oyster and found a perfect pearl. A young boy was trying on rubber sandals, much like the floppy ones on her own feet. Smiling, she marveled at how many couples wore matching Hawaiian shirts. Just then a man grabbed the woman's arm beside him, keeping her from falling, then they noticed the brick walkway was uneven. Watching a family piling Hawaiian leis around their necks, Jade-R smiled. Before long they covered the bottom of their chins. She listened to the Polynesian entertainment group located in the middle of the bustling place.

Continuing on, she thought, “How fun, but that’s a real tourist trap.”

It didn’t take long, another block, and there was the bookstore. She had never been in such a place. From an early age back home, her books arrived by mail. She gathered several, then sat in a posture chair and browsed through the pages. Before long she picked a couple of thick ones that would give her all the information she needed to know about California and Hawaii.

On the way back, the sound of spiritual rapture poured from the open doors of a small white church and drew her in. The preacher was saying, “We must forgive people that have done wrong to us! We must not keep that poison inside! Forgive them, for you are lost without redemption!”

When he was finished preaching, a young girl stood and said, “Turn to page seven in the hymnal.” A lady at the pipe organ played “Amazing Grace,” as the congregation sang.

An older man rose and gave the closing prayer.

As people were ushered out, Jade-R stayed seated and enjoyed the gentle breeze flowing through the open windows. It brought her back to the tranquility she had felt at the Gold Temple in Formosa. She suddenly realized this was the first church she had ever been in. The platform at the front was very simple with just a podium and a vase filled with local island flowers. Simple or gold, she thought: it seemed there was a calm feeling in any temple or house of worship.

Walking alone back to the hotel she stopped for iced tea. She contemplated the preacher's sermon about forgiveness and soon her head was spinning.

How could I ever forgive my father for drowning my mother? And how could I forgive him for wanting to cut my baby out of me?

The heaviness of her thoughts muffled the babble of voices in the outdoor restaurant.

When she got to the jewelry store window,

she saw no customers inside and decided to pop in. Mrs. Kamora smiled and quickly said, "This room is always a happier place when you come see us, Catherine! What do you have in your bags? They look heavy."

"Books, I like to read."

"So does Mr. Kamora. My husband always has a new book."

Mr. Kamora came out from his glass area. "Catherine, we missed you yesterday. You didn't stop by."

Smiling happily, she replied, "Thank you. I spent the day down by the beach." Then the realization came to her: no one had missed her in a long time. She was overcome with affection for these nice people. When she started to leave, Mr. Kamora said, "Be careful you don't fall. And don't buy any more books. I have plenty I will give you."

CHAPTER EIGHTEEN

A few days later, at the office to pay for her week at the Hawaiian Shangri-La, the man behind the counter was sniffing powder along the top of his hand. A skinny guy with a rakish laugh stood to one side. Looking up, he said, "Makes you feel good. Want some?"

At first she ignored him. Then loudly he added, "Answer me."

Quickly her words tumbled out. "No, thank you." She took her receipt and backed away feeling very disturbed by the desk clerk's behavior.

As she was heading out the door another guy in a red shirt darted under a strip of yellow caution tape near dirt piled by the street. A moment later he ran past her into the office.

Now it was late afternoon. With wind

churning the troubled sky, she stacked her clean clothes in a basket and turned toward the laundry room door. Next thing she heard was laughter, and the guy in the red shirt that had been near the office jumped in front of her. He couldn't hide the nervous twitch in his neck as he blurted out, "This won't take long if you don't fight us." The other skinny guy with jitters stood by laughing.

Feeling the early stage of panic, she dropped her basket and started to run, but the sweaty guy wearing the red shirt grabbed her and slammed her head into the wall. Just inches away, the other guy doubled up his fist and hit her in the face. "Look, bitch," he yelled, "We're going to your room and have some fun." Choking her around the neck and grabbing her hair, they started dragging her across the floor.

Out of nowhere a large man holding an ice bucket appeared. He dropped it and as the lid rolled toward the corner, he yelled, "Let her go, you punks!" Then calmly, he added, "Last time I'll tell you!" His face formed into a mean look. "I teach martial arts and I'm going to send both of you sick assholes to the hospital."

The guy in the red shirt stuttered, "Hey man, we don't want trouble!" Their drug-crazed eyes stared his way; then the two of them fled.

Jade-R fell to the floor with blood pouring down her face. The large man grabbed a towel, pressing it to her head. Carefully he helped her to a chair back in the room, then left. But minutes later he returned with alcohol and bandages. Looking up she recognized him as the muscular man digging through his suitcase early one morning, while his kids jumped on the bed.

"Thank you," she tearfully said. "I'm very grateful! How are your kids?"

"Napping. We've been at the beach all day!" Helping her over to the bed he said, "You rest!"

Again he returned, carrying her laundry basket tucked under one arm, and hugging an ice bucket with the other. He took one of her washcloths and filled it with ice and handed it to her. "Now keep that on your head! Sorry I can't stay; I have to get my kids up. We catch a plane in an hour! Maybe you should go to the hospital?"

"I'll be fine, she answered slowly. "And again, thank you."

Pacing the floor for a moment, he kept looking at her. "Okay, but lock the door behind me." He looked at her again. "Are you sure you can put the bandages on?"

"Yes," she muttered. "Go."

Standing at the door, he thumped on it. "Lock this," he said, then pulled it closed and left.

Overcome with emotion, she lay on the bed with her troubled thoughts swirling out of control. She had felt safe for a while and suddenly she wasn't. *How awful if that man had not come along? The clerk at the desk had to have told them where to find me, and he knows I'm alone. He probably has a master key to this room. What if they come back thinking I'll call the police?*

She got up and slowly dragged the chair across the floor, bracing it under the door handle. Feeling warm and confused, she became dizzy, and then worried she might have a head injury. Stumbling into the bathroom she added more ice to the washcloth, holding it to her forehead. If this was a concussion she knew it was dangerous to sleep. Drinking water, she continued walking around until she was exhausted. Adding ice to her neck, she remained still. By midnight, she realized for safety reasons she needed to leave. Fleeing far away again crossed her thoughts, but after this incident she realized there was danger everywhere in the world.

The night dragged on. Sitting on the bed looking at the picture of her mother, she asked her the question, "Where do I belong? Where do I go?" She missed the safety of her bedroom on Guam and her home on the hill. "I wish I could see the servants. I miss them; they love me."

Around four in the morning she showered and anxiously put a clean bandage on her forehead. The side of her eye was puffed up and now black with smudges of blue and green. Swiftly she pulled out her duffel bag and arranged books on the bottom along with shoes, then rolled up her clothes. Finally she tucked the black velvet pouch in her purse, and headed out the door.

Fearfully, she eased the door shut, and looked around, making sure no one had heard. Heading down the road, there was a sudden burst of noise nearby and then another. Shaking with fear, soon a coconut rolled past her, and relief crossed her face. She had read somewhere the safest time of the day was just before dawn. All the criminals and hoodlums were home now resting from the terrible things they had already done.

The duffel bag was heavy and her shoulders and arms were tired by the time she got to the corner. Sitting for a while on a bench she noticed the street was nearly empty. Only a bus passed and then occasionally a car.

Before long she crossed over to the sidewalk by the hotel. She noticed a man on a small tractor raking sand on the beach. The moon was still on watch and the ocean seemed restless. Looking at the water, then back toward the moon, she quietly yelled, "I miss you! I miss your warmth in my arms! I'm so lonely."

Her chest felt heavy, and she could hardly breathe. She put her face in her hands and said, "I don't know where to go." Gasping for air, she struggled to catch her breath. Then everything went quiet. She could barely hear the sound of the water lapping the shore.

Looking down at the sand beneath her feet, she remembered how her baby's tiny hand wrapped around her finger in the cabin on the ship that first night. She took her own hand and wrapped it around her finger. The memory gave her comfort and she looked back up at the fading moon. A hint of sun was beginning to glow at the edge of the horizon. Something felt wrong. She felt sick and soon realized she was dehydrated.

Approaching the drinking fountain by the hotel pool, she drank deeply; the water was cold and refreshing. Glancing up, in a restaurant through the open doors, was a beautiful grand piano. *Do I dare?* Wiping water from her mouth, she slipped quietly into the big room. No one was around and gently she ran her hand across the keys.

Softly she played an old Guamanian song and soon, she could breathe. That part of her life had been taken away, and quickly she became lost in her music.

Before long a waiter popped in the door smiling. Then a few early-rising hotel guests began filtering in. Their movements finally caught Jade-R's attention. Blushing, she grabbed her duffel bag and hurried away.

Her favorite little restaurant offered her a warm welcome with eggs and a muffin. While she sat eating, Jade-R realized where to go, and who to trust for good information. Two tall glasses of orange juice stood empty in front of her, and the pleasant coolness from the air conditioning seemed to have relieved the throbbing pain in her head.

Arriving at ten o'clock at the entrance of the jewelry store, she spotted a customer at the counter and started to continue on, but Mrs. Kamora came running out the door after her. "Catherine, stop. What happened? Come." She took her arm.

"I didn't want to disturb you when you're busy. I can return later."

"No, he's just here to pick up something."

Mr. Kamora was finishing at the register and looked her way as they came in the store.

When the man left, Mr. Kamora asked, "What happened to your head? Do you need a doctor?"

"Actually, I'm all right."

Again he asked, "What happened to you?"

"Where I was staying, a couple of men on drugs attacked me. But I was lucky. Another man scared them away. I thought maybe you might know a hotel where there's security? But not too expensive. I still have most all of the money from the buttons."

He looked at her and paused, then took his glasses off and turned to his wife. Together they said, "The coral tree house." Then both nodded. "We have the right place. Above our garage there are guest quarters we call the tree house. My wife will drive you. When you get there, young lady, rest!"

"I don't want to impose," Jade-R hastily said. "I will pay you for my room."

Adamantly, he shook his head. "Don't worry about money! It just sits there collecting dust. At least you'll be safe!"

Jade-R put her hand over her heart. "Thank you," she replied. "Thank you."

Mrs. Kamora beamed when they left the store. The drive was beautiful. As they headed toward the eastern end of town Mrs. Kamora pointed and offered, "There's the legendary old Diamond Head!" They passed large gated homes and then turned into a hidden oasis, almost sun free. Pulling into the garage Jade-R felt she was in another world.

As they climbed outside stairs to a narrow wood deck, a huge coral tree wrapped around parts of the walls, and huge beautiful lantern lights hung down from inside. While Mrs. Kamora unlocked the door, Jade-R could see a small strip of water. "Are we near the ocean?"

"Yes, dear. It's right across the street in front of those homes. There's an opening down that road." She pointed the way. "Our home is where my husband lived as a young boy. We inherited it from his parents."

They entered a large studio with pretty, light yellow cabinets, sink, oven and refrigerator. It was a simple room, unfussy, but airy and fresh. From every window she could see the beautiful coral tree. "I'll take care of this. I appreciate all you're doing for me."

Mrs. Kamora smiled lovingly as she turned on the ceiling fan and opened the windows. "The linens are fresh, but everything else I'm sure needs a good cleaning. My husband's sister moved from her room in the house up here. That is, once she was in college. Years later when she became a widow, she would come stay with us for months on end. This was her retreat. She always chose to be up here. She said it reminded her of living in a tree house.

"We were very close, even though she lived on the Big Island. Two years ago she passed." A look of sadness crossed her face briefly, but then she continued, "Here, you'll have privacy and be safe." She set a key on the table.

"Now I must get back to the store. My husband is right. With your head injury, you must rest. We won't disturb you, but ring our bell if you need anything."

Jade-R unfolded her dresses and hung them on nice white hangers. She looked at her one yellow shoe and set it on the closet floor asking herself, *Should I throw it out?*

Feeling queasy she lay down on the bed and slept until the next morning. She awakened still fully dressed.

Outside every window it was beautiful looking at the coral treetops. A pair of brown birds with short gray beaks lined up on a branch, and she waited for them to sing. But instead she heard the sound of a waterfall.

Waiting for water to boil, she checked under the sink and discovered coconut oil and rags. Rubbing oil on the small trestle table and octagon chair, she sipped her tea and looked around. After polishing the dresser beside the simple wood bed, she placed her mother's picture close to a seashell lamp. With a wet rag she wiped the window blinds and swept the wonderful old hardwood floor. The bathroom was clean and pretty with soft pink painted walls. She moved a dish with bars of soap shaped like palm leaves to one side and put her tortoiseshell brush and comb on the counter. Exhausted, she showered and laid down and slept straight through until the next morning.

CHAPTER NINETEEN

There was the murmur of water and voices through tall plants. Jade-R went out on the wood deck and called, "Aloha, Mr. and Mrs. Kamora!"

Mr. Kamora answered back, "Come, have black coffee."

Entering their garden, she was awestruck by its beauty. She passed soaring tropical trees and a group of planters with ferns and flowers in bloom. The floor was lava stone with moss growing between the pieces.

Mr. Kamora was standing by a waterfall cascading down to a group of colorful koi fish. Holding a dish, tossing food to them, "Here," he said. "Give them some lettuce. They also like watermelon."

"That white one, it's huge." Jade-R said, then smiled, admiring the graceful way they swim.

"Yes, the big white one, his name is Surf. And the red one, her name is Ruby. Surf is friendly. He comes up for his daily pat on the head. But his love is Ruby." Mr. Kamora added, "They've been together twenty years."

Intrigued, Jade-R said, "Please tell me more about your beautiful koi."

"They are descendants of carp. In the 1600s Chinese bred them, creating koi. The royal families immortalized them in art, et cetera. Even today you'll see them in paintings and embroidered onto silk hangings under glass. It was probably around 1900 they became desired in Europe and the United States when it was discovered they can become like a pet!"

She listened. Then finally asked. "Surf, is he considered normal size for a male?"

"He's a big guy, about three feet in length, and Ruby, almost two." With pride, he added, "Mine are considered on the larger side." He smiled. "With this filtration system, I could hold more, but I like lots of room for them to play."

Curious, she softly asked, “Do people eat koi?”

He smiled again. “Koi or carp meat is a bit tough. You could, and people have. But I don’t think it would be that good!”

“Have you always had fish?”

“I was in middle school when my father built this pond. Together it became our common interest. Through the years my father taught me everything. It was his hobby. Standing beside him, we’d talk and I learned to enjoy them as much as he did.” Pointing around to the ferns, he said, “We planted all this. Koi fish can get sunburned. So we created all this shade for them.”

Then he shifted his attention to Jade-R. “Say, enough about the fish. How does your head feel?”

“Much better; at least I have no more headaches. Thank you for asking.”

Mrs. Kamora came with a tray to the open lanai. “Aloha,” she said quietly, then pulled a tube of cream from her pocket. “Use this twice a day. We don’t want a scar on your beautiful face."

Several carved wooden chairs with green marble inlaid seats encircled the table. They were heavy and required tugging to pull them out. Mr. Kamora grinned as he said, "That's your exercise for the day."

Smiling, Mrs. Kamora added, "They're heavy. I remember when we bought them; now we're just used to them."

"Thank you," Jade-R said. "This breakfast is so good! I haven't had cereal in a long time."

"Cream of wheat with banana and sugar. It's my husband's favorite."

"Yes," he added. "With lots of brown sugar. Oh, and if you don't eat your plate of watermelon, don't forget the koi like it!" Even though it was the first day, she found sitting together with Mr. and Mrs. Kamora remarkably comfortable and easy.

"I noticed Diamond Head is close to here," Jade-R said. "I have a book about it, but I haven't read it yet. Have you been inside the crater?"

“We have,” he answered, “and when you get to your book you will find Diamond Hill was the name British sailors gave it. They thought they had found diamonds in the beach sand, it sparkled so much. But actually, it was really just calcite crystals around the bottom of the crater.”

Proudly Mrs. Kamora added, “My husband has his degree in geology. And since he is a jeweler, he also became a certified gemologist for gemstones.”

Mr. Kamora looked at Jade-R. “Can you tell she’s proud of me?” Adding, “When you read your book, you’ll learn that from the floor to the top of Diamond Head is over five hundred feet. Truly we believe the view at the top is worth going to see! It’s our big attraction in Hawaii. Sometime we’ll take you there.”

When they finished eating, Mrs. Kamora said, “I will drive you to the Food Store. You need groceries, and I’ll show you where to find the bus. Then you can go places if you wish. Oh, the washer and dryer are in the garage along with plenty of soap. Feel free to use them.”

"Thank you for everything." Jade-R politely said, as she watched a gecko run across the table while Mr. Kamora read the paper.

Somehow the day hurried past. Washing the windows several times she realized they were clean. They just had small, fine scratches. Then she scrubbed a teakettle with its insides full of lime.

By late afternoon a swelling of sadness overwhelmed her. She turned toward the ocean and knew she must go. Crossing the street she heard the lapping sound of water on the shore. There were miles of white beach in front of magnificent homes with endless views. At a turn in the shoreline, she soon found a more secluded spot. The mood of the ocean seemed different. As she sat on the beach looking at the waves, the glowing silhouette of the sun dipped below the horizon. She thought, *I'm sure mothers who lose a baby grieve in many different ways.*

She remembered Mrs. Ruvo telling her in the cabin on the ship, "Take your memories with you and keep them always. But find a peaceful place for them." When she stood, it seemed the moon she loved reached down to her and said, "It's been awhile; let's talk. Come walk with me!" She began to wander along the beach and a comforting thought suddenly filled her heart.

Maybe by now my mother has found my baby. And for them, a beautiful sand castle under the sea. And yes, Cherish may have a seahorse to ride!

In the daylight they could gather shells,
And fill vases with coral flowers.
And maybe in this magical fairyland,
She would have a little girlfriend!
A mermaid to swim with, laugh and play,
in this magical fairyland.
Out their windows they will see a colorful parade of fish go by.
I know at bedtime, my mother will hold my baby in her arms, and sing her a lullaby.
And for me they will always be together,
in their beautiful sand castle under the sea.

The night sky was serene when she looked up. The moon was smiling as brightly as a starburst, lighting a path across the water, and finally her heart was calm.

That night in the coral tree house brought her the first peaceful sleep since she had fled from the Island of Guam and her wonderful home on the hill.

CHAPTER TWENTY

The following morning birds again lined along the tree branch outside the window as Jade-R reached for a book.

Mr. Kamora called out, “Are you up? We have coffee!”

When she entered the garden, he was tending to the koi fish. “Here, pet Surf! Today we’ll give him peas! Look, he enjoys your attention.” Ruby dazzled them by swimming around as she waited her turn.

“Come, let’s eat!” Mrs. Kamora called.

Mr. Kamora turned to Jade-R. “My wife is like a dinner bell!”

Her dimples deepened as she smiled. “It’s warm out already. Muffins, fruit and coffee, that’s it today!”

Breakfast together became their morning routine, and quickly they formed a close bond.

At night, she enjoyed the enchanting beauty of the Japanese lanterns lighting the coral tree outside her windows.

One morning Mrs. Kamora called out "Jade-R," as she came through the gate holding her umbrella. "Come inside; it's cold and rainy."

The floors were dark mahogany and the kitchen cabinets a crisp shiny white. The walls were painted in soft lavender. A huge rolling cart held a colorful array of purple orchids, and trays of assorted island fruit. The coffee steamed from the pot while they perched on old cane bar stools eating hot cereal. It felt good being together, watching rain sweeping across the land and birds hurrying for cover.

Mr. Kamora took off his glasses and laid them on the counter as he picked up the newspaper, then seemed deep in thought.

Mrs. Kamora asked, "Did you forget something?"

"No, honey. I was just thinking about that

customer yesterday." He turned to Jade-R.

"This was interesting. About a month ago this German man, tourist, a complete gentleman, came to our store. He bought a very expensive gold watch, paid cash. Then he had a request. Could we hold it for a few days? Said he had to go out of town on business. We didn't ask 'Why don't you take it with you?' We were accommodating, just said that will be fine. Time went by and we tried to call but couldn't read the phone number he wrote down. We started to get worried about him. But yesterday, he showed up! Said he lost his receipt while traveling in Mexico and couldn't remember where he had bought it! Apparently he had gone to several other jewelry stores before ours. When he left, there was a big look of relief on his face and repeatedly thanked us. We were happy that story had a good ending."

Mrs. Kamora added, "Yes, we still have customer merchandise in our safe no one has come for and it's been years! Especially on repairs. Speaking of years," Mrs. Kamora said, smiling, "Tomorrow is our anniversary!"

Mr. Kamora added, "Yes, I'm a lucky man!

My wife has given me thirty of those filled with love and devotion!" Then he winked at her and went back to reading his paper.

"That's nice you've been married so long!" Jade-R replied. "Please sit and enjoy your coffee. You never let me do the dishes. It's only fair. You prepared all the wonderful food; the least I can do is the cleanup." She paused, and then added, "I have wanted to ask you this. I know how to run the vacuum and I can dust really well. Would you let me help with your housework? I could work with you and you could show me how you like things done." Mrs. Kamora looked at Carl. "That would be nice; I'd like your help."

For the first time that morning with rain falling, Mrs. Kamora waved her hand and said, "All right, mahalo" as Mr. Kamora smiled. Then he added, "We have noticed you rake leaves, hose the patio, and water everything around here."

Smiling, Mrs. Kamora said, "And don't forget, Carl, we know she sweeps out the garage all the time. It's spotless."

The sun was in full force as Jade-R took a seat on the bus and headed for the Food Store. She went down each aisle carefully selecting her items. Before long she was back riding the bus toward home.

When evening arrived, she heard the garage door open and hurried to light the last candle next to a cake. As the Kamoras came through the gate they both said, “What have you done? What a nice surprise!”

At the table Mrs. Kamora added, “Yes, all day has been a surprise! I always wanted a blue diamond solitaire to go with my eternity band.” She lifted her hand and the candlelight sparkled off her ring.

He chimed in. “And it was way past time, but also difficult keeping it a secret from her while I was making it!”

Smiling Mrs. Kamora added, “And this was wonderful. He closed the store early and took me to a small restaurant, one we always went to when we were young and dating.”

He laughed, “Fortunately for us, the food is still delicious!”

Admiring the ring, Jade-R said, "It's so beautiful! The design simple and elegant."

Mr. Kamora spoke up, "Wait before you cut the cake," and then hurried to get his camera to snap a picture of his wife's hand outstretched next to it. The evening was cool and the air was soft, like touching cashmere. Occasionally a leaf drifted down from the trees as they talked.

They were sipping coffee when Mr. Kamora sternly said, "And another thing, Catherine; we do not want you to call us Mr. and Mrs. Kamora any longer. It's too formal! We are Carl and Lum from here on."

Pleased, she answered, "Thank you. I like that." Then she asked, "How did you meet?"

His face shone with pride and love as he said, "Lum was working in a Hawaiian shirt factory, and doing the best she could supporting herself after her parents had died. Her older brother took off to go make millions somewhere out in the world. One day I came in and she waited on me. Instantly, I mean instantly, I was smitten. Right then I asked her out. At the end of that year, I finished college and we both knew this was it! We were happy when we were together." Looking over at Lum he gave her a special smile again.

Perhaps it was her exquisite blue diamond ring, along with their magnificent cake loaded with white frosting, covered in grated coconut and topped with fresh orchids that captured the evening. Maybe it was the romantic Hawaiian music that played as candlewicks flickered.

Nonetheless, when Jade-R turned to close the gate, she could see Carl take Lum's hand as they began to dance.

CHAPTER TWENTY-ONE

One evening, a knock at the door caused Jade-R to jump up, half asleep. The book on her chest slid to the floor.

"Are you accepting guests tonight... that is us, bringing chow mein dinner."

"Yes, most definitely," she replied, as they entered.

Carl set the food down and immediately said, "This looks nice. You moved the table over here!"

Jade-R quickly answered, "I hope you don't mind," while taking plates and napkins from the cabinet.

"No, it's better. This room seems larger."

Admiring the photo beside the bed, Lum asked, "May I?"

"Of course," she replied.

"Is this your mother, and you as a baby? She's gorgeous and you have her eyes!" Lum handed it to Carl.

Jade-R nodded. "That was taken just before she died. I was almost two and a half."

"How did it happen?"

At first Jade-R didn't know what to say. "It was an accident; she drowned in the ocean. I never got to know her. That picture is as close to a memory as I have." Then suddenly her eyes filled with tears. It struck her she had never talked to anyone before about that.

Lum quickly said, "I didn't mean to make you sad."

"It's a long time ago." Jade-R replied, and wiped her eyes.

"You were a beautiful baby and it's a wonderful photograph. Looks pretty next to the white orchids." Lum added.

While they ate, Carl glanced up. "I need to oil that fan."

Jade-R laughed. "I don't mind; it sings me to sleep at night."

When they finished she said, “Oh wait,” and began to dish bowls of mango ice cream.

Again he looked up at the squeaky ceiling fan moving the air and said, “This is a nice evening. I haven’t been up here in a long time.”

He reached in his pocket and pulled out a small box, which he placed in front of Jade-R. She looked at Carl and Lum and slowly opened the lid. Her gold-flowered buttons rested on velvet.

Quickly he put his hand up. “Wait, before you say anything. From the first day we met, we saw such sorrow in your eyes. Lum and I wished we could help. You’re a well-educated young girl, elegant and quiet. No one has a flawless life. We’re not here to ask for details as to what happened. It’s just...well; it brings us joy, seeing you feel better. We want you to know this will be your home for as long as you want.”

Her pale blue eyes filled with grateful tears as she touched her heart and said, “Thank you.”

CHAPTER TWENTY-TWO

Early one evening Jade-R heard Carl yell, "Catherine!" She hurried down the wooden stairs and through the gate.

"What is it?" she called. "What's wrong?" Lum was bent over groaning as Carl half-carried her toward the car. "I'm not sure what it is, but we're going to the hospital!"

"I'm coming with you," she insisted.

The drive seemed endless as Lum moaned, "These cramps are severe. I can hardly take it. I feel so nauseated." Jade-R held her hand tightly. Her creamy skin was pasty white as Carl threw the car in park at the emergency entrance.

Rushing in, Jade-R got to the counter and begged, "We need a gurney outside fast!"

Minutes later they watched as Lum was wheeled off. Carl's hands were shaking when he said, “All day I could tell she didn’t feel well, but when I’d ask, she’d say ‘I’m fine. Just tired. Didn’t sleep well last night.’”

Jade-R put her hand on his shoulder. “How could you know? But now she’s here! They’ll find out what’s wrong.”

When they glanced up a tall, important-looking young man was headed their direction. In a strong, confident voice he said, “I’m Dr. Garrett Eastman. I’m taking your wife into surgery immediately! Her appendix ruptured and she has a fever of 102. Has she eaten anything today?”

“No, “Carl quickly answered. “She wasn’t hungry. She never complains. She started getting nauseated and just thought it was the flu, so we went home early from our store.”

“What caused this?” Jade-R asked.

Dr. Eastman looked directly at her as he said, “She has a blockage and it causes a buildup of mucus, parasites and fecal matter. I have done many appendectomies. They’re prepping her now. I’ll come back when I’m finished. I will keep you updated.”

As he walked away, he turned and tilted his head with a reassuring nod.

A nurse said, “I’m sorry, we have one more paper for you to sign, Mr. Kamora.” She added, “You’re lucky he’s on call tonight! Dr. Eastman is our favorite surgeon and the best! We nicknamed him Top Blade! He’ll do a good job. Don’t worry.”

It was warm in the waiting room but the chairs were comfortable. Jade-R patted Carl’s shoulder several times as Carl dropped his head into his hands. As they waited he looked at his watch. “She’s been in there quite awhile,” he said, his voice cracking.

Finally Dr. Eastman appeared. “Everything is fine.” He smiled as he added, “She should recover without complications.”

Carl, trying to ease his tension, said, “I thought children had this surgery.”

Dr. Eastman answered, “They’re not the only ones.” He turned his attention to Jade-R. “You would be surprised! I have patients every age go through this.” He had not taken his eyes away from her when he added, “If she has no temperature tomorrow, I may remove the drainage tube and release her in a few days." He patted Carl's arm.

Before he walked away he said, "You can see her soon, but she'll be out most of the night. The two of you go home! Get some rest."

When they entered her room, Lum was hooked up to several monitors, with IV drips in both arms. Her eyes were tightly shut.

Wiping away tears, Carl clutched her hand and whispered something close to her face. He kissed her forehead several times before they left.

Jade-R awoke early the next morning. She hurried down the street to the bus and rode to the little coffee shop she used to go to. She bought a pineapple muffin and juice to go. At the convenience store next door, she picked out a small bouquet, and then waited for the next bus.

Lum's cheeks glowed with color and her dimples deepened as Jade-R walked through the door. “Aloha, dear. I’m happy to see you. How did you get here? Carl just left.”

“I rode the bus. These flowers are for you.”

“They are beautiful, dear.”

“Are you in pain?” Jade-R asked.

“Not really. But I need help walking to the bathroom. My doctor is great. He has come to see me twice already today. Oh, and he asked if you’re our daughter. I told him you are family. You are just like our daughter. I think he likes you.”

Jade-R smiled, “Did he say when you might get to come home?”

“I’ll know in the morning.” From a tray alongside of her bed, Jade-R fed Lum a few bites of orange gelatin and some juice.

“I haven’t had Jello for a while. It tastes good.” She wiped her mouth. “Dr. Eastman said I could have cooked chicken and rice soon. But today it’s everything bland!”

Anxiously Jade-R waited as their car pulled in the garage. Quickly she ran to open the door and assist Lum who was dressed in a silver-tinted robe. She squeezed Jade-R's hand tightly. They stopped for a moment to see Surf and Ruby at the waterfall. Soon Carl helped her to the living room. "I asked Catherine to stay and watch over you," he said.

"Yes, I want to help," Jade-R added.

"I'll be home early and don't forget what Dr. Eastman said. Stay off your feet, rest." He kissed her, then turned and stopped. He shook his head as he said, "Guess what, Lum? Our Catherine has been busy. She asked me yesterday if she could dust and vacuum the house. Then she rode the bus to the Food Store. Our kitchen is stocked for dinner and breakfast." Shaking his head again, he waved good-bye.

For a while, Lum and Jade-R sat drinking tea.

Looking around, Lum said, "You know we don't spend enough time in here." Glancing at the lavender marble Fu dogs on each side of the fireplace, she sighed. "It seems we watch TV in the den these days." She rubbed her hand over the beige sofa, then leaned back against the lavender and purple striped pillow. "Oh, how pretty! You put an orchid in that porcelain pot. It looks wonderful!"

"Thank you," Jade-R replied, "but in this room, it's your rug I love!"

Lum smiled. "Yes, I do, too. Especially against dark wood floors. Every time my sweet sister-in-law would come to see us, she'd say, 'Back at home I have the perfect rug with purple and lavender for this room.' Shortly before she died, we got this huge long thing rolled up. It was delivered with a note." Lum choked back tears as she said, "The note was simple but so special."

'Just think of me when you look at this rug, and I'll be looking down, thinking of you.' " Then Lum stared at the gorgeous rug.

Later, they walked arm-in-arm down the hall past a curved bamboo cabinet filled with treasures and through a double-door entry that led to the master bedroom.

Jade-R brought her a glass of water and said, "You probably need sleep. I'll check on you later. If you don't mind, I'd like to fix dinner.

When Carl returned home, he and Jade-R carried trays of piping hot beef broth and rice soup into the bedroom, where the three of them enjoyed a quiet evening together, telling stories.

Carl left early the next morning. Jade-R opened the shutters and moved Lum to a chair. She sat and watched as Jade-R changed the sheets. When she finished, Lum said, “It’s been days since I’ve showered.”

“I can assist you!” Jade-R said. When they finished, she handed her a towel, then helped her with a clean gown.

“That was good exercise. I’m tired, but I feel human again. Thank you, dear,” Lum said with a smile. Laying her head against the fluffed pillows in bed, she looked at Jade-R, and then spoke softly. “After Carl and I were married, we talked about having children. I miscarried twice in the first three years. Again I became pregnant. We had just opened our store when I was seven months along. One Tuesday morning, I woke up bleeding. I gave birth to a baby that afternoon in the hospital.

It was a boy! But our happiness did not last. A week later he died. We named him Cameron Carl Kamora. We tried, but I never conceived again." Then she was quiet as she wiped her tears.

Finally, Jade-R asked, "How did you get through that?"

"It was difficult. But we had each other. Later we planned on going to an adoption agency. However, Carl's mother became sick and died a year later. We were trying to keep our business going. Time just got away. I feel bad. Carl would have been a wonderful father, and I would have loved giving him a family." The room was quiet for a while. As she smiled, Lum said, "I must admit, my husband has been so happy having you here. I know he thinks of you as the daughter we didn't have." She took Jade-R's hand and squeezed it.

CHAPTER TWENTY-THREE

One evening it was just getting dark. Lum was preparing dinner when Catherine arrived. "We wondered where you were and just about to get worried," Lum said, while placing fish on a pan in the oven.

Jade-R looked at Lum, and then quickly toward Carl. "I need to ask you something."

"Of course," he said, taking off his glasses.

"You know every morning you give me the paper to read? Well, today I looked in the job section! I rode the bus to the White Sands Hotel and had an interview with the general manager. In the end, he asked for my identification. I showed him my passport and filled out a form. They want me to start work this Thursday! I won't unless you both approve." She was silent, looking at them hopefully.

Carl took a sip of iced tea. “Would you be a hostess?”

“No. They hired me to play the piano in the Orchid Room!”

Lum turned around from the oven. “You must play quite well.”

“Yes.” Jade-R answered. “I was given private lessons twice a week, for eleven years.” Nothing was said for a moment.

Then Carl asked, “How many days would this be?”

“It’s evenings for dinner.” Jade-R replied. He took a deep breath, then set his tea down again.

“What time do you start, and what time do you leave?”

“I must be there by five o’clock and leave no later than eleven. It’s Thursday, Friday and Saturday!” she answered.

Carl looked at Lum. Then said, “You must take a taxi from the hotel home. Riding the bus on the way there, that time of day is fine. But we insist you take a cab at night.” He smiled at Jade-R with pride. "If that's all right, we see no problem with you playing the piano in the nicest restaurant in Waikiki!"

During dinner Lum asked, "What type of music do you play?"

"My favorite song is 'Clair de Lune.' It means, 'light of the moon,' or 'moonlight.' But, I enjoy Beethoven! In fact, the greatest work he did was when he suffered deafness! Frederic Chopin, though, he loved the piano! His études are challenging but quite pleasing." Jade-R smiled. "Now, my teacher's favorite was Brahms. She's German and he was born in Hamburg where she's from. Naturally she was partial. But he did compose some of the most beautiful music in the world. At first I didn't like the fact that my teacher made me learn about the composers, as well as their music. Now I'm grateful."

They both looked at her, then Carl asked, "Is that what you'll be playing?"

"Only if requested. More likely it is 'Blue Hawaii' or 'Stranger in Paradise,' more American standards!"

Before dinner ended Jade-R turned to Lum and said, “I need to buy a few pretty dresses. Do you know where I should go?”

Lum’s face lit up as she quickly answered,

“Yes. It’s not a drip-dry or wash-and-wear place. This shop is very exclusive. It has the best. I’ll tell you what; at two o’clock tomorrow I’ll drive us. We’ll have fun picking your dresses out together. And oh, we must get you high heels.” She laughed as she added, “You like my Cherry Red lipstick. I’ll buy you a tube!”

Carl leaned back in his chair and smiled as he listened to them make their plans.

As Lum pulled into a space, Jade-R noticed the light pink building with tree ferns framing the front door to welcome arriving customers. Inside, three walls of mirrors encircled a platform where a woman stood admiring the dress she had on.

A saleslady said, “May I assist you?”

“Yes,” Lum replied. “We’re looking for

something very elegant." She took Jade-R's arm and added, "It's for her."

"The bridal section is in here. Would you like a glass of champagne while you shop?" the saleslady asked.

"No thank you." Lum quickly replied. "Just several formal evening dresses, please."

The saleslady smiled. "I'm sorry, I thought she was a blushing bride. Come in here. This section has beautiful dresses."

Satin hangers held a row of tea-length dresses in various colors. Lum pulled out a white dinner suit with black beads on the collar. "This is pretty. But maybe not quite youthful enough, probably more my style."

"Over here," the saleslady said. "This is our recent collection. It just arrived yesterday. New from Paris. Anything would be wonderful on you."

Jade-R had never seen a jacket with pink rabbit fur on the collar and cuffs. Lum smiled, then handed her a pale blue chiffon dress, with a high-banded waist. Dress after dress in several styles and colors were stunning on her petite figure. As Jade-R stood on the round platform with curved mirrors, other customers in the shop turned to "ooh" and "ah" with admiration.

Jade-R asked Lum, "Which two should I pick?"

"All of them," she answered.

"What? No. I only need two; besides, they are expensive."

Lum took her hand. "Carl and I talked, and it's our treat. We want you to have plenty of nice new clothes." She nodded several times and smiled.

Jade-R protested again, "But all of these will cost so much; two will be fine."

Lum shook her head and immediately said, "We'll take them all."

The saleslady arched her narrow brow, "You were right. A simple tailored look is the most elegant on her. And what you have selected will last for umpteen years."

They laughed and chatted all the way home, boxes stacked on the back seat, filled with the well-assembled look, along with a pair of the inevitable black gloves, and a bottle of French perfume in a fancy little sack. Included were lavish gold tubes of lipstick and nail polish, in various shades.

Jade-R said, “Thank you, Lum. I’m so grateful. It’s the first time I’ve ever shopped with anyone. This was so much fun! I will never forget today.”

Lum smiled again. “Neither will I; it was a good day for both of us, dear.”

CHAPTER TWENTY-FOUR

Jade-R stood calmly at the entrance to the Orchid Dining Room. Her black heels were high and the beautiful silver sheath dress accentuated her extremely tiny waist as she looked around at the entrance. She took a deep breath and gazed for a minute at the spacious room.

Big palm fronds dropped in vases of fresh water sat at each end of the bar. Pink sand-filled hurricane lamps, with candles lit, were underneath a huge mirror behind a row of liquor bottles: bottles that reflected the sun setting over the ocean. She carefully descended the three steps into the dining room, and then quietly walked between booths that resembled open clamshells, toward the white grand piano. Waiters were setting arrangements of orchids and night-blooming jasmine on starched white tablecloths. Walls of doors were folded open, allowing the gentle air to flow through.

She lifted the lid up on the piano and then from the bench, took out a thick notebook filled with sheet music. It felt natural as she stretched out her hands and began to play her favorite song, “Clair de Lune.”

The Orchid Room was dominated by romance! Before long a flurry of people were being served butter-crusted prime rib and mahi mahi with grilled pineapple. As the rhythmic sound of the tide gently rolling in accompanied by the piano, the night began.

An older, elegant black man in a white Panama hat and a grey suit headed to a table near the corner. He looked toward Jade-R, took off his hat and nodded. Instantly a waiter placed a drink in front of him. Later without ordering, he was served dinner and while dining she noticed he carefully watched her play.

Crystal from the chandeliers bounced light onto the ceiling as her fingers trickled down the keys and beautiful music filled the room.

The evening seemed to pass swiftly. She had just closed the lid of the piano and was putting away the notebook when the manager stepped up.

“You did great tonight! Everyone enjoyed your playing. Especially Mr. Davis. He’s the older gentleman that sat over at table 36.” He pointed toward the direction of the table in the corner. “He told me several times throughout the evening, ‘Do what it takes to keep that girl.’ ”

She smiled and said, “He sent me a request. It was to play the last three songs over again. So I did!”

“You will see him a lot and get to know him well. He’s a retired maritime lawyer and one of our favorite people. In fact, he lives here in the hotel. Has for years.”

He quietly added, “On the top floor!” He smiled again and said, “But what a gentleman and an interesting man. Maybe sort of eccentric, some say. He has this really big cat and walks it on a leash through the lobby to the grounds outside.”

Then the manager held up two fingers as he whispered, "He does that twice a day. But he's good to all of us. We are very fond of him." As the manager started to walk away, he turned back and said, "Again, you did great. See you tomorrow night."

She strolled with pride to the front entrance of the hotel. And to her surprise, Carl and Lum pulled up just as she stepped outside.

"We wanted to make sure your first night went well." Carl said, and as she climbed in, he pointed. "See, there's where the taxis are."

"Thank you, and thanks for picking me up."

"How was your evening, dear?" Lum asked.

In a happy voice she answered, "The time went fast. I enjoyed myself. Everyone is so nice, and I even made ...tips. If every night is like this, I'll have cab money and you won't have to worry about me."

CHAPTER TWENTY-FIVE

It was Saturday night. Jade-R straightened her tea-length coral dress across the piano bench and began to play.

The first request came from the very elegant Mr. Davis who personally walked up and introduced himself. He looked dashing with his silver and bone-handled cane hanging from his arm as he spoke. "I must tell you these are my favorite songs. I would enjoy it as the night ticks on, if you could play some of them." He handed her a small piece of paper.

She opened it, and then quickly looked up. "Most definitely. I would be delighted. And it's nice to meet you, Mr. Davis," she added.

"Thank you," he said. With a generous smile he headed to his usual table and the bustle of waiters who stood hovering around it.

In the middle of a song she was playing for

Mr. Davis, she glanced up to see a sophisticated-looking group of people just arriving. The maître'd began escorting them toward a long table set with fancy chocolates scattered around the flowers, place cards in front of dinner plates, and fan-folded gold napkins. Her breathing slowed and she missed a note as Connor Bodwen entered with friends and ordered a drink at the bar! He turned to the guests now seated at the table, then glanced over to the piano. His eyes widened. Then he gulped down his drink and gravitated toward her.

As he approached she still remembered his scent, and her heart trembled with conflicting emotions.

"Hi," he said. "Wow! You are beautiful!" The room seemed quiet, except for martini shakers in the background and the pounding of her heart.

He stood looking at her. Then he asked, "Do you know 'Stardust'?" Excitement rose inside of her as the memory of number 13 playing on the jukebox, and their romantic evenings in that little booth in the hamburger joint quickly returned. She was thrilled knowing he hadn't forgotten. But then he just looked at her.

Thoughts swirled in her head. *He's stunned. Over a year and half has passed. That's it. Should I speak first? I'm nervous. No. I'll wait for him.*

But still he said nothing.

Finally, she answered. "I do know that song; it's one of my favorites." Swallowing her emotions, she straightened her shoulders and began to play.

He glanced down at her once more, and then headed back to his buddies at the bar.

Before the song ended, he returned with drink in hand to stand near her at the piano.

"Have we met? I'm Connor Bodwen! What's your name?"

"Catherine Reign." She started to add, *but you knew me as*...but again, a voice inside told her to stop.

He raised his hand and said, "I know what it is! You have a striking resemblance to someone I once met. She also had pale blue eyes and dark shiny hair. That, I remember."

Jade-R's flawless skin was glowing, just thinking that he remembered.

She asked, "Was that someone special to you?"

He shook his head. "No, no way." Then repeated it. "No. I don't even remember her name! I just know it wasn't Catherine. Anyway, she's not important."

At that moment Jade-R's world began to crumble, and she felt sick inside, but her eyes kept smiling even as his words pierced through her heart.

She looked at the gold crest embellished with his initials on his suit jacket and answered, "It must be true. They say we all have a twin out there somewhere," then gathered all of her emotional courage and flashed him a brilliant smile.

Suddenly a pretty young lady with golden blonde hair wrapped her arms around Connor's waist in a familiar, tantalizing way. "Baby, are you requesting our song?"

"Hi, Hon." He turned and gave her a quick kiss. "Yes, I am, and she does know 'Stardust'!"

"Would you mind playing it for us?" She smiled at Jade-R, and then tugged at Connor's sleeve.

"I finished with the coordinator, and I hope to God she remembers tomorrow at our wedding. I'm really so tired of telling her about the seating. Come on, I need a drink."

Jade-R watched as they headed to the party table. Strained by those actions, suddenly her fingers felt numb and at that moment, she wanted to cry... but instead, she played "Stardust." With this heartache and pain, somehow, it came out more beautifully than she had ever played it before.

On her break she went to the restroom to deal with her tortured thoughts, but soon a parade of ladies was passing lipstick around, and touching up their beehive hairdos with puffer spray for hair in bottles.

The common theme was, "By tomorrow at this time you'll be a Bodwen!"

One of them laughed and said, "And believe me, it does take money to finance their love!"

Another one quickly added, "Well, she will

never worry about money again, that's for sure."

Then they all giggled as the room filled with the scent of scattered perfume.

Throughout the evening, there was endless toasting around the table as the group posed and the photographer snapped pictures.

Jade-R remembered all the secrets and details about his family that Connor had shared with her in Guam, especially about his sister and how his grandfather sent her to the finest school in Paris. When she returned, she had quickly married the tennis pro at their club. Occasionally, from pain and curiosity, Jade-R would glance their way. She could see similar features and identified his sister Cathy. Or little Catfish, as their grandfather so fondly nicknamed her. She was pretty and wholesome-looking, and actually appeared to be the most down-to-earth person in the group.

Connor's mother, impeccably dressed in a light gold suit, with her hair styled to perfection, stood and began telling a lively tempting story from her son's pampered childhood. Her hands moved around knocking against the lavish diamond brooch near her shoulder more than once. Then she would point to her son at times.

He listened intently to the nifty details, then shook his head and began laughing.

As the evening continued, Jade-R played several requests from their table. She watched as Connor joked, drank and stole the spotlight, with his bride-to-be sitting next to him pouting. Before long he whispered something in her ear and angrily she yanked away; then both of them gulped their drinks down.

It was late and finally the evening was drawing to an end. Jade-R wandered out to the terrace for a private moment during her break. Watching the faded moon standing still, she felt embarrassed and foolish. All those times in Formosa hoping at night, that maybe somehow he was thinking of her. Thinking he might even love her. Remembering back to the night they danced, and he said, “We are made for each other.” She recalled building that certain lovely, naive dream. But perhaps it was that dream that had helped her survive all the terrible loneliness.

She listened to the ocean pound the surf as

she looked out toward the dark sea and remembered her perilous journey and thought about how many lives had been shattered and damaged. Suddenly she heard someone behind her and turned. It was Connor! He tipped his head back and blew a smoke ring upward in the air, then said, "I think we should have lunch together, and see where this goes! I know you're interested. I saw you glancing my direction."

She stared at him with almost a blank look.

He added with confidence, "I bet we could have fun. I think lunch is a brilliant idea, don't you?"

Speechless for a moment, she finally answered. "But you will be married?"

"So?" he said with a boyish grin. "I won't tell anyone if you don't."

The moonlight was fading as he took his hand and ran it through his hair. Suddenly that gesture reminded her of every awful detail he had done on the beach that night, when he forced himself on her. Now there he stood. For a second, enslaved with anger, she was sick for revenge, but soon realized that it would only hurt her.

Finally she answered, “No.” Then quickly added. “That...will never happen.”

He gave her a smug look and returned to the party table and resumed his toasting. Before long, he and his bride-to-be were shouting angrily at each other.

Surprised by the disturbance, Jade-R turned their way to see the embarrassing display, and then quickly turned back to the piano.

Without her notice, Connor’s grandfather had moved to the table next to her. As she closed her notebook full of songs, Connor and his fiancée were snarling even louder. His grandfather saw Jade-R glance at them again.

“Noisy customers, huh?” he said. “They’ll run out of arguments soon, always do!” Out of politeness, she smiled at him.

Before long the bridal party headed to the bar for a last drink as some of the older guests stopped by, exchanging hugs before leaving.

Looking their way, Connor’s grandfather muttered, “I worry about you, Grandson. You’ll end up an alcoholic besides the bad marriage."

He glanced over at Jade-R. "I'm sorry," he said. "I guess I talk loud these days. They tell me I'm going deaf, or something." He waved his hand. "I apologize, didn't mean for you to hear that."

She smiled at him and answered. "I don't think I heard anything. Maybe I'm going deaf also!" He laughed and smiled back at her.

Finally Connor, with the help of his buddy holding him up, and his bride giggling with her girlfriends, walked out the door.

His grandfather turned his chair toward Jade-R at the piano bench. "Too bad, he didn't meet someone like you." Shaking his head, he said, "But the choices we make, we live with." She noticed that the twinkle in his eye had disappeared but the pleasant lines on his face still showed years of wisdom and humor. She thought to herself, *You would have loved your beautiful great-granddaughter, Cherish Bodwen Reign.*

A man looking like an older version of Connor called out. "Dad, are you coming?"

"Waiting for the bill, son, and finishing my cognac! Tell my driver I'll be out soon!"

Sitting quietly for a moment, Mr. Bodwen appeared in deep thought. Then he broke out with a laugh. "What do we know when we're young? Hell, when I was little, I just wanted to be a cowboy when I grew up! That was it. Then I came to Honolulu."

Looking at Jade-R, he changed the tone of his voice. "I never left." Laughing again, he added, "But I thought about this many times. Paradise probably beats eating dust and riding a horse all day!" As he puffed on his cigar he asked, "Are you married, young lady?"

"No," she replied, politely.

"Well, you have the road ahead. You're talented and gorgeous. I'll give you a bit of advice. Think long and hard what life you want."

Then the waiter brought his Diner's Club card back and he signed. She watched while he downed the last of his drink and tipped the ashes off his cigar into a small tray. "You play the piano beautifully." He patted her shoulder and dropped a huge tip in the glass jar before leaving.

That night when she got home everything felt stuffy. The air was stagnant and still in the coral tree house. She opened the windows and clicked the switch to the ceiling fan, then realized it wasn't the air. She was feeling bleak and tarnished. Pulling out a carved wood chair, she took off her high heels and nylons and sat down. Tears welled in her eyes as she thought about her past.

Back then, I was a young teenager captured by his charm, and simply took a walk on the beach with Connor Bodwen one night. And it changed my entire life, and the lives of others. Our precious baby was so innocent and I will always love her. But this evening, seeing Connor as he really is, a terrible cheat, I know I have been given a rare gift. The last few years have been devastating and the pain at times, unbearable. Now it's over and for my sake, I must go on and never look back.

Abruptly, she stood and wiped her tears, walked to the dresser and picked up the shell that Connor had given her, the shell she had saved for so long. Barefoot, she raced down the wood stairs, her coral chiffon dress flowing as she ran across the street, past the houses, to a secluded spot on the beach. She paused, breathing hard, with her heart pounding.

The moon was gone, but the bright starlight sparkled across the waves. She lifted the shell in her hand, stared at it for another brief instant, and then hurled it with all of her strength into the surf. As she watched the distant splash, she wiped her tears and screamed above the ocean's roar, "Good-bye, Connor! Good-bye Jade-R! Good-bye to both of you!"

Head high and shoulders squared, Catherine turned and walked confidently back to the coral tree house.

CHAPTER TWENTY-SIX

The next morning she pulled her hair into a ponytail and slipped on a soft cotton dress. Picking the yellow polka-dot tie she had bought from the tailor's shop, she wound it around her waist as her pretty belt.

The aroma of fresh coffee greeted her when she joined Carl next to his koi pond.

"Here, come feed Surf and Ruby; they're looking for a handout from you."

The fish swam close to the side as she tossed melon and patted their heads and watched as they delicately swam away.

During breakfast Lum said, "We closed the store and are taking the day off."

Cleaning his glasses, Carl chimed in. "Yes, it's been a long time since we've had a full Sunday to just go have fun. We're excited! First we'll head to the bookstore. Awhile back

I ordered a book on rare opals and finally it's in. Would you like to spend the day with us?" He said.

"Yes!" Catherine quickly replied. "That would be wonderful."

Lum added, "After the bookstore – well, we have the day planned. Thought we might drive around to Hanauma Bay on the east side of Oahu. It's tucked in a crater of an old volcano and protected from ocean swells. The surf is calm, and the sand is almost white. I think you'll like it, dear."

Carl said. "What I want to do is snorkel; haven't done that for years! It's a steep walk down to the beach, but so beautiful."

With bags full of books, they departed the store. The drive was relaxing as it followed the shoreline and every so often they could see a catamaran sailing just off the beach.

"I told you it was a steep climb down to this beach," Lum said as they made their way. Carl was worried and repeated every so often, "Be careful and take your time." Then he'd offer an occasional "aloha" to people they would pass, heading back up the hill.

Off and on in between reading, they waded in the water to cool off. Then Lum and Catherine watched as a Hawaiian man struggled to push his cart through a patch of sand, but finally made it to a concrete area. Before long he put out his sign. “Food, Open for Business.” Big kids and little quickly lined up. People kept walking by with shaved ice and drinks. “That looks refreshing!” Lum said, and then stared back at the line. “Come, let’s get our own. And I bet we get more of a breeze if we sit at one of his tables under the umbrellas.”

“Sounds good to me,” Catherine answered, as she jumped up and reached out to help Lum. Coming out of the water with hands full of snorkeling gear, Carl scurried across the burning sand, then stood on a towel and buckled his sandals. Waving with one of his fins at Lum, she waved back. The day and weather were beautiful as they sat talking and watching other people.

On the ride home they stopped at a small native restaurant near the road. Behind the counter a woman now dishing from a big brown skillet had just sautéed onions and spinach in vinegar and oil. A happy, heavyset, friendly Hawaiian man next to her, suddenly plunged mussels into water bubbling and boiling over the sides of the pan. A moment later the shells opened. He looked up and smiled, then handed Carl a loaf of hot bread. They sat on wood benches in the open air and stuffed themselves. Carl went into great detail sharing stories of snorkeling and the fish when he was young, and the difference between the fish he had seen in the blue water today.

The sun was setting as they pulled in the garage. It was the first time Carl gave a quick hug to Catherine as he said, “Glad you went, kid. We all had a nice outing!”

Lum whispered with her hug, “See, we are a family, mahalo.”

Catherine placed her hand over her heart and repeated, “Yes, mahalo.”

It was Friday night as Catherine walked

through the lobby and spotted Mr. Davis with a rich, tobacco-brown fur ball on a leash... his cat. The cat stood at attention with his tail pointed up straight. Then the cat's green-blue eyes glanced her way.

Mr. Davis smiled at her when she stopped. "This is my Gilligan!" he said.

"Well, your Gilligan is very beautiful! I've never seen a cat so regal looking," she replied with enthusiasm.

"That is bred in him," Mr. Davis answered. "He comes from a line of registered champions. Very rare, his breed, that is. I traveled all the way to England for him."

She kept admiring Gilligan, then said, "I have never seen a cat quite like yours. What is this breed?"

"They are called 'Havana Brown'," Mr. Davis proudly answered. "It's the result of a Siamese, Russian Blue, and of course ancient Burmese. A collected group of breeders fancied their color. As I said, they are rare."

Still petting him, Catherine asked, "How old is beautiful Gilligan?"

"He will be a year next month. He's just a young little boy," he added with a smile.

Mr. Davis beamed when she said, "I think you have the most attractive cat I've ever seen. I wish I had one just like him."

"Yes, he's affectionate, highly intelligent and this guy will quickly adjust to any situation I put him in."

As she stroked his soft mink-like coat, Gilligan stood quiet and poised as a passing hotel guest gawked in awe at them.

Soon, Catherine said, "Can you tell I like cats? Thank you for sharing your Gilligan with me."

Mr. Davis tipped his Panama hat and bowed. The silver and bone handle cane hung from his arm. "I will see you soon for dinner!" He pushed the button for the elevator and the door quickly opened. With his cat on the leash they strolled into the elevator and turned around. She waved good-bye to the distinguished pair.

The dining room was busy! When she finally took her first break, she turned and was surprised to see Carl and Lum. She headed to their open clamshell booth along the back wall. Delighted to see them, she slid in next to Lum as Carl stood to greet her.

"I'm so glad you're here." Catherine said.

"We wanted you to get comfortable before we came." Carl replied, as Lum squeezed her hand and said, "When you play, it's like you and the piano become one. It's beautiful!"

"Yes, she is right. Your performance is something! I see why the manager hired you immediately. It's obvious you enjoy it as much as the guests drinking and dining."

"Look who just arrived; it's your doctor, Lum."

"Yes, my very handsome Dr. Eastman!" They watched as he smiled at the waiter, and then turned to the older couple with him. The man was distinguished-looking, and Dr. Eastman shared many of his features. The lady with them was wearing a blue chiffon dress with a beautiful diamond and pearl brooch pinned to her wide collar. Her chestnut brown hair was curled softly and was extremely flattering around the petite bone structure of her face. Even from across the room, one could almost feel the kindness she portrayed.

Turning back, Catherine asked, "What did you order?" Just then, plates of chilled tomato filled with Hawaiian crab, dribbled with a saucy pink dressing, and a blue flower on top, were placed in front of them along with fresh-made crispy flat bread, piping hot from the oven.

She commented, "That looks good."

Lum asked, "Can you join us?"

"I wish I could. My first break is short, but I'll return!"

As she played, she noticed the long diamond earrings that adorned Lum's pretty face and almond-shaped eyes. Her evening dress in black taffeta was elegant. And Carl, wearing a black suit, looked so different than his island white linen, the uniform he usually wore. They were attractive as they sat dining, and it made her happy watching them while she played.

Then she glanced at Dr. Eastman. He caught her eye and smiled. As she continued to play, she looked his way again and smiled back.

At one point he headed over to Mr. Davis' table. From the easy way they were talking, it was apparent they knew each other well. Soon Mr. Davis and a waiter with his cocktail on a silver tray followed Dr. Eastman back to his table.

On Catherine's next break she returned to Carl and Lum. She had just slid into their booth and looked up to see Dr. Eastman heading their way. He shook hands with Carl, who quickly stood and said, "Remember my wife, Lum Kamora?"

"Yes, of course. You were my patient several months ago. How are you feeling?"

Smiling, she answered, "Thank you for taking great care of me. I have never felt better."

He turned to Catherine. "I could listen to you on the piano every night."

She answered with a smile, "Thank you."

He was impeccably dressed in his navy blue suit and red tie. “My parents are in town. This is my mother’s favorite restaurant. Mr. Davis, who is also my close friend, introduced me to this place. Actually, he lives in the hotel.” Looking again at Catherine, he smiled. “I won’t interrupt your dinner any longer; just wanted to say hello.”

Pleased, Carl said, “Thanks for coming over.” As Carl slid back in the booth, he said, “Now that’s a nice young man with a good firm handshake.”

Catherine watched Dr. Eastman as he walked back to his table. *Yes, he is a nice man*, she thought.

On her last break Lum said, “You must try the custard pudding with this apricot sauce,” and handed her a spoonful.

“Mmm,” Catherine agreed. “Delicious, you’re right.”

“Do you think, before we leave, you could play your favorite song?” Lum asked. “I believe it’s the one that means ‘Moonlight’?”

“ ‘Clair de Lune,’ ” Catherine replied.

“Yes, that’s it. I’d love to hear that, dear!” Lum said.

At the piano there were a few requests waiting when she returned. But as her fingers touched the keys, she looked at Lum and nodded. It was “Clair de Lune” that flowed gently through the room. Soon the waiter was tableside, between Mr. Davis and the other couple. Flames started shooting out of the pan as he prepared cherries jubilee. Gradually turning her attention again toward them, she found Dr. Eastman watching her, and he smiled.

When the evening came to a close she walked out to the terrace with Carl and Lum. They stood watching the ocean rolling along the shore. Over to their left on the large grassy area, the Hawaiian luau was still going on. They watched the dancing hula girls in grass skirts and native men twirling torches of fire in the air, catching them to the sound of pounding drums and the romantic tropical music.

Carl said, “It’s been awhile; we must come

see their show!" Lovingly, Lum put her hand through his arm and leaned her head on his shoulder.

On the ride home, Carl announced, "When we got ready to pay, a little birdie had flown off with our check! You should not have. But thank you, Catherine."

Lum said, "I don't remember the last time we dressed for dinner and went out like this. What a great evening. But most of all we enjoyed hearing you play, dear."

CHAPTER TWENTY-SEVEN

She could still hear rain coming down through the closed doors in the Orchid Room as she opened the lid to the piano. The manager said, "I almost called and told you not to come. It will probably be slow tonight. Our local customers don't come out in this weather! So I'm guessing you can go home whenever you want."

"I'll stay. We might get lucky," she replied.

"That's true. It's happened before." He tapped the side of the piano with his hand and left.

As soon as Mr. Davis showed up, he came straight over to Catherine at the piano.

"How is Gilligan?" she asked.

"He doesn't like this weather. He's tucked in, probably under my chair fast asleep by now. By the way, he told me to tell you hello and said he would like you to pet him again."

She laughed. "He said that?"

"He did."

"Well, tell him some time soon." She added, "I have come to know all your favorite songs, so this evening, you are my audience. I believe you deserve your own private concert."

"That would be wonderful, young lady." Jokingly he added, "Will you play them over and over?"

"I think I could do that!" she said smiling.

In his very elegant way he said, "I knew I liked you," then he took his usual spot over in the corner near the windows, looking out at the stormy ocean. Waiters hurried to his table with a drink, then stood around talking.

In the middle of playing a romantic song she was suddenly aware of someone beside her.

"That's the music I enjoy!"

She looked up to see Dr. Eastman standing there with an intrigued look on his face.

As the song ended, he said, "As hard as it was to get here in the rain, I bet they would let you have a drink with me?"

"I've never had a drink!" She immediately bit her lower lip in embarrassment, regretting her hasty response.

Quickly he replied with a grin, "That's even better! You must have your first drink with me!" She smiled and glanced down self-consciously for a moment. Still grinning, he said, "Now I'm going over to say hi to one of my favorite patients and my close friend, and when you're ready, I hope you will join me."

He walked across the room to sit and talk with Mr. Davis, and then eventually, was seated in a booth by himself. Playing a few more slow songs, she was intensely aware of his presence and finally, headed his way.

Without hesitation he stood as she slid in the opposite side. He looked at her a moment then said, "First of all, please call me Garrett."

She nodded. "And I'm Catherine."

"Good, we have that out of the way. Now, I've been thinking. What would be a good first drink for you? Not too strong, so that rules out a mai tai." With a mischievous smile, he added, "Or for sure you will think I'm trying to take advantage." His smile widened. "Yet, sweet, like you are." He looked at her and she smiled. "I was about to say, when you distracted me with your beautiful smile..."

The waiter suddenly stepped up to the table. Garrett turned and said, "Bring the young lady a piña colada with all the fancy little umbrellas and fruit, but go easy on the rum."

"I'm anxious to taste this magic mix," she teased.

There was silence for a moment. "Last week I wanted to introduce you to my parents. I looked up and you and your family were gone."

"Do they live here?" Catherine asked.

"No, they are from Ohio! That's where I was born, grew up, and went to medical school in Columbus, Ohio."

"How often do they come see you?"

"At least once, sometimes twice a year. Always they try to bribe me into returning."

"Would you ever go back?"

"No. I made up my mind how I want my life. But sometimes I feel bad, because I was their only child. My poor Mom cringes when I say this is home!"

"Would they move here?"

He thought for a moment, then answered, "I doubt it. My father's a doctor and wanted me to join him in his practice. But the snow, I'd had enough. However, my Dad did help me. His best friend is a vascular surgeon here and pulled strings. That made it easy for my internship. At first my parents thought I'd tire of island life, but when I learned to surf, that was it!"

As the waiter set her drink in front of her, he quietly said, "Bobby O, the bartender, made it extra special for you!"

"Tell him thank you," she whispered.

"We must toast!" They raised their hands and glasses together, clinking them gently as

Garrett said, “I’m honored this young lady is having her first drink with me! Hipalipa! That’s ‘cheers’ in Hawaiian.”

She sipped, and then sipped again. “This is delicious! Sort of a coconut milkshake!”

When they looked up Mr. Davis bowed his head, then waved good-bye to them, as he put on his Panama hat.

Sipping on her drink she said. “I feel very pampered right now. I’m sitting in this plush restaurant with a nice man and enjoying the flavors in this piña... What did you call this?”

“A piña colada,” he answered.

“Actually, I’m not sure I should drink all of this. Suddenly I feel warm inside. What is your drink?”

“When I drink I’m a scotch sort of man. It’s what my grandfather drank, my father drinks, and my friend Mr. Davis drinks. By the way, he loves to hear you play the piano.”

She smiled. “Yes, I know, and I like his cat. I’m sure you have met Gilligan?”

“Oh, Gilligan. That’s his baby.” He laughed.

"I make house calls for Gilligan. We just don't tell him I'm not a veterinarian. I'll make a house call free for some of Mr. Davis's ... old Scotch."

She looked at him more closely. His chin was square and strong with a dimple in the center. He glanced around the room. "Look, we are the only ones left." As they stood, she pulled out the fancy little pink umbrella from her first drink.

It was still pouring when they got to the entrance of the White Sands Hotel. The valet asked, "Do you want a taxi, Catherine?"

Garrett quickly replied, "No, I'll drive her." He turned to Catherine. "Can't have you in an old taxi riding around in this weather."

When his 1950s' woodie station wagon arrived, he laughed. "Guess my car is old too, and with the rain and mud, you'd never know I just got a new paint job!" When he opened the door he said, "Oh, look! Look at the new navy upholstery with the white piping!" He laughed again.

"It's beautiful," she answered. "I've never

seen a car with wood on the sides."

"Yes, well, this is the first rainy night it's been out since being painted. See, you're special for me to bring this beauty out." He smiled at her.

As they pulled out of the hotel driveway, he asked, "Which way is home?"

"Turn right toward Diamond Head!"

Driving along he asked, "Are you from here?"

"No. But I'm like you. This is now my adopted home. The place I want to live forever."

"Where did you attend school?"

"I was taught privately at home. I had an excellent teacher, Mrs. Walters, an older woman that came to my house. At least, like everyone else, I did get two months off in the summer." Garrett was quiet.

"I remember Lum telling me at the hospital you're family. So they're your parents?"

"Not my biological parents, but yes, I

consider them my family." Finally he turned on the radio to soft music. The windshield wipers seemed to keep time as they rode along.

She asked, "This car is nice. Have you had it long?"

"It was my father's. When I got to college he gave it to me and someday I'll give it to my son. It will be a classic by then."

Jokingly, she said, "What if you have two sons?"

"Well," he said as he laughed, "I guess I would cut this one in half. Tomorrow night I'm on call at the hospital, but Monday evening, would you have dinner with me?"

"Veer off toward the right. Soon you will want to go slow. It's the next driveway you come to."

He jumped out in the rain with an umbrella and opened her door. At the top of the stairs he said, "You didn't answer me about dinner, but I'll be here around six o'clock." He waved as he hurried back down.

The next morning, the rain was gone and the sun beamed through the trees outside the window. As Catherine came bouncing through the gate, Carl was cleaning the waterfall. "Got home late and didn't recognize the taxi!"

"It wasn't a taxi. It was Dr. Eastman that drove me," she said casually.

"Huh! I like that!"

Lum smiled, "Fresh Kona coffee and Carl's favorite cream of wheat is being served." She continued, "I find him very nice. Do you, dear?" She looked at Catherine.

"Yes, and he asked me out for dinner Monday night."

Carl smiled as he glanced over at Lum.

With one last look in the mirror, she checked the wide starched collar on her white blouse and fussed with the belt that cinched her tiny waist, then smoothed down her pencil skirt. A moment later, there was a tap at the door and she had to control the desire to run and answer it.

Garrett said, “You look beautiful! Let’s go have fun,” then stuck out his arm. As she took hold of his beige sports jacket he said, “Well, I guess we can’t go down the stairs together, they’re too narrow. I’ll go first in case you fall, I can catch you!”

Laughing she answered, “Or maybe we’ll both end up in a pile at the bottom!”

He turned and grinned, “But I know a good doctor.”

As they reached the bottom he politely opened her car door.

They drove toward the rainforest and then turned down a road protected by lush palms. Rows of tiki torches lined the long drive up to a quaint Hawaiian restaurant. They walked through grounds surrounded by magnificent botanical gardens, enjoying rare flowers and orchids growing wild.

Seated at a wood table by an open window, they watched as a man strolled around, playing the ukulele.

"This place is paradise," Garrett said. "I always feel relaxed when I come here. It's one of my favorite places. Well, except for the Orchid Room now." He smiled.

He ordered the special house drink in a large coconut with floating orchids. It was a drink for two, and it came with extra long straws. They dined on smoked chicken with a sauce of cut lemongrass and chili, topped with coconut foam and shavings. Catherine listened intently while Garrett shared some of his childhood stories about growing up in Ohio.

"Do you remember how old you were when you thought you might become a doctor?" Catherine asked.

Garrett laughed and said, "I had a golden retriever dog named Ginger; loved that dog. My parents were out for the evening. Ginger began acting strange. I know I was eight years old when this happened because my father still talks about it. I delivered my dog Ginger's nine puppies, while my babysitter watched over to one side, throwing up!"

During their lively conversation over a bowl of coconut and chocolate ice cream, they both agreed that they wished they had siblings. Catherine enjoyed the sound of his deep strong voice and light humor. Smiling at him, she noticed a small scar to the side of his cheek. He called that scar the trophy he came home with one day on a fishing trip with his father, when the big fish he had caught got away. Catherine thought it gave him a rugged outdoor look and added to his polished handsome doctor appearance. She watched his hands and marveled, knowing the good they did helping people.

On the ride back, she mentioned how low the big moon was hanging and how close it seemed to the car. Garrett said, “Yes, and look at the stars! When I was small I had a telescope and studied those every night! I’ve read a lot about the moon. I find it fascinating.”

She glanced over at him with surprise, adding, “Yes.”

“I’m sure you have discovered,” he continued, “Oahu has the best evenings!”

“They are beautiful,” she agreed. “I noticed you spoke Hawaiian to our server tonight. I read the original Hawaiian language has evolved into a creole, with pidgin elements. Was it hard learning?"

"Not as hard as you would think," he answered. "Their alphabet only has thirteen letters: five vowels (long and short) and eight consonants, one of which is the glottal stop called O'kina. Vowels come first, then consonants! You can pick it up fast! It helps to be able to speak to my elderly patients. It's just more comfortable for them."

The evening passed quickly and full of easy conversation and laughter.

When they pulled in the driveway he was quick to say, "Besides being beautiful, you're also smart. I had a nice time."

He walked her up the stairs, pausing at the door. The lights hanging from the coral tree glowed in her pale blue eyes. He put his hand up as if to touch her face, but stopped. Instead he said, "I'll see you soon!"

She added, "Thank you for dinner."

She watched as he bounded down the stairs, and drove away in his prized woodie. She sat down on the stairs thinking about the evening.

That night in bed she tossed and squirmed and moved her foot to a cold spot at the bottom of the sheets. Excited, she thought, *This is the first date I've ever been on.* Finally she told herself not to get too interested. He might feel different if he found out she had given birth.

It was late when she glanced over to the picture of her mother. It gave her comfort and she soon fell asleep.

At breakfast Carl asked, "Did you have a nice evening with Dr. Eastman?" Lum stopped pouring coffee to wait for the answer.

"Yes. He took me to a place called, 'The Green House.' "

"Oh, yes." Lum said. "That's been there since 1935. One of the best!"

Carl said, "Huh. That's a romantic place!"

"He's just a friend," Catherine quickly replied.

"That's how it starts," Carl answered, then went back to reading the paper.

CHAPTER TWENTY-EIGHT

Thursday evening the Orchid Room was buzzing with people; one large birthday group and an anniversary party. The requests never stopped. During one song she glanced around the room and there was Garrett. Her heart started swirling like her fingers across the keys.

When the evening ended Garrett sat alone waiting. "Come on, I'll drive you home." Walking through the lobby he whispered, "I've been on call and had surgeries all afternoon."

As he opened the car door, there was a package on the front seat and he laughed, "Oh, that! My mother makes me fresh peanut brittle at least once a month." As he moved the package and helped her in, he asked, "How have you been?"

"Good, but not as busy as you. Are you tired?"

"Not bad, I slipped home and grabbed a

shower."

She looked over and pointed, "You just passed the turn to my house!"

"I know. I want to show you something."

A few miles down the road he pulled up to a pair of rusted-out, old chain link gates. He took off his sports jacket and said, "Wait." He got out and the headlights spread a path of light across his broad shoulders visible through his linen shirt as he walked open the gates. When he turned and headed back to the car, she knew from the way he looked at her that something was different. They drove out on a flat vacant lot with a big sweeping view of the ocean.

"This afternoon my architect called and my house plans finally got approved! Come," he said as he opened her door, "Let me show you what I'm building."

She listened as he described it. "Here is where you will enter the foyer and look straight out to the ocean! The design of the home is old Hawaiian chic. Where you're standing will be a large room, kitchen-family room combination, facing the water. Everyone gathers in the kitchen, so I made sure it's huge." As they walked along he said, "Over here will be an open wraparound-porch, where there will be a long table for meals outside. And of course, to watch my kids play in the sand. Someday I'll teach them how to surf! I want to hear screen doors slamming and see a couple of dogs running in and out with the kids. All the rooms are big."

Excited he said, "Oh, this is neat. I have a patient that sells these fine hammered hinges and door handles. Some of them he buys when they tear down homes. When this home is built, this place will be beautiful!" he said with a proud smile. "But I also want it comfortable."

She listened intently to every word he said and was amazed at his confident enthusiasm and his clear vision of what he wanted. She could hear a whirlybird sprinkler watering an old banyan tree.

As she looked at him, suddenly he pulled her into his arms and kissed her! It was a long, meaningful kiss that held a promise of so many things.

When they got to the car they turned and looked back. She said, "Thank you for sharing your dream!"

"Sunday lunch. Mr. Davis invited both of us. Will you come?"

"That sounds delightful! He is always a gentleman and I'll get to see Gilligan!"

That night a beautiful song played in her heart and lulled her to sleep.

Sunday morning, as the sun peered through the windows, she heard Garrett's firm tread on the stairs to the tree house.

"You look so pretty," were his first words. "That's a beautiful dress."

"Thank you." she replied.

"I'm sorry to tell you this, but I won't be having lunch with you and Mr. Davis. I was locking the door of my condo when the phone rang and luckily, I went back and answered. It was the hospital. There's been a severe accident and they need all surgeons."

Worried, Catherine asked, "What happened?"

"A bus filled with tourists slid off the road.

People are seriously injured! I was looking forward to spending the day with you, but this is part of being a doctor. Plans can change fast. Do you mind going alone?"

"No. No, of course not. But do you think it will be all right, Mr. Davis will not mind?"

"Mind? He insisted you come. I'm guessing I'll be in the operating room till late. I won't be back to pick you up."

She smiled, "I know where to find the taxis."

She glanced over at his hands gripping the steering wheel. Soon they would be trying to save the lives of strangers.

"This is a busy week; tomorrow I'm on call, and Thursday I move." She watched as he talked.

"I'm anxious to be in my new office. I'll have twice the space and I need it."

He paused. "So how does lunch on Saturday sound? We'll have the whole day. Are you free?"

"Yes," she answered, then asked, "Where is your new office located?"

"Just around the corner from the hospital! I

can walk back and forth. No longer will I have to take my car, which will be convenient."

He seemed to relax for a moment as he said, "You'll enjoy getting to know

Mr. Davis. He's quite interesting. I've been to lunch at his place numerous times. He doesn't entertain much. So when he insisted I bring you, that says a lot." He smiled and added, "I know he enjoys hearing you play the piano. He has told me."

She smiled, and then asked, "You're his doctor; correct?"

"Yes. When I bought out the practice from Dr. Kane, who retired, Mr. Davis was not happy. But as soon as we met he was fine. Since then, we have become good friends. Enjoy your afternoon; I wish I could have stayed."

A group of bicycles veered back and forth unpredictably and Garrett had to quickly stop before pulling under the porte-cochere next to the stream of taxis lined up and waiting for fares. She quickly opened her door as the attendant came running.

"Thanks, Catherine, for understanding.

Remember, I'll see you Saturday. Pick you up at noon?" She smiled and nodded, then watched as he sped down the driveway and swiftly turned the corner.

As she exited the elevator on the penthouse floor, the door closed slowly behind. She paused to admire a pair of uniquely upholstered chairs. The fabric was brightly colored, with big green parrots covering most of the back. Slowly she wandered down the long, impressive hallway with its vibrant carpet, inlaid with huge tropical flowers. She couldn't resist touching the light green texture of the wallpaper.

In front of a pair of tall double doors that read "Penthouse A" in shiny brass letters, she pressed her finger on the bell. The door opened almost immediately.

"There's my favorite pianist. Come in, come in. I have been looking forward to this all week!" He took her arm to greet her. "Garrett called and explained why he won't be joining us."

She shook her head. "I'm sorry for those injured."

"I know, but at least they'll have the best doctor in town!"

"I told Garrett to take care of them, and that I will try to entertain you this afternoon." He patted her hand. "Don't worry, we'll be fine!" He took her purse and laid it on the credenza in the mirrored entryway. "Now, let me look at you!"

He stepped back to study her at arm's length. "Ah, you are even more beautiful in the daylight. I've never seen blue eyes so light, so I hope you don't mind if I stare impolitely. And one more thing; when you speak, you have a marvelous voice."

She smiled. "Such sweet compliments! Thank you." A furry tail brushed her leg. "Oh, hi, Gilligan," she laughed, then bent down to pet him, noticing a ball in his mouth.

Mr. Davis laughed. "He knows how to fetch. Throw it!"

With a quick flick of her wrist Catherine tossed the ball across the room and Gilligan came running back with the ball. Proudly Mr. Davis said, "See, I have a smart cat!"

Catherine laughed. "But how did you teach

him to walk on a leash?"

"Cat treats. First we walked down the hall to the elevator, and I gave him a treat. Soon he was curious like a cat. He wanted to go on. Once he went down to the grounds outside – more cat treats of course – when he saw birds and trees, that was it. Now he'll stand by the door waiting. Just knows our schedule."

Catherine laughed. "You're right…smart cat!" To the left entering the living room, she could see Diamond Head and the gorgeous ocean. For a moment, the endless blue water reminded her of home. When she turned around, her eyes widened in awe. A huge wall was covered with oil paintings. The varied sizes of abstracts were fresh and powerful, done in bright native island colors. They were mixed with the exacting imagery of ships that looked like they were straight from India in the 1800s.

"I'm almost speechless. The view out your window is spectacular, but this wall, it is the winner! Incredible. Who's the artist?"

With a humble smile, he said, "Come, let me show you around."

The hallway, too, was packed with stunning pieces. She stopped to enjoy, then said, “You have displayed each one perfectly.”

Finally he opened a door at the end of the hallway. The room resembled a professional studio. Tarps covered most of the hardwood floor. Two huge metal easels stood near a window and the abundance of light shone on a canvas, with work in progress. He looked her way as he adjusted it, balancing it better on the stand. It depicted a young Hawaiian girl holding a scruffy little brown puppy.

On the other stand the oil colors on the canvas were lightly faded and subtle. A camel was crossing the hot Sahara desert with a man walking in front dressed in white.

“Besides Gilligan, this is my passion. I’m blessed at my age to still have excellent eyesight.”

“I have always been fascinated with art,” Catherine replied. “I used to read books on how to paint, but I’m not sure I have any natural talent. Last week, I spent the day at the Hawaiian Art Museum, and your work matches anything they have. Do you ever sell these?”

He smiled. “No, this is my private collection. Please come, I’ll show you one in my room.”

A thick white velvety spread draped his immaculately made bed. Resting in the center was a decorative pillow, lime green with blue fringe.

A large round-mirrored table stood to one side and held an assortment of collectibles, including a small herd of perfectly carved elephants with ivory tusks. They were placed nicely under a huge white marble lamp. On the table was a photograph of a pretty woman. It was an elegant room, but one in which you would feel comfortable if you chose to sit on the bed.

Against the opposite wall of the room, she spotted his Panama hats neatly lined across a bench.

“You look dashing in those,” she said, pointing at his collection.

He smiled. “Some of those were my father’s.”

Walking past the white nubby chair and matching footstool, she saw an enormous oil painting. It portrayed a Hawaiian shack on a beach. There were several tall, thin palm trees, with a monkey climbing one that curved around and over the roof. It was fun and had a whimsical feeling. It made her smile. “That is my favorite!” Catherine said.

Looking over at the painting, he agreed, “I do believe it’s one of mine as well.”

In the small but efficient white kitchen, he poured something tropical into glasses. “I eat breakfast here and if I’m painting, lunch also. My maid Dorothy, that’s her name, comes in the mornings and faithfully leaves when she wants. She can do that after being with me close to twenty years.” He laughed. “Sometimes I think she’s my boss. Of course you know, at night I have the hotels on either side to dine at. My favorite is the Orchid Room. Something to do with the piano music, I guess.” He winked at her.

The bell rang and in came a stainless steel rolling cart from room service. “I thought we’d eat first, if you don’t mind? I’m an older man with strict habits.”

“I’m hungry,” she answered. “That will be fine.”

Adjusting her chair, he then dropped a white napkin on her lap. Her white plate had a gold and silver rim. "This looks delicious," she said.

"It's Black Stone salad, my personal favorite." He added. "It has a zingy French lemon dressing. Wait until you taste it. As you see, it's assorted lettuce leaves with tiny rings of pineapple, orange and grapefruit."

Catherine observed, as she picked up her knife and fork, "I like the layers. Garnishing it with bright red cherries reminds me of the refreshing colors in your paintings."

He smiled back and added, "I hope you enjoy the flavors. I used to make this myself. The dressing is easy."

As she took her first bite, he said, "If you ever want to try and duplicate this, it's simple. Just blend together fresh cream, the kind you put in coffee, along with Philadelphia cream cheese, and a pinch of salt. But I'll tell you the secret. Whip it stiff enough that you get a firm consistency so when you put it around the edge of your plate it stands up. Then garnish with, as you said, the refreshing maraschino cherries."

"Sounds easy, and tastes wonderful," she answered while delicately patting the sides of her mouth with the over-starched napkin.

Fascinated by his charming manner, she listened as he continued, "Now I always add caramelized walnuts and mint leaves. Today I forgot to tell them. But it's good anyway."

"So you like to cook?"

"I do. I used to cook all the time when I had my home. Oh, what a great kitchen that was!" He appeared to have a flashback, as a big smile covered his face.

Watching him, she remembered the first night he entered the restaurant and how aristocratic he appeared. Now up close, his features were clearly defined. His silver white hair had a slight wave. A deep dimple pierced only his left cheek. His straight chiseled nose added strength to his face. For his age, he was still handsome. *What must he have been like in those early years?*

Then she heard him saying, "I built my house on the side of a hill. In fact, looking down I could see this hotel. It was a good location, because my office building was just between my home and here."

"Do you still go to your office?"

"No. I was lucky and sold my Maritime Law Firm — that was the name of it — years ago to a lawyer who worked for me. Proudly I will add, just before it sold, I employed nine high-powered, full-time attorneys. We took international cases as far away as Saudi Arabia. The last one I personally handled was in Morocco!"

The doorbell rang. "I don't need to answer," he smiled. A key turned in the lock, the door opened again and the rolling cart from room service arrived. As the uniformed server collected salad plates, Mr. Davis said, "This is my favorite, table-carved duck."

Catherine watched the presentation, along with the pleased look on Mr. Davis' face, as plates were set in front of them. He requested the server add more cucumbers and scallions, and a bit more sauce. It was obvious the server, as he opened the bottle of Chenin Blanc and poured a small amount, knew Mr. Davis well. "Perfect," he said to the young man. "The pairing dances around being sweet and sour."

There were soft, delicious warm buns. “Catherine, dip them in the plum sauce if you wish. I do. Traditionally, hoisin sauce is made from sweet potatoes, but is somewhat salty. I have a fondness for this flavor.”

When lunch was finished Gilligan led them back to the living room. It was filled with dramatic off-white furniture and luxurious dark wood antiques.

“Here, I want you to have the best seat. You can enjoy the view of Diamond Head.” He escorted her to a white club chair. While he took his seat, she noticed an interesting array of uniquely carved pipes. They were lined up in a cut glass bowl on the side table near him.

“Do you smoke?” She pointed to the bowl.

He answered, “No. Those belonged to my father.” He picked one up and for a moment looked at it and rubbed the handle. “They are reminders so I keep them close. Actually, yesterday was his birthday.” He smiled. “My father was the most honest man I’ve ever known. And simple. Only had one job while I was growing up.”

“What did he work at?”

“Organized papers at a desk for the government. He enjoyed it.” His thoughts drifted for a moment.

“Have you always lived on this island?”

“Yes. Born and raised here. And as you probably know, Hawaii has a diverse population. In addition to the original Polynesians, there are Tahitian and Samoan mixed along with natives from Tongo. Then of course, you have the whites and Europeans, who are called Haoles. Blacks were known as Popolo. That means blackberry in Hawaiian. Blacks are the minority of the population. It’s small here so you get pushed together. If you’re nice and can find something in common, the racial divide is less.” He paused. “However, I did have a few bad experiences at the bus stop when I was young. The Davis family, we were the perfect neighbors. Polite and quiet, you couldn’t help but like us.”

“And your mother, what did she do?”

“My mom, she was very elegant-looking. A good homemaker that knew how to care for her family. Cooked, did all that.” He laughed. “Even made fresh pies for the neighbors. Both my parents were pleasant and enjoyed raising their kids. I had a sister who died at twenty from heart problems. My father and mother really never recovered."

Soon Gilligan wiggled around on the floor, then hopped onto a table near the window.

"That's his perch where he watches people sunning on the beach. Occasionally birds land on our terrace. It's a game. He bats the window and they fly off. He's my watch cat!"

She had just taken her first sip of hot Kona coffee.

He stood. "Coffee's good, but I think I'll pour myself some old Scotch." The bell rang, and with glass in hand, Mr. Davis headed to the door. She heard him say, "That's a great story. I'm glad it worked out for you," followed by a laugh. When he returned, a rather plump, older Hawaiian man was with him.

"Catherine, this is my longtime friend, Loka. He comes almost every Sunday at this time and plays the violin for me." He put his arm on his friend's shoulder and continued. "We met years ago at a club here in Honolulu. Back then he was head violinist with the Hawaiian Philharmonic Orchestra."

"Aloha," Loka said. Laughing he added, "Now I'm ninety-two years old. I just play for my friend. Glad to meet you."

"My pleasure as well."

Loka put his violin up next to his round face. He closed his eyes and laid the bow on the delicately made instrument. Out poured the most beautiful version of "Over the Rainbow" Catherine had ever heard. It was mesmerizing. Then he continued right into several classical pieces, finally ending with songs that had a Hawaiian bluegrass rhythm.

Clapping her hands softly, she said, "That was beautiful!"

Mr. Davis nodded in agreement. He turned to look at Catherine. "Loka, this young lady — may I add, strikingly beautiful lady — plays the piano downstairs in the Orchid Room!"

With the bow in one hand, Loka rested his violin on the bamboo print of his Hawaiian shirt. "Oh yes. I remember you telling me, it sounds like music from heaven! At least I think that's the way you described it."

"You're right."

Loka looked at Catherine. "I'll come hear you play. I love piano music! So does my wife."

"Then I will play for you!" Catherine answered with a smile.

Even Gilligan sat up and listened as he began playing the song, "Why Don't You Believe Me."

Catherine watched, and then glanced out at the huge clouds over the Pacific Ocean. *It would be fun playing a duet with him. Perhaps someday*, she thought.

He ended the private concert with "Flight of the Bumblebee," as Mr. Davis joined in, tapping his shoe on the floor.

When he said good-bye, Catherine replied, "This was a lovely surprise. Thank you for your music."

Mr. Davis picked up a small white envelope, and handed it to him as they walked to the entry.

The sun cast a comforting glow through the

window and for a moment the room was quiet, except for the ticking of the 150-year-old grandfather clock.

When Mr. Davis returned, Catherine said,

"Loka and his violin, that was special."

"It works," Mr. Davis said. "I help him with a little extra cash and get the pleasure of his music."

She watched briefly as Mr. Davis sat in his big comfy leather chair, sipping his scotch. "I hope I'm not being too personal by asking..."

He quickly interrupted, "My young friend, you may ask me anything."

"Thank you," she said. "I noticed a photo in your bedroom of a pretty lady?"

"Yes... Alani. We were married thirty-seven years. She was Hawaiian. Quite beautiful! Actually, she was much older than me."

He was quiet as he sipped his drink, then continued. "She played the piano. Now our favorite song, you play for me."

In a softer tone he said, "She developed a

blood disorder. I was in complete despair when she passed, aimlessly wandering alone at night in my big house. That's when I discovered I must talk to people. Some of us, well, when we get older, like to relive our stories."

Leaning over he almost whispered, "I believe it's an age thing." Then he laughed. "I'll never forget the night I looked down at the lights here in town. I knew I needed a change."

"So that's when you moved?"

"Yes. I had done work for this hotel owner, and he's a friend of mine. I called him and said, "Make me a good deal on a corner penthouse suite, one I can live in for years to come. Oh, and by the way, I want it empty." On the other end of the phone, he laughed and said, 'Are you joking?' It took a week or so, but we hammered out a contract. I put in the hardwood floors. I wanted to keep these beautiful Turkish rugs I collected from traveling. Just looking at them keeps those exciting adventures alive. Oh, I did replace the drapes. I like it dark like a cave when I sleep."

"Did you sell your house?"

"Leased it to Don and Kathy. He's a retired

executive from Scottsdale, Arizona. They'd like to buy it, but I built it for Alani. More likely I'll never sell. That's when I moved. I still have my personal maid Dorothy, plus hotel service, and a great view!" With a smile he added, "Around the corner, I'll soon be eighty years old, and I just signed another ten-year lease."

Looking at him, Catherine said, "Well, its apparent this penthouse holds your incredible art and beautiful antiques. Those are an extension of you. This place suits you!"

"Thank you," he said. "You put that nicely."

Then Catherine asked, "Do you have children?"

He paused. "Ahh," and sipped his scotch contemplating. "I haven't spoken of this in a long time. The only person that knew passed away. May I?"

Catherine nodded.

He sat straight in his chair and then leaned forward, resting his arm on his leg. "Early in life, I found that love comes in different ways and doesn't always work out." He stood and headed toward a uniquely carved box on a table. He ran his hand across a platinum frame as he sat holding it. At that moment Mr. Davis seemed far away.

"Back when it happened," he said, "this was a scandalous story. I had just started my Maritime Law Firm. I had modest ambitions, but I was struggling. One day I got this panic call."

He pointed to the floor. "Actually, it was this hotel. There was a bad accident involving one of their catamarans. Lucky for me their regular attorney was out of town and they couldn't stand his partner. I jumped in my car and headed straight here with legal advice. I hit it off instantly with the general manager, who later introduced me to the owner. He is half Hawaiian, part French and part black. We got along great! Much to my surprise, he told me he had three hotels. One is over on Maui. From that day forward I was busy. Before long I hired another lawyer, then advertised in the local newspaper for a receptionist. Fresh out of college and all enthusiastic, this young girl from Georgia called on the ad. She and her roommate decided it would be exciting to live in Honolulu.

"Her name was Susan Ann Kenner. And her

skin was as white and smooth as porcelain. She had pretty green eyes and natural blonde hair. She'd answered the phone in her polite, sweet little southern voice, and that girl could type 65 words per minute. Our clients were crazy about her. Smart, picked things up in a hurry. We'd pile on the work; she'd get it done on time."

Then his voice turned serious. "However, from the beginning I could tell she had a fondness for me. He held his arm out. My skin's a different color and I'm her boss. No matter how attractive she was, I never flirted or stepped out of line. Late one night I was working on a big case. I heard someone. Susan called out, 'Didn't mean to startle you; I forgot something at my desk!'

"Minutes later she came in my office, leaned down and kissed me. I was shocked. But I'd be lying if I didn't say it was wonderful! However, immediately I had second thoughts. I backed up my chair. 'Wait. Let's think about this. Sure, we are both young and attracted to each other. What about the racial difference?'"

He paused. "In my mind I simply knew better. However, it was when she said...but I love you!'

That was it. We tried to be discreet at the office. I had hired a second attorney. We didn't fool anyone. They knew. Just too much love pouring out."

Catherine noticed he wanted to go back to those moments.

He continued. "With her southern roots she had to have sweet tea. She spoke often about missing the fireflies back home. Every night we were alone in our secret world. By then her roommate had a Navy boyfriend.

"Almost a year passed. It was raining and close to midnight. I was awakened by a hard knock at the door. I grabbed a robe. She stayed in bed. When I answered, I knew immediately the couple standing there were her parents. I invited them in. Her father started calling me every awful word, then rushed into the bedroom and began screaming at Susan. Her mother stood looking at her naked daughter, then began crying. Susan quickly wrapped the sheet around her body and went to comfort her mother.

"Again the father said things I won't repeat. Out of respect, I let him. The shock and anger her parents were feeling, I understood. I said,

'Mr. Kenner, I do love your daughter.'

"He yelled back, 'I don't give a damn who you love. It won't be my daughter!' Then he told Susan to get dressed. She ran to my arms crying. 'But Daddy, you don't understand. I love him. My heart will break without him.'

"Angrily he said, 'I will disinherit you. Is that what you want, to lose your fortune? And think of your grandmother. You're her favorite. This will kill her!'"

Catherine noticed a look of pain crossed Mr. Davis face as he said, "Soon I could feel her arms loosen, as she let go of me. Leaving, she looked back as she climbed in the car. I was numb. The next day I went to her apartment. Her roommate said her parents had packed her things and taken her back to Georgia. In tears, she explained, 'I'm sorry I told Mr. and Mrs. Kenner where you live.' "

Mr. Davis got up and dropped fresh ice in his glass and poured more scotch. With his fingertip he swirled it around, then took a sip.

"Did you see her again?" Catherine asked.

"Six months later I got a call at home. It was

late when the phone rang. At first no one answered when I said, 'Hello, hello.' Someone was on the line. I was about to hang up, when I heard her voice. Crying, she said, 'I'm pregnant. I didn't know the night I left you... I still love you.'

" 'You're pregnant?' I repeated. She blurted, 'I don't want to do this but I have to. They're making me give the baby up for adoption and I don't want to.'

"At that moment I was numb, but I kept asking 'Where are you? Please tell me. I'll come get you. Don't adopt out our baby,' I begged. Soon I only heard a dial tone. I sat in shock."

Mr. Davis was quiet, his pain still real as he looked down at her picture.

With a whisper, Catherine asked, "Did you ever find her?"

"That week I caught a flight to Savannah, Georgia, rented a car and drove to their home. I remember the day was warm and strange. Like the air had decided to stop. I pulled up to their huge two-story house with white pillars running along the front porch and huge trees with moss hanging down. Pots clustered with flowers sat near the front door. I was impeccably dressed in a new light gray suit. I took a deep breath, but I felt like my red tie was choking me. When I rang their doorbell a colored man in a uniform answered. He stared when I asked for Susan Kenner. Then he replied, 'Ms. Kenner, she's not here.' Furious to see me, her father stepped to the door and dismissed the butler. He didn't yell. Pure, quiet hatred shot from his mouth as he said, 'You will never find her. And if you set foot on this property again I will have you arrested. Now get the hell out of here,' and slammed the door.

"Without thinking clearly I drove to town and found a private investigator." Shaking his head, Mr. Davis said, "That was my mistake. On the hot crowded flight home with a massive headache, I thought, 'Why did I do that? I'm a black man snooping on a rich white family in Georgia.' "

Reliving that moment, he said, "I had no appetite for danger. I was desperate. I would have done anything to find her. And that investigator was quick to take my money. With hope I waited, expecting a call. And he did, two weeks later. He had no information to give me. That was it.

"I was sick and could hardly work. I had a big case coming that forced me to go on. Finally I hired a professional man. He'd been successful finding witnesses needed for pending cases at my law firm.

"A week later he returned. 'I'm sorry,' were his words. 'She is definitely not living with her parents, and no one in town has seen her.' "

Catherine watched as tears filled Mr. Davis, dramatic dark eyes. "I knew the baby was gone. I'd never see it."

Silent tears ran down Catherine's face.

He cleared his throat and said, "Finally, three years later, clipped from a newspaper was a wedding announcement. She had married a wealthy businessman from Savannah. For the next few years, all I did was work." He shifted his attention and bent down to pet Gilligan for a moment, then took a deep breath.

Rather than set the picture down he gazed at Susan. "I worried for years, did my child end up with a good loving family? Kids at school, did they make fun of my girl or boy?

"I still wonder. Giving up the baby, did it haunt Susan all these years? Or was she able to forget and go on without guilt."

Looking at the photo, he said, "For her sake, I truly hope she found peace with that final decision."

Then he reached over and handed the picture to Catherine.

Under the glass the edges of the photo had turned crisp and brittle. The middle was breaking loose, beginning to disintegrate. But there was the faded image of a pretty blonde girl.

Catherine looked up at Mr. Davis. She knew it was long ago, but he was still deeply affected by his love for that young girl from Georgia.

"To finally answer your question, 'Do I have children?' Yes. I have one. And the beginning to that sad story happened forty-nine years ago this month." Then he stood and gently pulled tissues from a box for each of them. They sat in silence.

Before long, he said, "Come, let's go to the

kitchen and eat ice cream, lots of it. And I want to hear all about who taught you to play the piano so beautifully."

A taxi was waiting in front of the hotel when Mr. Davis escorted her down. He asked, "Did you say you live near Diamond Head?"

Catherine answered, "Yes."

"Make sure you get her home safely," he told the driver. The driver nodded as Mr. Davis handed him money through the open window.

With a hug and a good-bye, he said, "Young lady, we will always be close friends. We share my secret."

She answered, "Yes, thank you for confiding in me. It was a wonderful day." She smiled, and touched him gently on the arm.

As the taxi pulled away after dropping her off, she slowly began climbing the stairs to the tree house. Surprised, she heard Carl call out. "We hear you. Glad you're home safely."

Catherine turned back down the stairs and opened the gate. They were sitting at the table drinking hot tea.

"Would you like some, dear?" Lum asked.

"Thank you," Catherine replied.

Carl asked, "How was lunch?"

"Garrett took me to the White Sands Hotel, but had to leave."

Carl said, "We heard on the news there was a tour bus accident. We wondered if he would be called to the hospital?"

"Yes," she answered. "Did the news say how everyone is?"

"Five are in critical condition," Carl answered. For a few minutes they were silent, drinking tea.

"Did you enjoy lunch with Mr. Davis?" Lum inquired.

"He's authentic and the perfect host. I believe I told you about his cat Gilligan walking on a leash. Right?"

"Yes," Lum answered with a laugh.

Catherine smiled. "Mr. Davis paints. It's his hobby. And his work, I can only say it's beautiful!"

Carl pushed a plate of cookies toward her. "Have some. Lum made them when we got home. Shortbread with macadamia nuts. Really good," he added, biting into another one. The evening was warm. The sky was filled with stars and the crescent moon hovered at an angle.

Finally Catherine said, "I'm stuffed."

"Sleep well, dear." Lum replied.

Carl added, "See you for coffee in the morning."

That night as she brushed her teeth, Garrett was on her mind, along with all those who were injured.

Then her thoughts turned to Mr. Davis and the heartache and layers of life he had experienced. She was sure in her heart that he would always be a good friend.

Missing her own baby, Catherine unzipped the black velvet jewelry pouch as she sat on the side of the bed. Unfolding it carefully, she ran her hand across the birth certificate, and then continued staring. Thinking back again she remembered Connor telling her he had been rushed into surgery when he was a newborn. Something to do with his heart. Could that have been what she died from?

Looking at the date, this weekend Cherish would have turned two and a half years old. From the closet she pulled out the little white outfit and hugged it to her face, but the baby scent was gone. Tears welled in her eyes as she stared outside the window at the lights in the big coral tree.

CHAPTER TWENTY-NINE

The week flew by and soon it was Friday night. Catherine was once again seated at the piano in the Orchid Room. A gentle breeze drifted in through the open doors. Dimmed lights softened the glow on the chandeliers. The maître'd seated two men in army uniforms close to the piano.

"Thank you, General Rhodes, and General Allen, for joining us this evening," he said, and handed them menus.

As they dined she wondered about their lives. *What must they have sacrificed for their country to have that many colored ribbons and medals lined in rows across their chests?*

Turning pages in the notebook, looking for a certain request, she heard one of the generals say. "Did you know the governor of Guam is dying?"

The other answered, "I did. Cancer; right? Not expected to live more than a few days."

"Yes. I didn't really know the poor bastard, only met him once. But I can say, the guy looked well tailored and had charisma like no one I've met. You know, our government suspected him of skimming off buildings he had promoted the construction of."

The second general grinned, then added, "They thought he was involved in a lot of illegal things and investigated him thoroughly. In the end couldn't find a damn thing! If he did any of that, he covered his tracks well! Do you know about his background?"

"No. Tell me," the first general said.

"I read all the reports and it's kind of interesting. He grew up on the streets, only had that buddy who we knew for sure was evil. Always in trouble. Then the governor would bail him out."

"Yes, I think I heard. Didn't someone shoot him last year while he was in bed sleeping?"

"That's true. And whoever did it, even shot his dog next to him! He was in the hospital for quite awhile. But too damn mean to die. He lived!"

Shaking his head, the second general answered, "I know. But the people of Guam love him; they keep reelecting the guy! This morning my office got word the governor's now in the hospital with only a couple days left."

Catherine's hands started shaking as she closed the notebook and tried to play. At that moment only the loving father who doted over her as a child was with her; the father that tucked covers around her and kissed her good night. Suddenly she knew she needed to see him one last time.

When she got home she packed some things in the green leather duffel bag and wrote on white paper several notes.

"To my family, Carl and Lum:

When you took me in, I could cry again, it meant so much. Those were the toughest of times. It would have been hard for me to come away from what occurred in my life without your love.

I'm not sure I can ever repay you, so for now, thank you and I love you both, will have to do.

You have my heart always, Catherine."

When she went through the gate and past the koi fishpond, she could see Lum in the kitchen. Carl sat at the counter reading something. At her gentle knock, Lum opened the door. Carl looked up. "What's wrong? Are you all right?"

"I need to tell you something."

Lum set a cup of tea in front of her and pulled out the cane barstool.

"I'm leaving tonight. I'm not sure how long I'll be gone. My father's in the hospital dying. We're not close, but I must see him."

"Where does he live?" Carl asked.

"He's the governor of Guam!"

Carl took off his glasses and looked at her in shock, then turned toward Lum. Still in shock he sputtered, "He's the governor?"

"Yes." For a moment there was silence. Then she said. "I told the manager at the hotel that I'm sorry to leave so abruptly, but it's an emergency. He understood. Then I had the concierge at the hotel book me a flight. They said I could pay for the ticket at the counter. Also, I was to have lunch with Garrett tomorrow. If you could, please see he gets my note?" She handed it to Lum.

Quickly Carl asked, "Do you need money?"

"Thank you, but no. I saved all my paychecks from working." For several minutes there was silence again. Finally with tears building in her eyes Lum said, "We understand, dear. You must go."

Carl drove deliberately slow on the way to the airport. "Will someone pick you up in Guam?" he asked.

"Yes. I called my father's driver."

From the backseat of the car, she could see Lum wipe her eyes with tissue, and again, it filled her heart with sadness.

When they parked curbside, Carl and Lum both got out. Lum was the first to kiss her cheek and hug her good-bye. Carl took off his glasses and asked again, “You will return?” He hugged her tightly.

“Yes. I left the picture of my mother holding me for you to keep. I will come back.”

She handed them the note she had written. “This is important to me. Please be sure and read it!”

Buckling her seat belt she realized this was her first flight! She clutched her armrest and held her breath at the rush of taking off and enjoyed the experience as the plane climbed into the sky. From the air she could see a city of beautiful lights and thought about Garrett. She told herself it was only a kiss. Yet it was a kiss that meant something. She reassured herself, the concierge would deliver the note she wrote to Mr. Davis. She would never want him to think it rude, that she didn’t say good-bye. With the darkness outside her window and the steady humming of the plane’s engines, she tucked her head next to the pillow, pulled up the blanket and went to sleep.

CHAPTER THIRTY

Seeing light on the horizon, she watched clouds drift by the window and could feel the plane slowing. As they got lower there was Guam! From above it appeared very small. When the plane circled to land she could see patches of green jungle across the island. Then she spotted a huge cargo freighter pulling out of the harbor and it brought back frightening memories.

It was hot and more humid than she remembered as she stepped off the plane and walked down the stairs. In the open air, Napo, the chauffeur, who had known her since she was a baby, greeted her with affection. Oddly enough as she climbed in the back seat of the car, it almost felt normal. "It's good to see you again," she said. "Thank you for not telling anyone I was coming."

He nodded, "I did what you asked," then

turned his head toward the back seat and smiled. “It’s good to have you home.”

She had always felt safe and comfortable with Napo, and it was as if she had seen him yesterday.

The ride to the hospital was short. But looking out the window she became worried, realizing before long she would see her father. What would it be like?

Nervously entering the hospital, she took a deep breath and paused, then felt a rush of emotions, and once again for a moment, that dreadful image appeared in her mind.

Two people struggling in the surf. A man and a woman. A wave knocks them over. The woman gets up and runs toward the beach.

Will that horrifying image ever leave me? she thought.

Taking another deep breath, she headed down the long corridor. A guard in a uniform stood at attention by the door and as she started to enter, he took her arm.

“I’m his daughter,” she said. The doctor in

the room looked over to a couple of men standing there. One motioned that it was all right, then they moved to a corner in the room. Moments later she stood beside her father.

Light streaming through the window fell across the bed. Her father's face had lost that powerful look and his thick dark hair was now gray. It was the first time she had seen him since that lurid night several years ago. His eyes, transfixed with terror, looked up at her. Then suddenly, clenching his fist he began gasping for his last breath.

With a feverish chill she reached out and touched his arm. Soon the nurses removed his breathing tube and IVs. Quickly a thought flashed through her mind as they covered him with a white sheet. *Will the gates of heaven or hell be waiting?*

She wiped a burning tear as it rolled down her face, put on sunglasses and walked out of the hospital to the black limousine waiting.

Official flags fluttered on the front of the

car as they sped through town toward home. People stood, silently watching, in the blistering heat.

Heading up the long driveway, again there was the mansion, and she smiled.

Napo set the green duffel bag down as she glanced around. The living room still seemed enormous. The view through walls of glass to the tropical turquoise sea was stunning, just as she remembered. In the dining room, flopped across a chair was her patched tabby cat named Max. She touched his head and whispered, "You grew up to be such a big boy! And so beautiful!"

Making her way to the kitchen, she found the faithful servants listening to the radio, just as the announcement was made, "The governor is dead." Stunned, both servants looked up at her as if they were seeing a ghost. She hugged them, and they cried, then stood completely dazed again and stared at her.

In her beautiful room, everything looked the same. Piled high on a table next to a swivel chair were stacks and stacks of unopened books from her different book clubs. As she stared at them, she was certain all those years of reading as a young little girl had helped her survive alone out in the world. Suddenly the memories of that gruesome night flooded over her. She told herself, *It's because I just saw him, and he just died. That's why I'm afraid!* She thought, *Maybe at the hospital with his eyes filled with terror when he looked up, maybe it was still anger toward me! Or maybe, one last time he saw the look on my mother's face, just before he drowned her in the ocean. But then again, maybe it was just fear, knowing it was his turn and he was dying!*

While sitting on her closet floor she spotted her other yellow shoe, smiled and picked it up. Viewing the rows of beautiful custom clothes, it popped in her mind, *No kid needs this! I would have traded it all for just one friend my age!*

She felt tears rising and before the next teardrop fell, she quickly wiped her eyes. It had been an emotional day. Finally she told herself she must quit remembering the terrible things and how it all began. Now it was time to get up and continue on, whichever way life went.

From the living room she made her way out to the swimming pool. But that empty feeling of always being alone rushed across her again. Now her cat was sunbathing on a lounge chair and she scooped him up into her arms. Max fussed a little, then settled down and began to purr. “One day soon,” she said, “I will tell you the story about another cat I met. His name is Gilligan.” She hugged him. “You were just a kitten when I left. I thought about you.” She kissed his head.

She lingered at the door and then finally opened it to her father’s room, feeling almost guilty as the cat went running. His wood and jade carved bed was still impressive. And now there was something new. A large portrait in oil hung on the wall. His hair was still dark, and he was wearing one of his many beautiful custom-made suits. He looked so important, seated in his favorite dark green leather chair, holding his usual Cuban cigar in his left hand. He was handsome, but his eyes frightened her and she quickly turned away.

On the table near the sofa was a photograph of her parents' wedding. Her mother had on a beautiful simple white dress, so innocent, so pure-looking with her face glowing. Catherine said out loud to the picture, "What hopes you must have had that day!"

In his closet, she looked down at the shoeboxes and lifted a lid. Inside were shoes, no money. Then she remembered as a young girl snooping around, and pushed on a secret door to a small closet. Stacked were boxes and shoeboxes that ran halfway up the walls. She lifted several of the lids. All were stuffed with money, and she wondered where it came from. Uncomfortable, she dropped the lids, closed the door and slid his clothes back in place.

In the kitchen everyone seemed to have settled down and were extremely happy to see her. They kept touching her, kissing and pinching her checks. It was nice and before long she was sitting with the servants just as she had done when she was growing up, eating pot roast, chamorro style. It reminded her how often she longed for the flavors of this island food. It was good having them call her

Jade-R; it had been so long since she had heard anyone say her birth name.

Looking around the kitchen brought back the memories of her life growing up in this house filled with happiness and loneliness at the same time. For a moment the maids were talking and she couldn't understand. It bothered her she barely knew a few words of ancient Chamorro, the Malayo-Polynesian language of her native land. Looking at them, she remembered back to when she was little. One morning they were teaching her how to say "milk" in Chamorro, when her father walked in. What he said still rang clear, as if he were standing there in his beige suit. He pointed his finger at the servants, "I demand you only speak to her in English. That is proper for her."

Now it was dark outside the tall window in her room, and the moon was faintly smiling. She looked down at the docks remembering her frantic desire late one night to get aboard a ship going anywhere just to save her unborn baby. It felt so long ago. When she turned around, she could almost see her pink blanket spread across the end of the swivel chair and for a moment, it left her body weak. She sat on her bed and whispered, "Cherish, for you I would go through all of that again. I love you and I always will."

It was the bed she had slept in for years, but it seemed different. The down pillows, as always, smelled fresh and were fluffy. The pressed Egyptian cotton sheets were soft. But soon she found herself missing the coral tree house with the branches wrapping their arms around the walls, protecting her. She thought about Carl and Lum, Honolulu, and being with them. And that seemed more like home.

Whether she liked it or not, life had changed again and there would be lots to think about. With the heaviness of it all she fell into a deep sleep.

By midmorning the doorbell rang. A middle-aged man said, "Hello, I'm Peter Tamong, your father's attorney. We didn't get a chance to talk at the hospital yesterday. May I come in?"

"Of course, please." She led him to a chair near the fireplace.

"Has anyone told you about the funeral?"

"A little while ago, I called my father's office and his secretary was rather vague. Finally she told me all arrangements were handled. The service is tomorrow at ten o'clock; then she abruptly hung up."

He smiled. "You probably don't remember, but we met when you were small. I'm glad you are home. When I saw you in your father's room at the hospital, I knew that was a private moment for you. I didn't want to interrupt. But I thought I should make sure you know when the funeral is."

Handing her his card, he continued, "I hope you can come to my office Tuesday morning? We have things to discuss." He stood.

She shook his hand and said, "I'll be there Tuesday."

Before leaving he smiled. "I'm sure I'll see you at the service."

CHAPTER THIRTY-ONE

It was early when she awakened to the gentle drumming of rain. She slipped on a black dress. As she buttoned the P for Princess inlaid with only diamonds, she remembered these buttons were solely designed by her father and quickly shook her head and took a deep breath.

Even in the turbulent rain the drive to the cemetery didn't take long. Napo, the chauffeur, held a large black umbrella over them, offering his arm as she walked next to him. Occasionally the heels on her black shoes sank into the wet grass.

A large tent sheltered the closed casket and several rows of chairs. Draped with the Guamanian flag, the casket sat on boards over the open grave. Behind it a hand-framed, hand-painted Seal of Guam sat on a stand surrounded by dozens of floral arrangements.

Most of the chairs were already occupied; all by people and faces she had never seen. Right up front she spotted her father's secretary in a brown dress. The woman stared at Jade-R with disdain through the drooping lids of her brown eyes. Saliva gathered at the corners of her mouth giving her the appearance of a vicious dog. Eventually she turned away.

Looking further down the front row Jade-R thought, *Is that Ditch? He has changed.* For a moment she wasn't certain until she saw his profile. He kept wiping his nose. Feeling uncomfortable, Jade-R moved closer to Napo as she stood among strangers outside the tent, rain pouring off the edges of their umbrella.

A middle-aged lady with a strong voice began singing an old Guamanian song. People were emotional and kept wiping their eyes. The song was touching, but Jade-R thought, *Why can't I cry, even listening to that song?*

Next, a man with a thick mustache got up with his notes. He fumbled through them. "As we know," he finally said, "Our governor had his own unique style. Everything he did brought comfort and light to the people of

Guam. He advocated good education and reached new heights while rebuilding most of our schools! It took courage promoting the construction of new restaurants and hotels that would bring jobs and money to the people.

"He was a devoted husband, and we watched him suffer when he lost his beautiful wife Reign and experienced other kinds of…" he stopped speaking as he shuffled his notes around, finally enumerating awkwardly other family heartaches.

"But he carried on with courage. He set an example for all of us. You couldn't help but smile when you heard his laugh. He was blessed with the gift of being able to tell a story or joke, better than anyone! You that knew him well would agree.

"And there wasn't anything he wouldn't do for someone in need. He was a great man.

"We will miss you, Governor. But you will be enshrined in glory forever on this Island. May you rest in peace."

Next, the former lieutenant governor, now

governor, said a few kind words.

When the service ended Jade-R still felt nothing.

A heavy-set, older-looking man, with a rather frail woman beside him, came from under the tent and quickly opened their umbrellas. “Sorry, Napo, for your loss. I know you worked for him a long time.” The man patted him on the shoulder.

“Thanks,” Napo said, and then quickly added, “This is the governor’s daughter, Jade-R.”

Instantly she felt uncomfortable with the man’s restrained handshake.

However he soon replied, “Yes. I remember Jade-R.” With a strange look he added, “I was your father’s doctor for years. We had a talk late one night about you!” Then a shadow of coldness descended on him. Abruptly, he excused himself and the lady with him.

As they walked away, her father’s lawyer Mr. Tamong was standing there. After the normal polite hello, it was quiet as they watched people. Then, looking around, Mr.

Tamong said, "The service was nice. Your father would approve!" Casually he added, "You know, I think rain is good at a funeral! Maybe it washes away certain things and let's us move on with life."

Turning, he said, "I'll see you in the morning at my office."

"Yes. Nine o'clock," she answered, as he walked away. A man wearing a red shirt and tan sports jacket that made his island print tie stand out, headed toward them. Napo introduced Jade-R. "This is Mr. Lewis. He leases one of the governor's liquor stores." The man looked at her, almost bowing. She thought as he shook her hand, *If I had on my father's jade ring, I think he would kiss it.*

Turning to leave, they heard a rough loud voice say, "Stop!"

He drew closer, and Jade-R was surprised at how much weight he had lost. Now aged and very weathered-looking, he still gave off an unholy mean spirit as he approached.

Ditch said to Napo, "Here we are. He's dead." Then he looked at Jade-R.

"Where the hell you been?" he spurted out.

She stood silent.

Quickly Napo said, "Good service. The governor would be proud."

Napo took Jade-R's arm while saying, "Ditch, he would want us to go on with life." Right then the sound of dreadful thunder cut across the sky. "Gotta go. See you, Ditch."

Napo escorted Jade-R toward the limousine with the official flags no longer on the front, with the governor's death.

That evening she still felt uneasy, in fact, awful. She studied herself in the mirror. She knew her father's doctor; he was the one, the one who would have come to the house to cut out her baby. Then she remembered the last scorching words her father ever said to her. "You are a disgrace to me."

She marched with fury down the hall to his room and looked around as if to face that demon. But those words could never be taken back. His death was final and his grave was deep. Turning toward his portrait on the wall, she fell to her knees and chanted, "You're a hero to so many people out there, yet... you completely destroyed your own family!"

CHAPTER THIRTY-TWO

The sun was brilliant and the weather balmy as she entered the elevator. When the doors opened, Mr. Tamong was waiting to greet her. His private office was tastefully decorated with everything blue: Walls, drapery, and furniture all in different tones. He offered her a comfortable upholstered chair, then sat behind a bamboo desk.

"Let me start by saying your father was my only client for over twenty years. He was a very intelligent man. This is a copy of the trust I set up for him when you were three years old. Please note that your father named your trust fund 'The Guamanian Princess.' That's how he saw you. Because he was the governor, he had the land legally entitled in your name. After you read everything you will see upon his death, the trust provides that all income goes directly to you. Here are the documents that show I have had Limited Power of Attorney over land deals for you that go into that trust. Your father told me long before he was governor, the first dime he made he saved and started buying land in Agana Bay. In total, it is now over one hundred acres. There are twenty businesses that pay land fees monthly into your trust. Now that your father has died, I am obligated to relinquish my power of attorney back to you.

"First. Your private home on the hill, he paid to have it built. The government does not own that. That's his personal property. The same with his automobiles. And the building we are sitting in, he owns.

"The Agana Bay Hotel he built and owns out- right. In fact, Tony Louhon's restaurant is located in that hotel, and is the best place for dining in Guam. You'll see another small hotel on the list. It has thirty rooms, lobby, bar and kitchen. The navy guys all stay there. A side business to do with women is run out of there. I have everything printed out for you, all properties are in your trust."

He was quiet, then leaned back in his chair. He looked at her. “Do you know Ditch?”

“Yes, I remember him. He didn’t come to the house very often, but yes. I saw him briefly yesterday at the funeral.”

Mr. Tamong said, “He runs the small hotel where the navy guys that come in and out of port stay. There are several small liquor stores and a few grocery stores in Tinian and Rota. They have a boat going back and forth delivering goods daily between the islands.

“Also, the governor and I had an agreement for years. I managed the other tenants here in the building in lieu of rent. Monthly we give him an accurate account on all the properties, who’s paid, repairs, etc. That is, Margaret, the C.P.A that works for me, does. It’s a full-time job for her. But she knows everything about every building and tenant.”

As he handed her an additional file, he said, “If you need money, this bank, which is right down the street, has an account that was opened in your name years ago. So you can get checks or draw whatever you need.”

"Thank you," Jade-R replied as she looked at the stack of documents, then at Mr. Tamong.

He paused, then said. "I was curious, of course, as to what happened and why you left. But I never asked. It's not my business, and your father never discussed it. As his lawyer and friend, I want you to know he tore the island apart looking for you. Even went to the Marianas searching. After that he was never really the same." It was quiet as he looked down at his desk.

Finally he added, "He didn't know if he would ever see you again but never changed his will and that is the way he wanted it. You are the sole beneficiary.

Oh one other thing. He did leave twenty-five thousand to a church. It's a priest he knew growing up. I have already dropped off that check. Actually, it was the same priest that gave the closing benediction at the service.

When you go over everything, you'll notice there's a separate account with your father's name and mine. He opened it when he became sick. I'm able to pay taxes on the house and all his properties and payroll to the help. The governor said to me, 'There's enough to cover it for years; after that I'm sure this cancer will have grabbed me and I'll probably be dead. Give everyone money to live on for at least ten years, including yourself. The rest, I don't give a damn.'"

There was silence for a while. She looked at him, and then asked. "Have you always been an honest man?"

He leaned back in his chair thinking, before he answered. "The governor gave me my start."

He turned his head and rubbed his hands across his face and sat thinking for a moment. "I was fresh out of law school and had just passed the Bar when I met your father. He hired me with no experience. He said he had faith in me. Early on I did a few things for him I'm not proud of. But I felt I owed him! Today I would never do anything to be disbarred."

He pointed to a framed photo on his desk. "See my wife and children in that picture? They mean the world to me and I always want their respect."

He looked at her. "But that's an interesting question. Why did you ask?"

"Probably because you worked for my father for so long! But I do appreciate your answer," she said, smiling at him.

He took a deep breath and looked out the window. "I'm going to tell you this because I think it's important. Over the years, I got to know the governor quite well. He personally told me not long ago... in fact, right in the chair you're sitting in...how he grew up. Do you know the story?"

Jade-R shook her head no.

"Never had a pair of shoes until he was seven. His mother had no idea who his father was! It sounded like he would have almost been better off without her. She was mean to him. Then he found Ditch, lying wet and filthy, in a ditch!" Smiling he said, "That's how he got his name. More than likely he had just been abandoned. Your father figured he was probably around three years old. He cleaned him up with a neighbor's garden hose. Heck, they said he still messed his pants. Then your father's mother died, and they couldn't sneak back into the dumpy house to sleep any longer. So they were completely on their own on the streets doing whatever it took to survive." He added, "It's hard for me to think about those two young kids living that way!"

He shook his head several times. "I'm still amazed. But the difference is your father was ambitious, extremely smart and very charismatic! As for Ditch, well, he's a little off in the head and your father knew that. The guy always had problems and your father would fix them. He was the only person Ditch ever trusted. When he was shot, he was too tough to die. I don't know what he'll do now with no one to keep him even halfway balanced. It was a strange relationship. But there was a certain bond between them. Probably because they only had each other growing up."

Again he looked out the window at the ocean. "I didn't always approve of everything the governor did. However he always treated me more than extremely well."

Jade-R sat quietly. At last with a gentle smile she stood. "I guess I have a lot to think about."

"It's what I'm here for, if you want to run something by me."

"Thank you for the information. I will be calling you."

He shook her hand and said, "And thank you!"

Puzzled, she said, "For what?"

"For not asking me right away, how many millions of dollars you are now worth!"

She smiled.

Outside, Napo was leaning against the limousine, warming his face as he looked toward the sun. Quickly she hopped in the front seat. He said, "Oh, you need to be in the back."

"No... I need a friend," she replied.

As they rode along she asked, "What would you be doing if you had not worked for my father?"

"Well, let me see. I always liked driving. It's relaxing to me." Then he smiled and said,

“Maybe I’da had a taxi!”

They passed the Dairy Queen. Quickly she said, “Let’s go back. We need an ice cream.”

“Sounds good,” he said. “Just like when you were little; you always liked your ice cream.”

As they ate their hot fudge sundaes, she inquired, “Would you happen to know where Kimea lived? I’d like to meet her son.”

“Sure, I drove her home when she had time off.”

“Good. Tomorrow if we can, I’d like to go there.”

On the way home Jade-R quickly looked as they passed the place once called Island Burgers. “We guarantee the best burgers on the island.” The spot where it all began one night was no longer there! A new dry cleaner’s had moved in. She thought to herself, *Everything has changed. Even that little place didn’t make it.*

CHAPTER THIRTY-THREE

The hot sun beat down on the pavement as they drove along. Jade-R had never seen this part of the island and was amazed how beautiful, how green. She sat up front talking with Napo and it was easy, like tossing a ball, or riding her bike again. His straight brown hair had a wiry gray streak at the part. Then he smiled and a fond memory popped up.

"When I was little, I remember asking why do you wear that gold cap on your front tooth?"

He smiled again. "And I'd tell you, that's where I hide the banana bread the maids give me. Your father would shake his head, and you would always giggle."

She smiled, "Yes, that would make me laugh. I remember you have kids?"

He replied, "Three."

"Tell me about them."

"My girl, she's the oldest and married." He smiled. "And about to make us grandparents! Ben, our first son, works at a garage. He's their number one mechanic! He has big dreams, one day he'll buy that garage." Then he laughed. "I'd get home and my wife would be ready to wring his neck. She'd say, 'See what he did?' The lawn mower or something would be in pieces on the patio floor. But he could always put it back together. Just had that knack for fixing."

"And your other son?"

"He's in his second year of college. A good young man; he is going to be a dentist."

She could see a proud look come over his face just thinking about his kids.

As they passed Tumon Bay, a young boy, barefooted, stood on the corner with stalks of green bananas resting on his head. Tearing one off he waved it at their car.

Curious, she said, "He's so little, and that pile's so high! Do you think his mother knows where he is?"

"Sure." Napo answered. "She probably put

him there, then left."

They turned onto a dirt road where tall grass mingled with native plants and ran wild. Most of the houses had tin roofs that hung over roughly sawed boards, and everything looked shoddy. Clothes on the line were blowing; some appeared to have been hanging for days. Close to another house they waited for a truck to move. An old man caught her eye as he sat on a wooden stool, batting flies and watching the woman next to him yank feathers from a dead chicken.

Pulling in front of a brown house in need of paint, they stopped. In the yard, half grass, half dirt, children were playing with a worn-out hula hoop. Napo spoke to them in Chamorro. Turning back to Jade-R he pointed, "Ton's inside."

A pretty young lady holding a little boy said, "Come in," as she opened the screen door.

As she entered, Jade-R looked down at a table covered with family photographs. A handsome young man soon entered the room. All he could say was "Hello."

Then he stared at her. “I know you.”

Putting out his hand to shake, he said, “I’m Ton, Kimea’s son. I hoped someday we’d meet.”

Jade-R quickly replied. “Your mother talked about you all the time. I remember when you got your dog Curley.”

He smiled. “My mother talked about you too. She said your eyes were as pale as clouds in the sky.”

He turned. “This is my wife, Rose, and that’s our son. We have another one out front somewhere.”

Rose picked up a black and white picture and handed it to Jade-R. Kimea was holding Jade-R’s hand as the two of them stood under a tree when she was little. Ton said, “If you like, you may keep that. I have others.”

She drew it to her chest. “I don’t have a picture of your mother. Thank you.”

An old woman sitting next to a small television kept saying, “Haf Adai-” she smiled.

“This is my mother’s sister, my aunt,” Ton

announced. The woman smiled again and kept saying, "Gat Bo Gat Bo!"

Ton explained. "She's saying you're pretty." He offered Jade-R a seat on the clean but very worn sofa.

"So many times in the last few years I have thought about your mother. I feel bad I was with her most of the time and you only saw her on weekends growing up."

"Don't," Ton said. "I had a wonderful grandmother always with me. We were all scared when my father died. Definitely scared, especially my mother. We didn't know what to do. We had no money. I was proud when she went to work taking care of you. I'd tell my friends that she works for the governor! She's important! We had plenty of food and lived in this nice house. My mom, she wanted me to get an education. The governor was kind and paid for my school."

"Did you finish your education?"

"Yes. I'm a teacher. So is my wife. We met at the University."

"Do you work close by?"

"Not far, maybe five miles." He stepped near the window and pointed to a group of buildings across the street. "We're saving as much as we can. We have a plan. The man that owns the property wants to sell. We want to open our own school. Plus, there are two small houses. My aunt can have her own place. Right now she's in with our boys. It's crowded, but we manage. The other house, maybe homeless kids will come."

As she watched him talk she could see expressions from his mother and also his charitable soul.

Rose asked, "Would you like to stay for dinner?"

Jade-R could smell the delicious aroma of meat cooking and answered. "Thank you, but I'm sure Napo needs to get home. Another time." She looked around the small room and there wasn't much furniture but this was a home filled with tremendous love.

When she was ready to leave, Ton and Jade-R stood alone by the car. "Is your mother's grave close by?"

"Yes, just down a mile that way."

"Do you have the time to show me?"

"Sure," he replied.

In the car Napo said, "I remember I went to her service. It was nice. The governor wanted to attend, but that day he didn't feel well."

The cemetery was very simple, with tidy rows of white-painted wooden crosses. In the middle of one row a beautiful green marble headstone stood out. Proudly Ton said, "Your father had her white cross removed and put this in place of it."

She knelt in front and laid her hand across the chiseled words "Kimea Batingo." To herself she whispered, "Thank you for everything; I miss you."

She was silent on the ride back, while Napo and Ton spoke about the changes going on in Guam.

In the driveway at Ton's house he started to climb out of the car, then turned to Jade-R. "Don't ever feel bad; my mother loved me. I was never jealous. I was glad she loved you too. I grew up happy!”

That night she looked at the small picture of Kimea holding her hand and knew that the huge difference that lovely woman had made in two children’s lives would be with them always.

CHAPTER THIRTY-FOUR

Soon after breakfast she heard loud voices outside.

At the door Napo was holding the arm of a woman with stout legs and dark hair, who was jabbing her finger on his chest. She turned when she saw Jade-R. In a mindless state, her eyes bulging, she started lashing out.

"I was the only one that really cared about your father. Me, his secretary! Not you. You went running off. Just had to go have your fun, you disgusting brat! I came for the oil portrait of the governor. I found the artist and your father said I could have it. It's mine. I want it!"

She yanked away from Napo and stared at Jade-R with the same disdain as the day of the funeral.

Jade-R said, "If the governor said you could

have it, please Napo, will you bring it out for her?"

While he was gone Jade-R asked, "Would you like a glass of water?"

The woman started to cry, then fought back, jumbling her words. "I want nothing from you. Even talking to you irks me. You're the one that hurt him." She turned her attention to Napo as he put the painting in the back of a truck. Nothing else was said. Hurriedly she backed up, popped the clutch and tore off down the drive.

Napo shook his head. "I will tell the guard at the gate she's not welcome here anymore." Watching him as he started down the road, Jade-R thought, *My father's secretary thinks she knows what went on. I wonder... were they lovers? No, I doubt it. She's probably still doing what she has done for twenty years. Defend the governor with her unfailing loyalty.*

That day her morning included trying to telephone Mr. Tamong several times, but the circuits were busy. Finally it rang through and she was able to go immediately to his office.

She sat in the same chair.

He smiled. “You have a serious look.”

She opened a notebook. “I’ve given this a great deal of thought. I have no intention of staying in Guam. I hope you can help me with these things.”

He answered, “That’s what I’m here for.”

“First, I have this address. I would like you to contact the owner and pay what he’s asking for that property.”

He answered, “I’ll negotiate and see what I can do.”

“That sounds good, but in the end I want to make sure we get it.” She handed him a sheet of paper.

Puzzled, he glanced down as she continued.

“My second question, what does Guam need? I mean, is there anything they’re thinking about... library, museum? That’s what I’m trying to ask.”

He leaned back in his chair. After a minute of thinking he said, "A couple of years ago, your father was looking for land to build an additional hospital. But it was going to cost a lot to bring water and electricity to the location he found. Why are you asking?"

"I'm thinking, with the beautiful view on the hill and the house, it would be perfect for something. And it has all that land around it to build on, with room for plenty of parking."

He lit up. "That's right, and all utilities are in. Are you thinking of selling it?"

"No. I would donate it. But let me ask you this. I would want a guarantee; it can only be used for a good cause. I'm not giving it away, and then have it become some official's personal home. But if it's used for the public to benefit, I'd be glad to do that."

He looked at her. "You could sell it."

"I know," she answered.

He paused. "Okay. I'll contact the new governor and a few other people and speak on your behalf."

“That would be good. Thank you.”

Concerned, he said, “Today I telephoned Ditch again. I told him according to the will, he must buy the hotel he runs. He has plenty of money. He cussed at me and then hung up. I will notify him in writing. I’ll give him one week to respond.”

CHAPTER THIRTY-FIVE

As she climbed out of the big pink marble tub, she remembered it was the one thing she had missed the most in Formosa, soaking with bubbles up to her neck. Patting her skin dry, she splashed on after-bath, and then wrapped a towel around her. For a moment, she started thinking about how blessed she was. Glancing out the window, clouds seemed to bounce across the exquisite sky. She pulled her shoulder-length hair into a ponytail and slipped on white pedal pushers with a blue cotton top. Max strolled past her meowing several times as she dabbed perfume on her neck. She picked him up and headed to the living room as the phone abruptly rang. It was the gate calling.

"A Dr. Eastman is here to see Jade-R."

Quickly she interrupted, "Let him in." She spotted the car winding up the long drive to the front.

"Aloha!" he said, as he removed his sunglasses.

Stunned, she repeated "Aloha back," and threw her arms around his neck as they hugged. "Come in. How did you find me?"

He smiled. "Even at the rent-a-car they knew where the governor's mansion was. It was here that I had trouble. I told the gate I came to surprise Catherine Reign. It's my birthday! The guard said, 'Nobody lives here by that name.' I asked, 'Do you know where I can find her?'

'I told you that person is not here!'

"Finally I asked, 'Do you know someone with pale blue eyes and dark shiny hair, really beautiful?'

'Oh, you mean the governor's daughter, Jade-R?'

'Yes. That's who I mean.'

"That's how I found you." He grinned.

She smiled. "Did I hear you say it's your

birthday?"

"It is. Yesterday while making my rounds at the hospital I thought, the only person I want to see is you."

She smiled again, saying, "Come in to the living room."

He stood looking out at the view as she studied him intensely. "This is quite a home you grew up in, and that's ... now, that's a view!"

"It is nice. I never get tired of it. Tell me, how's your home? Have you started building?"

"I have. The foundation's poured and they are framing." He grinned. "My contractor said I'm the typical owner. I just added another room last week. Thought I needed a library."

"Library, that's great."

There was a moment of silence as they stared into each other's eyes.

"I'm happy you're here. Let's get you something to drink." When they stood, he picked up a picture.

"Is this your parents?"

She nodded.

"Your father was a good-looking man, and your mother... beautiful! You have her eyes."

He looked around. "Five years ago I would not have noticed much in this room. Now that I'm building a home, well," he grinned, "this place is furnished beautifully. I like the carved wood pieces mixed with bamboo."

In the kitchen the servants looked up. "This is my friend, Dr. Eastman, from Hawaii." Jade-R made the introductions, and when she finished pouring him a glass of iced lemonade, she dug out a huge pan and started dumping flour, sugar, eggs and other ingredients.

"What are you doing?" he asked.

"Making you a cake. You can't have a birthday without cake! I think you told me your favorite was pineapple upside-down, right?"

"You have a good memory." He leaned near her against the counter as the mixer splattered some batter on his shirt. She laughed and said, “Sorry.” Then laughed again. He dipped his finger in the bowl, and she gave him a reproachful look.

“Well, it is my cake, my birthday!”

As she closed the oven door she asked the cook in the kitchen, “Will you watch that, please? And he’ll be staying for dinner. Come I’ll show you around.” They headed down the long hall to her room.

“This is your bedroom?” he asked. “You have a great view out your doors.”

“I spent most of my time when I was young in this room.” Suddenly, it really hit her. He had come all this way and was standing there. “How long are you here for?”

“Only until tomorrow. That gives me a day. I have an important surgery on Friday.”

“You came all this way for one day?”

“You’re worth it!” Grinning, he put his arm around her. In the entry they started climbing wide wood stairs that curved and wrapped around. “What room are we heading up to?”

“The library,” she answered. “But it was

also where I went to school. My teacher and I would spend all day up here."

At the top, the wood floors were highly polished. One huge wall was covered with shelves filled with books. A double-sided desk with a leather top sat near the windows. She rubbed her hand across the leather, her pencils squarely placed near the ruler.

"See, this was my side looking out at the ocean."

"Not bad, not bad. Wish I had this view in school," he replied.

"Well, someday I want my kids to go to a real school and have lots of friends. In the evening they can do their homework at this desk!"

He grinned. "Have you read all these books?"

"Most of them, I guess. Follow me, I'll show you the wing where you'll stay."

"Oh, no, no. I have a room reserved at a place in town called the Agana Bay Hotel."

She smiled to herself, *Agana Bay Hotel! I*

own that!

“Oh, this is much better for you” she said. “Besides, we’ll be up late talking.”

“You’re probably right!” he agreed.

When she opened the door to the guest bedroom he said, “Wow, I don’t think I would get this in town. Did you have lots of guests growing up?”

“You are the first that I know of to ever stay in this room.”

They sat on the sofa. In a serious tone she asked, “How are Carl and Lum? I have only telephoned them twice.”

“They’re good. Actually, I see them once a week. We eat together. I’ve gotten to know Carl. He’s an interesting man. Very smart! Sure likes his koi fish. But they miss you.”

She lowered her head, “I miss them too.”

He could see she had lost her smile, and quickly said, “Ask me about Hawaii.”

She smiled again as he continued. “It’s good. Part of coming up here reminded me of home."

She nodded, "I know, especially the weather. It can be raining on one side of the street and sun shining on the other."

"Remember, I'm a guy from Ohio and I've always found that interesting, but strange."

At dinner he looked around, then at her. "This is wonderful. I hoped we'd have the day alone. I wanted to tell you, I was sorry to hear about your father. Were you close?"

"When I was small." Softly she said, "I read something the other day. Failures keep you humble. I didn't see my father in the last few years. I saw him only beside his hospital bed minutes before he died." Then she looked down at her plate and was quiet.

Still watching her, Garrett said, "Life is certainly a journey. Sometimes it takes awhile to understand what we think are failures and reevaluate them later and see them more clearly."

Then he changed the subject. "How big is

Guam? From the plane it didn't appear too big."

"It is actually around 12 miles wide and 30 miles long and you probably know it is approximately 3,950 miles west of Hawaii."

"No. I didn't."

"We also have our own time zone. It's called Chamorro Standard Time. But the down side, other than typhoons and hurricanes, etc., we get earthquakes. We're on the edge of the Western Pacific Plate and near the Philippine Sea Plate."

"I don't really know what you are talking about." he said jokingly with a smile.

"Well, it's like a trench paralleling some islands near here called the Mariana Islands. It marks the fast-moving Pacific Plate that moves against the slower Philippine Plate. One is usually under the other." She tried to explain with hand motions, then could see he was teasing her.

"I'm probably not explaining it right." She laughed. "Well, it's not important and hopefully we'll have no earthquakes while you're here."

"That sounds good!"

"However, I just thought of something. There is one thing you would like. The surfing is good on Guam! But I'm not sure which area. Wouldn't want you to go where the stingrays go for breakfast!"

"That's nice of you." He grinned as he finished his curried spareribs.

Max slowly walked through the dining room swishing his tail. He looked around, wanting to plunk down on his favorite bamboo chair. He appeared upset that it was being used.

"And who is this?" Garrett inquired.

"That is Max."

"What does he want?"

She looked at Max, then said, "I think you're in his chair. He's not even-tempered like Mr. Davis' very smart Gilligan. But he's an interesting cat. Speaking of Gilligan, how is wonderful Mr. Davis?"

"Every time I see him the first question,

‘When is Catherine returning?’ The Orchid Room hired a pianist he isn’t fond of.”

Smiling, she asked, “And what birthday milestone is this for you today?”

“I’m thirty-four,” he answered.

She said “Ah,” then excused herself. Minutes later she came out from the kitchen holding a cake with sparklers blazing and singing “Happy Birthday.” When she finished her song, she said, “Bet you can’t blow these out.”

“And I won’t try,” he answered. “But you have a nice voice and I liked your version of Happy Birthday.”

She smiled, “For that compliment, I’ll cut you a great big piece to go with your coffee.”

In the soft light, she looked into his eyes. They were so hazel they appeared almost gold. Finishing the last bite, she asked, “Did you bring a swimsuit?”

“Never go to an island without it.”

Her legs were long and tan, and the water was velvet soft as it brushed their skin. Evening stars twinkled and the moon smiled down at them. They traded stories as she floated around watching him swim several laps. They listened to slow jazz on the radio. She looked at him in wonder, as he told jokes, sitting on the side of the pool and laughing. She was blissfully aware he was teasing her, as now and then he'd touch her leg while talking. There was a certain amount of glamour as she blinked at him too hard, and too long!

Typically, out of nowhere, rain began pouring. He held a towel over her as they headed inside. With a kiss he picked her up and climbed the stairs. In the guest room she could feel his hard body as he held her close. She felt his warm breath against her ear as he murmured, "I missed you." She melted in his arms and whispered, "I missed you too."

He removed her wet suit and gently laid her on the bed. She felt no shame, only how much she craved him. He kissed her hard nipples and down her body. Finally he lay on top of her as she opened her legs. His slow penetration pleased her and soon they were drenched in love. Just the thought of him made her weak, and the scent of his skin caressed her as they spent the next few hours feverishly wrapped together.

Finally she lay resting in his arms. He said, “Do you mind if I tell you a secret?”

She asked, “Will I like this secret?”

“I believe you will. I have something for you.” He handed her a long velvet box. She opened it and there was the strand of south sea island pearls she had admired so many times.

“I went by Kamora Jewelry and Lum told me you were drawn to these.”

Excited and no longer guarded, she exclaimed, “I love them!”

He grinned. “But do you love me?”

Her eyes widened with surprise, and she answered, “Yes.”

“Good,” he replied, as he helped her fasten the clasp. “They are beautiful around your neck. Now, when are you returning to

Hawaii?"

"My lawyer is finalizing some business for me, and let's see, movers arrive week after next to pack the furniture, take it to the docks to be put in containers and shipped to Hawaii for me."

"So how long before you come home?" he asked again.

"I'm not sure exactly. Why?" she said, looking at him with a smile.

"Why?" he said as he kissed her neck. "Because I have an insatiable craving to do this again, and soon. It would be a little hard, as you pointed out, being 3,950 miles apart."

He kissed her cheek. "Now, do I call you Catherine or Jade-R?"

"You call me Catherine. Jade-R Jewel Ponce is on my birth certificate. Catherine Jewel Reign is on my passport."

"Where did you get the name Catherine?"

"I gave it to myself. One of the first important books I ever read when I was young; the girl's name was Catherine. I admired her and read the book many times. My mother's name was Reign Jewel. I reversed her name. Catherine Jewel Reign."

He said, "Why did you change your name?"

She paused a moment. "Another time I'll tell you why my name got changed. When I leave here, my birth name, Jade-R Jewel Ponce will stay in Guam. Something else. I just turned twenty-one. My passport shows I'm twenty-four. Thought my real age is important. I should clear that up."

"All right for now," he replied pinching her cheek, "but I want to know someday."

With no sleep, dawn arrived quickly. She scurried down to her room. The very hot shower felt revitalizing. She scrambled fresh eggs, fried potatoes, and sliced fresh baked bread, then dropped it into the toaster.

As Garrett entered, she smiled and touched her pearls. Steam billowed from the coffee as she handed a cup to him. While they ate breakfast, Jade-R smiled. "I'm very happy this morning."

"Good," he replied and grinned. "When you get back to Hawaii you will be even happier."

They stood by the car. He looked at her with concern. "Don't work too hard moving. I wish I could stay to help, but you understand, right?" He tossed his small overnight bag on the front seat as she nodded her head. He wrapped his arms around her tiny waist, and they shared a passionate good-bye kiss. They looked at each other in lingering silence. He leaned over and kissed her neck, gathering with him the last hint of her perfume. "I will call you every few days," then he smiled. "Maybe every day." Then he slowly drove away.

She touched her creamy pearls and watched until his car was no longer in sight.

That night at the piano she played every romantic song she knew, and her thoughts were only of Garrett.

CHAPTER THIRTY-SIX

From the living room Jade-R watched the sunset drop into the ocean. Her thoughts were of Garrett and the love she had for him.

In the kitchen she grabbed hot pads and took her pecan pie out of the oven. Sitting with the servants for dinner at a small table near the refrigerator, she got up to pour milk in her glass.

Suddenly the screen door flew open. Ditch, along with two other guys, rushed in. His hair slicked down with pomade, and he was dressed in a faded, wrinkled gray suit with a shirt that looked like it should have been thrown out long ago. One of the men was fat and bald, the other looked Filipino. He was short, wearing a tee shirt that said USA on the front, and had a cigarette hanging out of his mouth.

Immediately Ditch grabbed Jade-R, causing

the glass in her hand to go crashing to the floor. He yelled at her, “I ran the hotel with the girls. Your father should have left that to me. He had me combing the island for months looking for you, you little bitch. Now you show up and take what’s mine. My hotel!”

From his hip pocket he pulled a knife and waved it in front of her face. “See this? You won’t be the first girl I left my initials on.”

Flushed with anger he yelled again, “Get your ass down to the lawyer and sign that hotel over to me. You don’t know what I’m capable of doing.” He slid the knife close to her cheek as he said, “You won’t be pretty, all carved up with one of your eyes missing. Don’t think I won’t!”

From his mouthful of crooked teeth, he shouted, “Sign the papers!”

As he backed away, the older servant got up from her chair and stepped in front of Jade-R.

Ditch laughed. “Nobody, not you or any one else, can protect her, you silly old woman!” He pushed her to the floor. Jade-R scrambled to help.

With his knife still in his hand, those evil-looking eyes turned toward them again. "You don't want to see me or my boys back here." Heading out, they laughed as the screen door slammed shut.

Blood raced frantically through Jade-R's body as she ran to the living room in time to see them leaving past the guard gate. Instantly she phoned the gate to the man on duty. "Don't let Ditch back in. Take him off the list of people that have access to enter. Call the police if he or his buddies come near this property again."

Running from room to room, she made sure all doors and windows were locked.

In the kitchen the servants were huddled together, shaking as Jade-R bent down and hugged them. "It's all right. They're gone." She boiled water for tea. The freshly baked pie sat on the counter uncut. No one wanted a piece.

Later, in her room, waves of fear rushed through her again. She had not felt this unsafe since Formosa and the Shangri-La hotel. Rubbing her head to sooth the tension, she tried to forget locking eyes with Ditch and reliving that moment of private hell.

During the night she wandered through the house flanked by fear and checking doors.

Early the next morning when Napo arrived, the servants told him about Ditch. When Jade-R walked into the kitchen, his first words, “We’re calling the police. That guy’s not right in the head. I’m worried. I never trusted him. Sometimes he would show up here drunk and the governor would tell me to drive him back to the hotel. He’s dangerous.”

“Yes, I found that out,” Jade-R replied. “Please take me down town to Mr. Tamong’s office as soon as he calls back. We’ll get his advice.”

Pulling into the parking lot, her lawyer stood waiting, then got right to business. Jade-R looked at Napo and motioned for him to come along.

“After we talked, I went over everything again, even my notes prior to drawing his will. Nothing was outlined and left to Ditch. I know for a fact he has plenty of cash to live on for the rest of his life. Period. It was the governor's wish for you to inherit everything. That's why he put the properties in a trust years ago. They are already yours."

"How many rooms does that hotel have?" she asked.

Mr. Tamong glanced at Napo. After a moment he said, "I believe around thirty rooms. It has a lobby, good-sized bar and small kitchen. I've only been there once, years ago when your father first bought it."

"Maybe I should go there? Is it nice?"

"It could use a lot of paint. But until we get some kind of restraining order...it is not safe for you to be there. From what I know, girls offer their services for a price. As I said, it's a favorite for the navy guys. That's what Ditch turned it into, if you catch my meaning."

"Is that legal?"

"Well, the police look the other way for a fee."

"It's a rowdy place," Napo added. "You don't want to see that!"

Quickly Mr. Tamong added, "Napo's right."

He picked up the phone and began dialing. "My brother-in-law is a retired cop. He and another retired cop do private work. I'm hiring them to stay at the mansion around the clock until we get Ditch handled. Here's his name. Give it to the gate."

Napo quickly asked, "Shouldn't we also call the police?"

"You could, but until Ditch commits a crime, more than just threatening you, there's not much the police can do. I'll file a restraining order so he can't go near the Palms Hotel – that's the name of it – or near the governor's mansion. That should really set him off. None of us will be safe after that."

Looking at Jade-R, he humbly said, "Your father would want us to protect you."

Agreeing, Napo nodded his head. The ride home after that was quiet.

Finally Jade-R asked, "When my father went out every night, is that where he went?"

"Not that hotel," Napo quickly replied. "He

was at his big luxury one, the Agana Bay Hotel. He socialized in the restaurant and listened to live music in the bar. I know, because I'd hear him talk about it. Ditch runs the other place, and I'm told, he treats the girls badly."

"What do you mean 'treats the girls badly?' "

Napo paused, thinking. Then he explained. "The lobby and bar are actually nice. Everything looks respectable. Most of the second floor is for working girls, and most all of the other rooms are filled with navy guys coming and going. 'Badly,' means that Ditch has a violent side to him. It's simple. He can't stand women."

Napo looked out the rear-view mirror and added, "I'll say no more. You're young and don't need to know all that stuff."

It was quiet in the car. Jade-R was still thinking as Napo waved to the man on duty and waited for the gates to swing open at the governor's mansion.

At the top of the long driveway she said,

"Please come in the kitchen. Let's have some pie with the servants and talk. They'll feel better knowing we'll have security around here."

That evening there was no moon out as she anxiously waited for Garrett's long distance call. Hearing his voice was calming and for a moment she seemed to forget the last twenty-four hours. He did most of the talking. She winced when he asked, "Is everything all right?"

"Yes, I miss you," she said.

Then his last words were, as always, "When are you returning?"

She whispered, "Soon, I hope, soon."

It was early morning when the phone rang. On the other end of the line, Mr. Tamong said, "I know it's barely daylight, but can I come over?"

Mr. Tamong had a more relaxed look as he entered. "I called Napo. I wanted both of you to know... we don't need to worry about Ditch; he's dead. Seems he fell off a balcony and broke his neck. It happened at the Palms Hotel around three o'clock this morning. My friend, the police chief, called me knowing I'm still the lawyer for the governor's estate. The story is that Ditch was beating a fifteen-year-old girl. According to the chief, he beat her rather badly, then pulled out a knife. She ran and he started chasing her. She moved to one side and that's when he went off the balcony."

Napo sighed with relief, and then sat quietly.

Nothing was said. It was silent for a long moment.

Looking up, Jade-R finally asked, "Is the girl going to be okay?"

"I think so. I'll find out."

"Please, and if you could, where she is." He nodded.

"By the way, the other thugs usually with him just got arrested. They robbed a tourist. The police have two good eyewitnesses."

Pulling her cardigan sweater over her shoulder, she said, "Thank you for all your help!"

The clinic sign was dimly lit. The modest, very small, wood building was faded white. The woman sitting behind the counter, writing, smiled as Jade-R walked in.

Jade-R politely asked, "Which room is Gloria Cabrera in?"

"The only room we have," she said, pointing down the hall.

Gloria's face was disfigured from the many blows. She looked up with fear in her blood-filled eyes. Such a young girl and life had already been so cruel. Jade-R asked the woman sitting on the foot of the bed, "Do you and Gloria speak English?"

The middle-aged woman answered "Only me."

"My name is Jade-R."

The woman answered back, "Hi, I'm Maria." She pulled her hair back on one side.

Not the entire ear, just the bottom of her lobe was missing. Jade-R caught her breath and tried not to notice, but for a moment it took her back. *Dora,* she thought. *Yes, Dora,* while putting her hand slowly to her mouth.

"Are you related?" she asked.

The woman said "No." Appearing embarrassed, she answered, "We work together," then looked down at the floor.

Gloria had become calm watching Jade-R talk in her soft, kind voice, and she reached over and touched her arm. Then she tried to smile. Jade-R held her hand. For some time it was quiet in the tiny room.

Taking a chance, Jade-R asked Maria, "Do you feel safe working at that hotel?"

Tears quickly fell from her cheeks, as she shook her head no. "Ditch was always mean. Someday he would have killed one of us. I'm glad he's gone. Us girls called him 'The Devil.' He was always beating us. One night for fun, he tore my earring out, then didn't like how my ear looked. He took scissors and cut it straight across. Laughing he said, 'That's better.' "

Jade-R gently asked, "How long have you and Gloria worked at the hotel?"

"I didn't want to go there, but my husband died a year ago. I have children and a mother to feed. Gloria, she's nice and so young. I've tried to watch out for her. She started there about eight months ago."

"Does she have family?"

"Her stepfather kicked her out. She has nobody."

Jade-R looked back at Gloria. "Will she be going home with you?"

"Yes, she has no place else."

That night, watching the stars from her window, Jade-R began thinking. *Those women were trapped in their horrible lives with no escape, except for a bad ending. That mother was willing to do whatever it took to care for her children.* Remembering that feeling with Cherish, she wiped a tear before drifting to sleep.

CHAPTER THIRTY-SEVEN

With shirtsleeves rolled up, a small army of movers started to pack. Jade-R asked the easygoing Napo to bring boxes to her father's room. Waiting, she stood in his closet and looked at all the spit-shined polished shoes. A thought came over her. *Perhaps he had so many because he never had a pair until he was seven years old.*

Then she opened the drawers by his bed. His large gold and imperial jade ring, the one he wore daily, rested next to his gold watch. Jade-R sat on the side of the bed and looked at them. Napo entered, dropping boxes all over the floor.

"I bet these suits would fit you, and maybe one of your sons. Sort through and take as many as you wish," she kindly offered.

"Thanks. The governor, he used to give me his shirts. We were the same size."

"Good. The rest, I guess we'll take to the priest down at the church."

Napo nodded his head and agreed. "I've noticed you can figure things out. You know what to do, just like the governor."

She looked at him.

The two-story church was painted a stark white. As they pulled up to a back door, bells were ringing from the tower on top of the steeple.

"Napo, while you unload I'd like to go inside."

He nodded, "It's my church; it's wonderful." Then he smiled.

As Jade-R entered, her focus was immediately drawn to the huge crucifix emphasizing the figure of Christ nailed to it. That sacrifice had a spiritual impact that grabbed her attention and pulled her down to the front row. She sat on a simple wood pew and stared. Soon footsteps from behind echoed up the sterile white walls. A gentle hand touched her shoulder and a man said, "I wanted to meet you." She glanced up to a clerical collar on a black short-sleeved shirt. "I am Father Feland," the man said in a gentle tone, "and you are Jade-R Ponce?"

Surprised he knew her name, she answered, "Yes."

He sat beside her. "The governor was not a member of my parish, but we were friends. He'd stop by; we'd visit."

"How did you meet?" she asked.

Meekly he answered, "I stole his wooden box of food when I was six, he was eight, and he beat me up. Broke my nose. My mouth was cut, and a few ribs."

Her eyes widened. "You became friends after that?"

"We were young; none of us had guidance. But your father did come back late that night. I was hiding beneath a bunch of trees when he found me. He brought me something to eat." He smiled as he said, "It didn't feel good when he shoved small pieces of fabric up my nose, but it helped the bleeding. It wasn't the last time, but probably the first, that he ever showed mercy."

She noticed deep pockmarks on his face. He pulled a handkerchief from his pocket and wiped the dots of perspiration gathered across his brow. "Your father spoke fondly of you. Especially when he became sick." He folded his hands across his lap. "You were the most important person in his life."

She looked at his light brown eyes, and there was an inward calmness, and she was impressed with his straightforward manner. "How did you decide to become a priest?"

He smiled again. "When I was almost thirteen, a nun took me in. I was always helping carry groceries or doing odd jobs for her. She was very kind to me, and that kindness changed my life."

Jade-R looked at him curiously. Finally she asked, "Did my father ever go to confession?"

He smiled. "Regretfully, as a priest, I wouldn't divulge. I did tell him, you might have secrets; however, God knows everything. But personally, knowing him, confession isn't something he'd likely do. He would just go direct to the Almighty." "By the way, your father was very proud of how well you played the piano." Again, she was surprised he knew so much about her. "I can tell you he did pray that wherever you were, you were safe and he'd someday see you again."

It was the first time Jade-R started to weep and put her head down. Father Feland reached over, putting his hand on her head. "Tears rinse the soul. We all have sorrow we live with, but God gives us the choice to be forgiven and forgive others. When we reach out, He'll always be there."

About then a nun hurried in saying in a low voice, "A young pregnant girl just arrived. She's been knocked around badly, and she's bleeding."

"You will have to excuse me." Standing up, Father Feland said, "We are getting more of these children of God every week. We somehow find room for them in His kingdom here on earth." He smiled as he politely said, "Come see me anytime. I look forward to talking with you." Jade-R watched as he hurried away with the sister.

That evening, staring at the moon and stars, she thought, *I hope before my father died he went direct to God and asked forgiveness for what he did to my mother.*

Jade-R worried about the beaten girl giving birth at the Catholic Church. She thought about what the priest said: “We are getting more every week and somehow find room for them.” Her thoughts wandered to Gloria and Maria. That night, no matter how peaceful and pretty the stars were, she had trouble sleeping.

CHAPTER THIRTY-EIGHT

Jade-R stood to one side of four big corners. Looking toward the east a small hotel, in need of paint, now sat completely empty. Natural landscaping was plentiful, traveling up the sides of the two-story building that once had navy guys coming in and girls waiting. A wide gravel drive led to the large covered entry. She stood watching men hoisting a sign in place on the wing attached to the left side of the vacant building.

Slowly heading back, she leaned against the car next to Napo. "It's better," he said. "I'm proud, you're doing a wonderful thing." Jade-R glanced back at the sign. It said, "Dora's."

Later she could hear the ocean roaring as they pulled up, and a young valet quickly opened her door. The grounds at the Agana Bay Hotel were lush with tropical greenery and flowers. The bustle of brass luggage carts filled with suitcases, rattled as they were being wheeled in different directions. Ladies coming out of luxury gift stores were laughing and saying, "These prices are better than the duty free shops we went to yesterday." On the way to the Turf Restaurant they passed "Tony Louhon's Fine Dining."

Jade-R peeked in. Huge fish swimming in a giant aquarium divided the elegant dining room from a beautiful tropical bar. Soft lights shone down as liquor bottles glowed and lava lamps bubbled slowly. A platform with drums, marimba and a grand piano sat waiting for another enchanting night of dancing and fun. In the dining room, palms in big pots were scattered among the tables covered with white linen. Crystal goblets for water and wine were waiting to be filled. It had glamour, a place in which anyone would enjoy spending time.

Walking down a wide, open-air hallway, large, glossy, split-leaf philodendron with birds-of-paradise plants were being watered. A soft breeze greeted them at the Turf Restaurant. Servers seemed to know Napo and expressed how much they would miss the governor. They were quickly seated at a table near a large window where Mr. Tamong was waiting. Looking out at the Pacific Ocean, they lunched on lobster with baked vegetables and were entertained watching kids scurry the short distance from the pool to the beach.

A strong voice rang out "Hello!" Looking up, Napo and Mr. Tamong quickly stood to shake hands with a man at their table.

Mr. Tamong turned. "Tony, I would like you to meet Jade-R."

Tony had the dark, ruggedly handsome look of a movie star. He was wearing khaki pants, a flowered print shirt and straw hat. In a charming tone he said, "I wanted to meet you; just missed you at the funeral."

He shook her hand. Invited to join them, he rolled his chair toward the table. "I knew it must be you. I heard a beautiful young lady with pale blue eyes came through the lobby with Napo. I'm Tony Louhon."

She smiled. "You have a wonderful restaurant! I hope you don't mind, I walked through it."

"Good, I'm glad. I wish we were eating there, but it doesn't open until five o'clock. I used to joke around telling your father, it's his restaurant... I'm simply his tenant. I considered him my best friend. Great guy, always had the finest cigars along with a good joke. Hell of a governor, just had that business sense. He did a lot for Guam. Even more for me."

He was quiet for a moment. "I want you to know this. The first time I met him I had drawn up some plans for a restaurant here on Agana Bay," he pointed, "but down a ways. Thought he might go in with me. He owned the land; I figured I'd get a loan for the building. He was so mad he tore up my plans. Said nobody was ever going to build anything on his beach. He almost threw me out of his office. Well, close to a month later he called me back to come see him."

Laughing, Tony said, "He sort of apologized the only way he knew. Offered me the main dining room spot here. Said he was building this hotel. It was much fancier than I was planning on. Back in those days I wasn't sure I could afford it."

Mr. Tamong spoke up. "I remember. But he wanted to make sure you succeeded."

Tony nodded yes and added, "I tried to from then on pay him later, but he wouldn't hear of it. I made sure he never had a bill for a drink or dinner. Your father did not charge me rent for nearly a year just to get me started. Didn't press me for a cent. I will never forget that."

He laughed. "Almost nightly he would come in the restaurant and have a few drinks with me. Then he became more serious. In the last few years he started walking on the beach before he'd leave. Sometimes he would stay down there for hours."

He looked at Jade-R and smiled. "I saw you once when you were little. You were eating ice cream with you father and Napo at Dairy Queen. You were your dad's little princess! He'd say 'the pale blue of the sky matches my daughters eyes.' "

Listening to him, Jade-R thought he was a pleasant man with a great sense of humor.

When he was about to leave, Mr. Tamong said, "Napo, do you mind walking out with Tony? I need to talk to Jade-R." Napo stood and nodded.

Watching them talk as they walked away, Mr.Tamong said, "That man was your father's closest friend," then he looked out the window. "There are over twenty businesses along this beach, and as I told you, they pay land fees monthly into your trust." He pointed: "See those hotels further on down? You own all the land. That amounts to thousands a month. I invited you for lunch to make sure you realized how large your trust is. It will create revenue forever. Unless, of course, you were to sell, which I would advise you to never do. As I said earlier, the governor was a shrewd businessman when he started buying land."

Jade-R looked at him. Fixing the collar on her gold silk blouse, she finally spoke. "The first day I came to your office, you said my father was the only client you had ever worked for." He nodded his head. "I want you to continue running everything the same for me."

Smiling, he answered. "That's good. I hoped everything would remain that way. I know the full business, well... that is, along with Margaret, my C.P.A."

He smiled at Jade-R. "I know you were raised with manners and to call someone older Mr. and Mrs. However, if I'm going to work for you, it's time you call me Peter."

She smiled back, "And it's time you give yourself a raise. You're an honest man. Whatever you think is fair. Hawaii is not that far away if you need my signature. I'm sure your wife would like to come along."

He grinned, "Yes, she would enjoy that."

Out front of the hotel, Napo and Tony Louhon were still talking when Jade-R appeared. Tony said, "Do you have a few minutes? I'd like to show you something."

"Yes, I do."

He repeated, "I loved the governor. We were close."

Down a side path to the beach they walked

for a while. “As I said, your father would come in the restaurant almost nightly, especially the last few years. Faithfully before he’d leave, he’d wander along the beach. One night, he took an unopened bottle of liquor with him. I watched. He drank, then paced back and forth. Later when I looked down, he was gone. It was late, maybe around two-thirty in the morning. I had closed the restaurant. His snazzy truck was still sitting out front. I thought, ‘I better check on him.’ That’s when I saw this.” They stopped and he pointed to a large concrete cross standing eight feet tall.

Jade-R walked over and placed her hand on it.

“Has this always been here? It’s beautiful.”

“No. It just appeared overnight. You can’t see it from anywhere else unless you are right here in this place. That night, there was a full moon. The bottle of liquor was empty on the sand. I heard him yelling. He was in the ocean, up to his waist in water. You know his expensive clothes? Still dressed, suit, tie and his Bally shoes yelling ‘Reign, I love you! Jade-R, I miss you. I’m sorry for what I did.’

He came out of the water and knelt in front of the cross. I asked him why he was doing this? All he would say is 'I lost my wife and now my daughter is gone.' "

Tears rolled down Jade-R's face, then she hugged the huge cross. Tony put his arm around her shoulder.

Finally he said, "Over the last four years I saw the deep pain he fought inside and how he suffered. He told me many times how much he missed you and that he'd give anything to have you back. When he came down with cancer, he said 'My daughter needed me.' He never said what it was, just that he had deep regrets he wasn't there for you. I was at the hospital when you came in the room. Just knowing you were alive and he got to see you, even for a moment, was very important. I wanted to make sure you knew how much that meant to him."

That night she sat, quietly thinking about her father. Wandering into his room, she picked up her parents' photograph from on top of a box. This time she stared at them both. Jade-R remembered him saying, "Your mother is the only woman I will ever love." As she was growing up, she remembered he hugged her all the time and he didn't seem to be troubled. Now, knowing what he had done, he must have lived his life with horrible guilt from that sin. She had so many questions, but one thing she knew for sure, that huge cross that he had placed on the beach was for her mother.

CHAPTER THIRTY-NINE

It was humid and had rained until mid-morning. She was floating around in the pool. Max was near the steps, curled on her towel. She rubbed his big head. “I will miss you,” she told him. “You are a nice cat. Did you like the story I told you yesterday about Gilligan?” He looked up and swished his salt-and-pepper tail.

As so many times before when she was young, she picked a bouquet of flowers from the bush. In the kitchen she made cupcakes for the servants and anxiously waited for Garrett’s call.

That night she went over everything in her mind as she stared at the happy moon outside her window and felt at ease.

Papers were spread across the dining room table at the governor’s mansion as Jade-R and Peter Tamong sat together. He said, “I wanted to go over everything, it's finished and ready for you to sign. My notary should be here in about forty-five minutes. I locked it in writing that you are guaranteed the mansion you are donating to Guam will be used as a hospital. If it is not used that way, there is a clause that it will legally revert back to you.

"They plan on doing huge renovations. The city has already pulled the original plans. At least part of it will open in a couple of months. The building of a new wing will begin as soon as possible."

Jade-R smiled.

"Everyone is grateful and excited. They named it 'The Governor's Hospital.'

"This should really please you. The huge beautiful living room will be the permanent lobby!"

She looked up with surprise and thought, *I guess it is appropriate to name it after my father! After all, it was his home.*

Noticing the look on her face had changed, Peter asked, "Do you have any questions so far?"

"No," she replied. "Please continue."

"Effective immediately, they'll start paying the day guard and the night guard down at the gate. They certainly don't want any vandalism to occur with it vacant."

"Next, the building with the extra houses." He paused as he pulled that file.

"Yes?" she asked.

"Here it is. The owner was eager to sell. So we did well. I drove out there and spent time looking around. It's not much when I walked it with the man. The last house you bought connected to this property is where he and his family lived. It's vacant. They moved a week ago. I checked. We reimbursed him for all the paint he had just bought to fix it up. He was going to use it for a rental. I feel the price you paid for all the houses was fair. Here's the deed and title the way you wanted. I had them recorded.

"Recently a very respectable Japanese man, Mr. Ito, called me. He has a couple of grocery stores and a liquor store on Tinian and Rota not far from the ones you own. He wants to know if you would sell."

"Who is in charge now?"

"Right now the manager, but I think you should consider selling those. They're on different islands and it would be hard for me to keep a watchful eye on the managers."

She looked at Peter. "I agree. Now I have had many talks with Father Feland. He knows you."

"Yes, I take my family to early morning Sunday mass. How can I help?"

"One thing has been on my heart as I see women and girls in trouble, pregnant, physically abused and desperate. Like the girl beaten by Ditch. To the point I'm trying to make, I have experienced my share of pain and sorrow. I never thought coming back to Guam I'd be in a position to do what I'm offering. I have a huge box filled with money for you. Probably dirty money. It's to pay for things that need to be done. I guess I'll never know for sure, but I assume it probably came from that business, the one Ditch ran. I want you to help coordinate with Father Feland and the sisters at the Catholic parish; they are going to use that hotel for as many years as they want. No rent. I will pay the taxes. It is to be used for unwed mothers, and a children's shelter and orphanage. They can name it what they want. We have that understanding. But the right wing is to be called 'Dora's.' "

Peter Tamong looked surprised. Then he said, "The small hotel that is vacant was my next question. I had some ideas for you, but your idea is by far better."

Jade-R smiled. "It needs fresh paint, new furniture and some fencing. I want it clean and safe. Father Feland is very pleased and has agreed on the Dora's sign I already put up."

"Who is Dora?" Peter asked.

"She was a woman that risked everything to help me. In the end it cost her her life." Brushing away a tear, she said, "I would appreciate it if you handle whatever is required on that building. If they need more money, give me a call."

Peter sat speechless as she continued.

"The sisters are excited. They know a couple of older women that will volunteer to cook in the kitchen. You'll be happy about this. Remember Gloria Cabrera, the fifteen-year-old that Ditch... well, you know."

"I recall," he answered.

Jade-R said, "She will be attending the Catholic school soon. Gloria, and her friend Maria, will work cleaning or whatever is needed to help the sisters. They will be paid."

It was quiet as they sipped their iced tea. Jade-R could see Peter was busy thinking. Finally he said. "I commend you. You're a wonderful young lady. I'll take care of everything."

When the notary left, he added, "Keep me in mind; someday I'd like to buy the building I'm in."

Jade-R nodded. "You would be the only one I will sell it to."

"Great, and meanwhile, I have your address and phone number in Hawaii. We will be in touch. I do strongly suggest we draw up some papers for you and Father Feland on the hotel building. It will protect you and the church. Now one last thing: Yesterday when we went to the bank, do you feel comfortable about what he told you to do?"

Jade-R smiled. "When I got home I went over the papers again. In Honolulu, I will choose a bank. I'm to ask for the president and have him call the bank president here. He will explain how I'll be transferring money from my trust, to my checking account in Honolulu."

"Good," Peter said. "By the way, I should tell you, maybe all that money wasn't dirty. The grocery stores paid your father in cash."

Then his voice deepened. "You have a very kind heart. You're young but catch onto business quickly, like the governor did."

As he stood to leave, his brow pinched together with concern. "I'm not trying to get in the middle of anything. But I know this. Everyone has secrets. Whatever happened between you and your father... he loved you."

CHAPTER FORTY

The white clouds were larger than ever as Jade-R and Napo drove along. Finally they pulled into a dumpy, dirty shop. A weathered old man with several missing teeth said, "It's ready. See, I told you the other day at the hotel, I can weld anything but a young girl's broken heart!" He smiled at her as he and another man with blood-red betel juice in his hair loaded a sign in the back of the truck.

Traveling down the road Jade-R admired the chrome dash and plush tuck-and-roll upholstery with fancy piping. "This is a nice pick-up!"

Napo laughed. "Sure is. This is what your father tooled around in when I wasn't driving him. I'd see him around town on my days off."

They turned down a dirt road and again, the young boy was on the corner with bananas piled on his head.

Jade-R said, “Stop!”

The boy smiled when Napo picked the half-bruised pile from off his head. Jade-R handed him the money. Barefoot and smiling, he turned and ran.

Later they passed the old man rocking on the front porch, batting flies, but this time, a puppy playing in the yard held his attention.

They pulled in front of the brown house. Kimea’s son Ton answered the door. His mood was somber.

He said, “Please come in. You must excuse my wife and me. We just found out the man sold the property across the street.” There was the smell of potato bacon soup coming from the kitchen as Jade-R handed him the recorded deed. He stared at it, and then gave it to his wife.

He looked at Jade-R. “You bought it for us?”

“Yes, children need you and Rose. Please, come help Napo with some boxes. I cleaned out my library and these will be great for kids to read!”

In the back of the truck was a long iron plaque.

"This is for you."

The iron sign read, "Batingo's School." Ton stood speechless for a moment.

"I want you to help others. Kimea would be proud."

Ton looked at her as she pointed to the other small house next door. "It's also yours. It sits so close to this property I thought someday you might want to expand. Meanwhile, you can rent it out."

Napo spoke up. "Call me if you need anything."

Wiping his eyes, Ton said, "We'll never forget what you have done."

Rose shook her head and whispered, "Thank you."

With a smile, Jade-R explained, "Movers are delivering some furniture. A sofa, tables, bedroom set, other things. I thought they would be good now that you have more space."

Finally Ton found his voice. It was with deep emotion he answered. "My mother would be proud of both of us."

Jade-R said, "I wish we could have played together when we were young."

Napo set down a small box with several shoeboxes filled with money, while Jade-R handed Ton a slip of paper. "Here's my address in Hawaii. This box, well, it should help you get started with your school."

It was noon when Jade-R hugged the maids in the living room. "No matter where we are, these affectionate ties will always last. I'm glad you're happy to be going to live near your family."

One of the older maids answered, "We wanted to go for a long time, but couldn't leave your father."

Jade-R reminded them, "Don't forget the furniture you picked will be delivered." Wrapped tight in bags, she handed them each several shoeboxes. "I have a request. Please open these tonight before going to bed."

She held her cat for the last time as they walked to the car, and then handed him to the oldest maid. “I love you, and I thank both of you, for all you did for me as a child.”

They embraced tightly as many tears flowed. Rolling down the car window, again she patted Max’s head, as he sat on the maid’s lap. Wiping tears, she waved good-bye as they slowly drove away.

CHAPTER FORTY-ONE

The house was now empty and everyone was gone, but it was the first time she had not felt lonely there. An army cot dressed in sheets for her bed was near the huge window facing the endless sky and ocean. She was glad they would keep this room as the hospital lobby. Now many would enjoy the breathtaking view and perhaps it would give comfort to those in need. She started thinking about her father and suddenly it seemed words echoed around the room, words from that preacher in the little white painted church back in Hawaii; words that called to her, "We must forgive people that have done wrong to us! We must not keep that inside! Forgive them, for you are lost without redemption!"

Then she thought, I *hope someday I forget those filthy words my father said, and the malice that poured from his tongue that terrible night. Actually, I wish he had never told me the truth about my mother. The truth that is still scorching inside my heart.* Adjusting her pajamas she looked down at the beautiful marble floor, then thought, *But I have learned a lot about him. He was tough to the core, always trading evil for evil.*

Again, she was overcome by sadness as she remembered wandering the streets of Formosa alone and scared, and all that happened after. *I had to grow up fast, and I experienced some awful things. The feelings I have toward my father are so mixed and hard for me to understand.* Finally staring at the ocean, a moment of truth hit her. *Poverty and greed motivated his life. Maybe he would have been different growing up with a loving family. Perhaps that dark side of him wouldn't have been there.*

Hours passed and she realized it was the last sunset she would ever see from that spectacular vantage point. She told herself, *I am now sure when I was at the hospital by my father's bed, the terror in his eyes when he looked up and saw me was knowing he didn't have time to ask forgiveness for what he did to his family.*

That night she could almost feel Garrett's arms wrap around her as she touched her pearls and thought about all their long distance calls. Excited she would see him very soon.

Guam was clear and beautiful on Jade-R's last morning. Napo loaded her suitcases, as she walked from room to room through the house. In her bedroom she looked down at the cargo ships at the docks and felt peace at last. In the kitchen she admired all the stainless steel and remembered the servants teaching her how to make cakes and cook, and it brought warmth.

She walked out to the huge swimming pool. As the filter swirled the water, she now had good memories to think about. In the end, there was someone special to swim with — Garrett, the best friend she could possibly have. Before turning the lock on the door, she took one last look at the enormous living room and then whispered good-bye to the house on the hill. Outside she took the lid off a little glass jar, bent down and scooped up some earth, then placed the lid on tightly. She picked two flowers from a hibiscus bush she and her father had planted together. At the bottom of the gate, she looked back up at the house, then asked Napo, "Will you take me to the cemetery?"

This time the grass was dry as she stood at her father's grave. His towering marble headstone was larger than the casket he was in. The deeply carved engraving read, "Governor Ponce, may you rest in peace. The people of Guam love you. Born August 14, 1905 and died November 9, 1963."

Her heart was calm as she said out loud, "I will never forget the horrible thing you did to my mother or understand. But I forgive you. That terrible night when I told you about my baby, I didn't mean to hurt you."

With tears in her eyes she said, "I'm sorry this is how life turned out for us. The father you were when I was little I will always keep in my heart and love." She looked at both of the yellow flowers in her hand, then placed one on his grave and wiped her tears.

Napo was waiting by the car and smiled as he opened the front door.

Minutes passed as they rode along quietly. The silence was finally broken when Napo cleared his voice and said, “You took your first steps in the kitchen one morning. I was there. I put together your first bike with training wheels. Your father and I taught you how to ride around the driveway in circles. And I saw you cry all day when your pony Oatmeal died.”

His voice was cracking and filled with emotion when he said, “I woke from a sound sleep many times at night for almost a year when you were gone.”

The sadness she could see in his huge brown eyes made her feel bad, as he cleared his throat again “I’ll miss you, and I miss your father. If you ever need me, just call. I’ll get there.”

She patted the rough skin on his right hand. “I thought about you also when I was gone. Thank you for everything. You were always good to me.”

In front of the airport Napo started unloading luggage, then picked up a sealed box from the back seat. "No," she said quickly, "That is for you. It may help with your son's college tuition and some extra to live on!"

Then she handed him a large envelope. "I thought this could start a taxi or limousine service. You can't fly the official flags on the car, but with the official seal embossed into the seats, well..." she smiled. "Don't forget all the great stories you have to tell the diplomats and executives you will drive around!"

Out spilled the keys to the pickup and both pink slips. "I don't believe this! I don't believe it!" he beamed.

Smiling she said, "Now, I must go."

He waited as she started to walk away, but soon came running back and hugged him. Leaving again she looked back, as he called out, "If you ever come back, just call 'Napo's Limousine Service,' ask for your Uncle Napo! I'll be there."

Smiling, she replied, "I know."

As she buckled her seatbelt on the plane, a thought crossed her mind. Growing up she had believed she had no friends; now, she realized she had many.

When the plane took off, she looked out the window down at the island of Guam. It was at that moment she felt completely different, and she slowly said good-bye to her birth name, Jade-R Jewel Ponce.

CHAPTER FORTY-TWO

Butterflies fluttered inside her as the plane landed in Honolulu. She almost ran toward the luggage claim. Waiting were Carl and Lum. With joy he said, “We’re glad you’re back,” while Lum piled plumeria flower leis around her neck. Lum’s dimples seemed deeper and her almond eyes sparkled brighter than ever as they tightly hugged.

Unlocking the car door, Carl insisted Catherine ride in front with them. Lum reached over to hold her hand and Catherine was moved by the sweetness of that gesture.

“Did Garrett know you were arriving tonight?” Carl asked.

“No. I thought we’d just spend time together.” They smiled.

Finally Lum said, “He’s crazy about you, we can tell. I see you have on your beautiful pearls."

"Yes, sometimes I even sleep with them on," as she rubbed her hand across the strand. They laughed together.

"Garrett said Guam is beautiful and very green like here."

"It is. There are things that remind me of Hawaii. The flowers are very similar. I was surprised and pleased to see Garrett on his birthday. What a long way for him to come."

Carl, always cool-mannered, observed, "That's real love, to travel that far!"

Proudly, Lum added, "When he got back, I fixed him dinner. Garrett told us it was the best birthday he'd ever had."

As the garage door opened, Catherine breathed in, "I'm home."

Carl added, "Yes, Lum, our girl is home."

The tree house was cheery, with all the charm and coziness she missed. Her suitcases now lined the floor as Lum said, "We got you fruit, ice cream and juice! You must be tired, dear. We'll see you in the morning."

Catherine wandered around the room for a few minutes, then picked up the picture of her mother. She rubbed her hand across the glass. That picture had given her comfort on the long journey so many tears ago. Now she felt safe and for a different reason she held it to her heart. She opened her purse and took out her father's large, imperial jade ring and gold wristwatch, laying them on the table next to the wilted flower, like the one on her father's grave. Someday, she would know what to do with them.

Opening the first suitcase, the other yellow shoe rolled out. Slipping into both of them she looked down at her feet and walked around the room smiling. But soon she glanced over to the green leather duffel bag, now faded, with lots of scratches. It was beaten and weathered, like she had felt so many times. She touched that worn and cracked shoulder strap, and only for a moment, that awful image of moonlight bouncing off the tumbling waves appeared. Then as quickly as it came, it was gone, and she smiled, knowing that forgiveness in her heart had truly helped.

Looking at lights in the coral tree she thought about Garrett and her heart was beating with love, knowing he was not far away.

It was late when she climbed into her fluffy bed, and the sound of water falling in the koi pond was soothing as she fell asleep.

The sun was up and bright as she came through the gate. As usual, Carl was feeding the fish.

“How are Surf and Ruby?”

“Good, getting big! Eating too much, like me! How did you sleep?”

“Wonderfully,” she replied, and watched the koi swim gracefully by as if to say “Hi... you’re back!”

Lum said, “Aloha, dear, hot coffee’s waiting!”

During breakfast Carl said, “This is our late evening at the store, remember? But I’m sure you’ll be busy tonight!” He winked at her and went back to reading the paper.

Zipping her white cotton sleeveless dress, she put on round-toed flat shoes and dabbed perfume on her neck. Anxiously, she watched out the window and finally the cab arrived. On the ride she crossed her fingers, hoping he would be there and not at work. When the cab pulled up, she wasn't sure it was the right place. Plastered entry walls and huge impressive wood gates with large rusted looking pineapple lights on each side greeted her. Then she spotted his woodie station wagon.

In the entry she could see straight through to the ocean with water lapping the shore.

The ceilings were high and the smell of new wood permeated the air. She found Garrett in the kitchen. For a moment her heart stopped as he turned and saw her. She ran to his open arms and he kissed her.

"With a kiss like that, I guess I'm not dreaming, you're really here!"

"I am!" she smiled.

The buzz of power saws and the pounding of hammers bounced through the empty house as he showed her each room. “I didn’t think I’d mess up if I ordered everything in neutral tones! Right?” He looked at her and grinned.

She couldn’t take her eyes off of his gestures as he spoke. He whispered to her, while showing the master bedroom. “I think the sound of the ocean will be great at night! I put two bedrooms nearby for kids when they’re little, and four on the other wing. I remember from experience, teenagers also like their privacy.”

They wandered out to the beach. He picked up a handful of sand and let it drift slowly through his fingers. Looking at her, he asked, “Are you hungry? I am.”

She nodded her head.

“Good,” he said, “Then let’s go have lunch!”

They sat outdoors on a small patio and ate oriental food. He stared at her, then reached across the table and held her hand.

“Soon I want to ask you something important. Would you be ready for that?”

She blushed. “I never thought it possible, to

feel this way."

"That's good! I would take you to dinner but one of the doctors called. He's headed home sick. I told him I'd cover the emergency room. But tomorrow evening, will that be okay?"

Dropping her at home, he kissed her several times. "Your pearls are beautiful against your skin." Kissing her once more, he hurried down the steps to his car.

That night she realized she could never marry him without telling him about the baby, and then suddenly felt scared that he would feel differently. But she knew if she didn't, it would haunt her always. Like the sweet and sour flavors from their lunch, she thought, *That's how my life is right now. Will it end up sweet or sour?* Then she remembered what her lawyer Peter had told her. "Everyone has secrets!"

No, she thought. *If I want a peaceful life Garrett must know. If I respect him, which I do, then he deserves that.* With hope, she held tight to her beautiful strand of pearls. Then for a moment became frightened again. *What about the rest of this hideous mess? The brutal part, do I explain my motherly instincts were my guide, telling me I must do anything to protect my baby? Even stab a terrible man to death, a man who came to steal her and sell her to those people? That dreadful hell in my life is over,* she kept thinking. *But is something that traumatic, is it ever really over?* She paced the floor again, finally saying out loud, "I lived that nightmare and did what needed to be done at the time. I have no problem looking in the mirror. I was sixteen, trying to survive. Yes, for me it's over."

Pacing back and forth, she picked up her mother's picture. "And what about you? Someday do I tell him what Father did to you, my own mother?"

She fought the moral conflict for hours, reliving that private hell, then realized she was the only one that knew. It was late when she came to a final decision. She would only tell him about her baby. That was it. No other gruesome details. Everything else she would take with her to the grave.

CHAPTER FORTY-THREE

It was early morning, but darkness still hovered around the windows as Catherine sat thinking, *When I tell him, will the love he has for me still be there?* Then she became scared, and pulled the covers over her head.

At breakfast Lum asked. "Is there anything new?" Carl eagerly looked up.

"Yes. I saw Garrett yesterday and the beautiful home he's building. Then we went to lunch. Tonight he's taking me to dinner!"

"That's good," Carl replied. Pausing, he said, "How many seasons does Guam have?"

"Just two. But I noticed while I was there, the sun is more direct. Even with lotion, if you don't watch out, you can burn."

Still curious, Carl asked, "What's the normal temperature?"

Suddenly her thoughts went to Garrett. Trying to concentrate, she finally answered, "Average at sea level...it's about eighty-five Fahrenheit."

Lum smiled as she said, "I was just thinking, I've never had a sunburn!"

Carl quickly replied, "And keep it that way. I have. It doesn't feel good."

Catherine smiled and looked at the beautiful flowers in the terraced planters cascading down the lava wall. She glanced at Carl and Lum and was happy to be back with them.

They hugged her. "It's good having you home." Those were the words they used in place of good-bye, as they left for the jewelry store.

The day seemed endless waiting for Garrett. All she could think about was how this would end. She wandered around cleaning imaginary dust in her immaculate tree house, feeling nervous.

Tan and so very handsome, he arrived in lightweight tweed slacks and a white linen shirt. He complimented her. "Your dress is beautiful. I've never seen diamond and ruby buttons like that!"

She smiled.

"I'm taking you somewhere special!" he announced with a grin.

"How was your night at the hospital?"

"Only a couple of small emergencies," he answered as they pulled up to a restaurant called "Blame It on the Moon!"

He grinned, "Good name, right?"

She smiled as he opened her car door. "Yes, I like it." Interesting moon-shaped steps led to the entrance as he held her hand.

The interior was plush, but small and dimly lit. They were seated in a cozy leather booth that gave them a feeling of privacy. He kissed her hand and looked at her lovingly as he sipped on his scotch. She stirred her piña colada with a long chunk of pineapple. He told a joke he had heard from a fellow doctor, and together they laughed. The waiter explained the specials for the evening. They enjoyed the grilled swordfish on an extraordinary bed of rice with mint and basil. Catherine felt nervous, presuming this might be the night, and gathered up the courage ready to tell him just as… Flames blazed from their dessert now placed in front of them. They finished the last of the cherries jubilee, and again she hesitated. *No, this is not the time. I'll wait.*

It had been a lavish evening with much laughter. At the door he kissed her, then said "Dinner tomorrow night. I'll be here at eight o'clock."

The next day dragged on. Again she thought, *Will there be a happy ending?*

Finally it was evening when she heard voices. Carl and Garrett were talking by the garage.

"Doesn't she look beautiful?" Garrett said. As she gracefully came down the stairs, he reached out, taking her hand.

With pride Carl replied, "She always looks

beautiful."

Catherine was puzzled and felt something different as she looked over at Garrett. They drove up to his huge wood gates. Like a gentleman he helped her out of the car. "How incredible!" she said. As candles flickered at the front door he found the wrought iron keyhole. He led her through the large living room where rows and rows of candles lit the path down to the beach. A table was set with flowers and more candles.

"This is the most breathtaking" ... Putting her hand to her heart, "I have never seen anything like this. It's magical!"

"I wanted this night to be unforgettable for both of us." Beneath the moonlight he opened a bottle of champagne, then handed her a piece of paper.

"It's a deed," he said. "I had my lawyer add your name to this house, our house. I want you to have half of everything I own, along with all of my heart. Will you marry me?"

At that moment, this great love she felt inside leaped up and touched the romantic moon. Then she looked at him, and fell to her knees in the sand, sobbing. "This is the most wonderful evening of my life, but it's important you know something."

She glanced at the dark ocean. Garrett bent down on his knees beside her. Tears flowing, she said, "Look what you want to give me, and tonight the truth is what I must give back."

He wrapped his arms tightly around her. "There's plenty of time in the future to explain whatever terrible thing happened. No matter what it is I will love you. But tonight..."

He looked at her beautiful face in the moonlight and wiped away her tears. Smiling he said, "You didn't answer. Will you marry me?"

"Yes, oh yes!" she replied. He kissed her and as the waves rolled along the shore, she felt loved and safe in his arms.

CHAPTER FORTY-FOUR

The giant sun was warm, and the row of palm trees fanned out, swaying in the gentle breeze. Garrett and Catherine were excited as they entered Kamora Jewelry to select their wedding bands. Lum beamed, congratulating them again with kisses as Carl went to the safe and pulled a special tray of 18 karat gold bands. Their decision was quick. They both pointed to the same simple design. Lum nodded. Carl added, “That’s a nice choice.”

Suddenly the door flew open. Rambunctiously, a couple entered. Hearing the man’s voice, Catherine quickly turned her head away using her wide-brimmed hat as a shield while thinking. *Honolulu is not that big. I expected to run into them somewhere, but why this day?*

With a smile, Carl politely said, “I’ll be right with you,” as the smell of liquor reeked from their mouths.

Impatiently, he answered back, “We’re in a hurry. Can someone else wait on us?”

Carl answered. “We’re almost finished.”

“We’re not pressed for time,” Garrett quickly said to Carl. “Go ahead, take care of them.”

Connor’s wife pointed at a display counter. He said, “Okay, I’ll buy you that diamond necklace.”

His wife snarled, “Don’t think that after what you did with my girlfriend, you’re getting off the hook that easy.” She leaned her elbow across the counter while she removed her sunglasses. Her right eye was swollen almost shut.

Holding his wallet, almost bragging, he said, “I get a discount! My parents buy all their jewelry here.”

“Who are your parents?”

Slurring his words he answered, “The Bodwens. From Bodwen Shipping and Cargo.”

Carl nodded. “Yes.”

Connor pulled out a credit card and tossed it on the counter as his wife added, “Maybe that pair of earrings too?” then snarled something under her breath.

Looking at her with disgust, he said, “Be rational; you have enough,” then pushed her arm off the counter, sloshing the word, “Bitch!”

Embarrassed, he looked at Carl. “Excuse us. It’s a family thing.”

Catherine glanced up. Connor was having trouble standing. Turning too quickly, and wobbling to one side, Connor grabbed Catherine’s arm to hold onto, her hat falling to the floor. Face to face he stared into her eyes and said, “Jade-R!” At the door he looked her way again as they left.

“Sorry for the interruption; they’re a mess,” Carl said while taking off his glasses. “I hope they’re not driving.”

Garrett picked up Catherine’s hat and gently held her hand.

In the car it was unusually quiet as they drove along. Pulling into an area overlooking the beach, Garrett said, “He called you Jade-R! What just happened back there?”

She got out of the car, and Garrett followed. They sat on an old wood bench. “My baby’s out there,” She pointed toward the ocean, and began to cry.

“That man in the store came to Guam; that’s how we met. I was young, just sixteen. It was my first dance, the only boy I had ever been around. One night alone he kissed me, but then he wouldn’t quit. I begged him, please stop, but he forced himself on me.”

Sobbing, she poured her heart out. “I was pregnant, and he had left. I could only hide it for so long. Worried sick, I didn’t know what to do! My father loved me, but when I told him, he flew into a rage and his anger was scary. Immediately he was going to have my baby cut out of me! Terrified, all I could think about was fleeing! Late that night I snuck aboard a freighter. In Formosa I delivered my baby girl. On my way here to Hawaii, she died. Only five days old, I buried her at sea.”

Still sobbing she said, "Time has now passed. I understand what my father must have been going through. A governor's daughter pregnant? His little princess!" She dropped her head in pain, reliving those moments, as Garrett put his arm around her.

It was quiet. They looked out at the ocean and watched white caps from a distance. Finally she said, "I'm sorry you had to hear all of this."

Always strong and sincere, one of the things she loved most about him, Garrett answered, "I was just thinking. If that had not happened, you would still be in Guam. We never would have met. It makes me feel bad what you went through alone. That's what bothers me the most."

He turned her head toward him. "Our new life is waiting, and I want to spend all of it with you!" The look and kiss he gave her at that moment were far more meaningful than ever before.

CHAPTER FORTY-FIVE

Two months later, on a Saturday afternoon, silver streaks of clouds ran across the bright blue sky as the ocean rolled ashore. A small group of family and friends sat in white chairs on the beach in front of their home. Loka played the violin, with another man playing the ukulele. Catherine was regal in a simple white gown, worn slightly off her shoulders. Holding a bouquet of orchids and gardenias, she touched the pearls around her neck and then glanced down at her mother's emerald and diamond ring, and the matching bracelet. Lum kissed Catherine.

She took Carl's outstretched arm as he said, "Such a stunning bride. You are the most wonderful daughter we could have ever wished for." He walked her slowly down a white runner, rolled across the sandy beach. Orchids and gardenias were loosely tossed on each side, some on the sand, a few on the runner. With her chin held high, she kept her smile and focus on Garrett as he stood waiting. This time her tears were honey sweet. He put his hand around hers as a woman sang the "Hawaiian Wedding Song." Catherine whispered words from that song to Garrett ..."Yes, I will love you longer than forever."

Fluffy clouds lingered, floating over them as they repeated their wedding vows. The wedding kiss was short, but the look into each other's eyes lasted longer.

Dr. Edward Eastman, an older version of Garrett, with wisps of gray at his temples, introduced them. "I want to congratulate our son and his new bride, Catherine Eastman."

Garrett said, "As fate would have it, here we are on this special day. Thanks to all of you for being a part of it." Catherine watched her new husband, thinking how blessed she was as her eyes danced with happiness.

The immediate reception was held on the wraparound veranda. Waiters with white gloves carried silver trays of tall crystal glasses, bubbling with fine champagne.

Carl and Lum Kamora stood together as Carl said, "This toast is for our beautiful Catherine, and her new husband Garrett. May your life together be fulfilling, as you so deserve. We love you both."

As guests wandered around the house, the center table in the entry held an exquisite wedding cake. One of the waiters stationed nearby was heard patiently repeating, "The bottom layer is pineapple upside down, and the top layer is scrumptious coconut cream." Then he would smile.

With pictures out of the way, everyone was seated at small white tables, in the unfinished family room. Elegant vases held towering orchids, with small chocolates sprinkled under them. They dined on hearts of romaine and old-fashioned chicken potpie with young vegetables, catered by the chef from the Orchid Room. A lady played the harp during dinner. Later after the cake was cut, guests danced to a small Hawaiian band in the soon-to-be finished living room. Then Garrett asked everyone to join them out front. Catherine looked at him with surprise.

Outside the open double wooden doors sat a big white convertible with red leather upholstery. Woven through the huge bow wrapped around the windshield were orchids and gardenias. Garrett said, “I hope you like your wedding gift!” Everyone laughed when he added, “And, of course, driving lessons. No more taxis for my wife.” With excitement, she threw her arms around his neck and gave him a big romantic kiss.

As the sun was beginning to set, they waved good-bye to the last of their guests. Garrett swept Catherine up in his arms and carried her out on the beach. He rolled up his pants and she gathered her dress to one side as they walked along hand in hand. They sat resting on the warm sand to watch as the last drop of sunlight disappeared.

He whispered, “I love you!”

EPILOGUE

Looking at a whimsical oil painting of an old shack on the beach, with a huge monkey climbing a thin curved palm tree over the roof, Catherine thought, *We have had that almost twenty years. I will never forget the first time I saw it at the penthouse for lunch! The uniqueness captured me. It was his favorite, the one Mr. Davis said he could never part with, was delivered here on our wedding day. How fast time goes and what a great life!*

They had that large family they both wanted, two really good-looking boys and then tried for a girl. Blessed, they got darling identical twin daughters! Their home turned out comfortable, casual and breathtaking. The hardwood floors throughout are now filled with the scuffs and scratches from kids and dogs and have real character.

When the children were little they built

sand castles on the beach outside their doors!

In the evening the big wide veranda was a favorite spot for reading stories, eating ice cream and family time. As they grew older, their dad taught them how to ride the surf.

Watching her children doing homework at her double-sided old school desk or putting a puzzle together, the heritage of that makes her glow with happiness.

At night before they go to sleep, with the sound of the ocean rolling ashore, Catherine and Garrett look at the stars and the moon. Garrett takes her hand and says, "I'm the luckiest guy on earth."

Granddad Carl shared his knowledge with the boys, about the joy and serenity of caring for koi fish. As the twins got older and would spend the night, they always begged to sleep... yes...in the coral tree house!

Carl began having severe medical issues, so he and Lum decided to sell the jewelry store to two young men; one from Japan, a gemologist who could not speak any English but quickly learned, and the other young man, from a wealthy family, half Japanese and half Hawaiian. Both had previous experience in the jewelry business. Carl thought the two men were a good fit for the store and his customers with their impeccable style and excellent taste. In the sales agreement, they kept the name, Kamora Jewelry Store. When Carl would come home after visiting the store, he would say, "Those two young men sure like each other."

The sad news: Carl passed away after a prolonged illness. Sitting with Lum one afternoon, enjoying a glass of wine, and talking to his beloved koi fish, he slumped over, dropping his glass and without pain, peacefully went to sleep.

Shortly after, Garrett and Catherine asked Lum to come live with them. "That would be nice, I'd like that, but I could never leave Carl's koi fish!" Loneliness spread across her face as she tried to smile.

During construction on a new addition to their home, they said, "Oh we're building a playroom for the kids."

Lum's dimples were deep with expression and her almond eyes sparkled as they surprised her! It was a guest wing, with bedroom, bath and living room large enough to hold all her treasures including the lavender and purple rug, a gift from her sister-in-law. Right outside glass doors was a beautiful new koi pond with a stunning waterfall, just waiting for Surf and Ruby!

With Grandlum's guidance the twin girls have learned how to cook many of her special recipes.

One night, Catherine tucked covers around Lum and kissed her forehead. "When I was scared I had no one and no place to go. Carl and you took me in. You gave me a home and comfort. We are a family and now it feels right that we are all here together."

Before long the elegant and wonderful Mr. Davis will turn ninety-eight years old, and for his age enjoys extremely good health. He still lives at the White Sands Hotel on Waikiki Beach but never misses Catherine and Garrett's Sunday brunch. When first arriving he spends time in the entry. Leaning on his silver and bone-handled cane, he gently touches that huge monkey painting, while studying the choice of oil colors he used on that great work of art. That's also the day Catherine plays the piano, and all his favorite songs, just for him!

Brunch is casual but held in the formal dining room at the big bamboo table; the one from the mansion Catherine ate at when she was small. The enormous chandelier with blue crystal prisms intertwined with huge pieces of natural coral hangs above the table, adorning the room. A few years ago she found a woman to hand-paint a white coral motif around the ceiling. It's now her favorite room, and the charm and beauty it has always makes her smile. The table holds eighteen and there is rarely an empty seat. With plenty of food, it is open to all, and usually their children's friends show up and keep the table lively with youthful conversation.

P.S. Mr. Davis's twenty-year-old cat, Gilligan, died. They had a special little funeral service and the kids helped bury him under their old banyan tree near the kitchen. When

Mr. Davis comes to lunch, they make sure there are freshly picked flowers on the cat's grave.

Peter Tamong, her attorney, has been extremely good handling the business. He and his lovely wife have traveled to Hawaii many times. Catherine and Garrett have gotten to know them well. The Governor's Hospital now has two large new wings. The original living room is still the main lobby with the polished blue marble floors and breathtaking view of the tropical turquoise sea.

By airmail, a very impressive large embossed letter arrived. It was stamped with the official Gold Seal of Guam, thanking her for donating the governor's mansion to the people. It has a wonderful tortoiseshell frame and hangs in a prominent spot on the wall in their library. Right below on a wood table Catherine has the little bottle filled with earth from her birth land that she scooped up the day she left.

When it comes time for vacation, they always head to the farm in Sunberry, Ohio to visit Garrett's parents. The kids ride horses, catch fish in their private lake, and have learned how to milk a Jersey cow! They enjoy experiencing the way their father grew up. But someday soon, they will take their kids to the Island where she spent her childhood, and stay at the beautiful Agana Bay Hotel.

Napo's Limousine Service is the only one on that island. Several times a year, (and it always comes addressed to Jade-R Catherine Eastman), he sends a short letter or post card. She looks forward to introducing her children to her Uncle Napo.

Dora's Wing has been successful providing women and children a good home with the Catholic nuns who truly care. A few years ago Catherine received a letter from Father Feland. In it was a note from Gloria Cabrera, the young fifteen-year-old girl badly beaten by

Ditch, thanking Catherine for all of the financial help. She is now a registered nurse working in the emergency room at the Governor's Hospital.

Every year, Batingo's school is filled with students eager to learn. Ton and his wife Rose have raised five children, who had been dumped on the streets. Three of those kids will graduate from college soon. Ton's mother, Catherine's governess Kimea, would be proud.

One-morning headlines in the newspaper read:

"DEAD! HEIR TO BODWEN SHIPPING!

WILLIAM CONNOR BODWEN III, died on impact in head-on collision."

Further down, the article said he was forty-three years old, not married and had no children. Police were investigating the night's events. Catherine continued reading. He had wrecked his car and been arrested one year before on drunk-driving charges.

With sadness, she sat thinking, *If his grandfather is still alive, he will be heartbroken. Connor was a young man who had everything and every opportunity. And now, this is how his life ended.*

As for her parents, photographs are placed around their home and her children only know the good stories. Her father was the governor of Guam and her mother drowned by accident. Occasionally she pulls out her father's imperial jade ring and gold watch. Touching them makes her feel close to him as she recalls the happy times, the father he was when she was little. That terrible image of moonlight bouncing off the tumbling waves has never returned. That horrific thing he did late one night can never be taken back. Then she thinks about that huge concrete cross on the beach back in Guam, and it brings her comfort. For she is certain, alone while kneeling in front of it, he did ask forgiveness for his sins. In the last moments of her father's life, she truly hopes he found peace, seeing her and knowing his daughter Jade-R, was standing close... beside his bed.

Often she has thought about the way life turned out. When she looks at the ocean, it reminds her of her gorgeous American mother. The hours spent talking to her picture on that long terrible journey, somehow brought them close. She felt she got to know her and always says "Thank you for taking care of my baby." She knows it's not real, but holds it tight in her heart and keeps a vivid memory of them happy together in their beautiful castle under the sea. And she whispers, "You were my first precious baby. Even though it was so long ago, if I close my eyes, I can still see your darling little face and feel you in my arms.

"Cherish, I love you and I always will."

Philippine Sea
Guam
VIA AIR MA
Pacific Ocean

Dana L. Evans is an American romance novelist who now lives in Newport Beach, California with her husband, Joe, a retired veterinarian.

As a young girl, she climbed palm trees, danced and played in the sand of the countries she writes about, and always tucked handfuls of air in her pockets when leaving.

Her events and characters are completely fictional, enchanting readers with murder, sex, tragedy, and love ravished with mystery.

Her next novel, *Sugar Palm Hill*, debuts in Summer 2019.

To my readers:

I hope you enjoyed reading this as much as I enjoyed writing it.

Made in the USA
San Bernardino, CA
14 March 2019